DATE LOANED

APR 18			
MAY 23			
JUL 18			
JAN 28			
JUL 29			
SEP 16			
OCT 14			
DEC 7			
MAR 13			
JUN 8			
MAY 16			
OCT 8			
APR 8			

THE TROUBLED MIDNIGHT

Rodney Garland

THE TROUBLED
MIDNIGHT

Coward–McCann, Inc.
New York

gift

Copyright, 1954, by Rodney Garland

THE TROUBLED MIDNIGHT

Book One

1

I OUGHT to have remembered Hogan's habits, but it was some time since I had last seen him. He would give me an appointment for a quarter to nine, which meant that, getting up late, I would have practically no breakfast and would arrive out of breath in Queen Anne Street. He would then talk for half an hour about his exotic fish in the large tank between the window and the X-ray machine. An amusing dissertation on their sharp sense of hearing, their love life, their various illnesses, an operation he had performed on a sick Shubunkin, or a large green and gold Nippon. Then, having exhausted the fish as a subject, he would ask what I was writing, a purely rhetorical question, because he would at once begin to talk about the book he himself was reading, and all this, as far as I was concerned, on an almost empty stomach, anticipating pain or bad news.

On this particular morning, to make matters worse, it was raining and I had brought neither raincoat nor umbrella. Hogan must have sensed my impatience, however, because he soon walked away with a sigh from the fish and went to his desk. "Well now," he said, holding an X-ray photograph not much larger than a postage stamp in front of the four blue bulbs hanging above my head. "You can see quite clearly, there's a small decay under the filling." I saw nothing, but I was pleased we were getting a move on. "If neglected it will spread down . . . here . . . and attack the pulp and later the root. Luckily, we've caught it just in time. I'll take the old filling out; then we'll see.

There's a nine out of ten chance I can save it. . . . Open wide, please."

Some ten minutes later he turned the drill-arm away and with slow care placed some dressing into the tooth. "Next Monday?" he said, turning to his engagement book. "At the same time?" He was looking at me with a mysterious smile. "Did I ever tell you about the Abbey Theatre? Many years ago now. . . ." But his bell began to buzz. "My next patient." He broke off with deep regret. "Remind me to tell you on Monday. You may be able to use it."

I walked across the black and white tiled floor, past the fake Regency sideboard in the hall, and out of the front door. I ran as far as Wigmore Street, but by the time I had reached the corner the rain had become a torrent. I just had time, before getting thoroughly soaked, to dash into a little café I knew. I might as well in the circumstances have a proper breakfast. But the dressing in my tooth made the tea taste like angostura and the scrambled eggs like fishpaste. It was still raining slightly when I left. As I hurried to the bus stop in Oxford Street I felt a headache coming.

I somehow knew that the rain would stop the moment I reached my doorstep. In fact, as I got off the bus at Queensway the sun was already halfway out, and when I reached Portobello Court it was shining as if it had been blazing away for hours.

On the broken marble top of the hall table was my morning mail: a publisher's advertisement, my laundry bill and a postcard to remind me that the book I had borrowed from the Paddington Borough Council Library was overdue.

The book in question was Dressel's *Interpretation of Canonical Law,* which I had taken out two or three weeks

4

earlier, hoping to find a reference I wanted for the book I was writing. I was concerned at the time with the subject of miracles, and as I walked up the stairs I thought I ought to try to get what I could out of the book before returning it in the afternoon. Hogan, it occurred to me, was probably a Catholic, and the type of man, moreover, likely to have had some views on the subject, but we had talked instead about tropical fish. I decided in any case to work that day, no matter what happened. If the headache got worse, I would take something, but I was determined to work; I had done nothing much for the past two days.

The first thing I noticed as I unlocked my door was a brown canvas bag lying on the hall chair. There was a square yellow football-pool envelope placed where I could not possibly miss it, on the clean side of which was written: *You left it at Piraeus Restaurant called this morning you were out.* Under this was printed in block capitals: NIKKI PAPADATO.

The Piraeus, I vaguely remembered, was a restaurant in Soho to which I had once been taken to lunch. It was small, good and expensive. But I had never left this or any other bag there, because I had never owned one.

It was one of those bags with a zipper—red-brown canvas and rather worn. What had led the man to think it was mine? I opened it. At first I saw just two parcels, one square and the other long and slim, almost as long as the bag. The small parcel contained a box of *Piker's Best Marshmallow,* the other a musical instrument, some kind of flute, of black wood.

It was then that I noticed the orange-yellow folder lying at the bottom of the bag. I took it out, and saw that on top of it were three lines typed on a little adhesive tag:

J. B. Edmonton,
37 Portobello Court,
Queensway, W.2.

That was certainly my name and address, so the mystery was solved at least to the extent that I could understand why the bag had been brought to me. But I had never seen that folder before. I undid the tape which was tied across it.

"*No. CA-87531*"—I read the first sheet:

"*Edmonton, J. B., writer. Born, Poona, India, 1913. Parents dead, one married sister. Education: Tonbridge and New College, Oxford.*

"*Income around £500 p.a., derived partly from books and freelance journalism, partly from investments (probable value £3,000). Bank balance usually around £100, repeatedly overdrawn. Apparently no debts.*"

2

For the third time now I was reading the typewritten sheets in the folder. The first mingled feeling of curiosity and shock was over and I felt more and more disgusted. One has sometimes been the subject of malicious gossip, or the victim of unflattering opinions and untrue accusations, but this was the written word, impersonal, merciless, almost inhuman, like an anonymous letter. I could not decide which was more shocking—the deadly accuracy of some of the statements, or the equally deadly inaccuracy of the others.

"*A member of the Communist Party since 1931. . . .*" I read this for the fourth time. Yes, it was about then, in the autumn or winter of that year, that I had begun to attend their meetings—round about the time of the General Election. When was that? Probably November. But it was only a phase such as many of us passed through at that time, and I had given it all up soon after I had come down from Oxford. I had attended no further meetings and paid no subscription. Never at any time had I been "active," as the report said.

I turned quickly to another page. Yes, I remembered correctly. *News from Abroad* was not even mentioned. This seemed quite typical.

In 1939 I published my novel *News from Abroad*, in which I attacked Communism. The book was a flop, but it was quite widely denounced by the left-wing Press. Yet the dossier remained significantly silent about that.

On the same page, however, which dealt with my books, my first novel *Bombay Duck* was described as "subversive." I was twenty-one when I wrote it; a shamefully sloppy, sentimental book, which was very kindly received even by the conservative Press.

"Managed to get out of the R.A.F. in 1943 and became employed in the Ministry of Information, where his most intimate friends were Communists."

Managed, indeed! I had been brought back from North Africa in 1943 and had been in and out of Service hospitals for several months, when an impulsive medical board decided to discharge me. My friend Dunkley said at the time that the specialist had made a faulty diagnosis and that the Board thought I would need lengthy psychiatric treatment. "So they discharged you to save money. But you don't want to complain, do you?"

It was true that after I came out of the Air Force I got a job at the Ministry of Information for the rest of the war, but why should anyone think my intimate friends were Communists?

My most intimate friend at the time was Patsy, with whom I had an affair, and she was certainly no Communist. I was also on very friendly terms with Vernon Maxwell, who had no political views whatever. As to the people with whom I worked, they were Waterton, an elderly Conservative M.P., and Plunkett Moynihan, who, before he got himself killed in a railway accident a year or two ago, was a Roman Catholic poet.

"After the war was regularly employed by the Plaistow

Metropolitan Studios, many of whose executives are known Communists."

The Plaistow people had bought my novel, *The Last of Edwina Probyn,* and I wrote the script. Payment was spread over two years for income tax purposes, so my name may have figured in their books for two years, but there was no question of regular employment. As a matter of fact, I had asked them for some script job once or twice since, but it had never got beyond an offer to "bear my name in mind."

"Under various names, such as 'Russell Anderson,' wrote and published a number of semi-pornographic novels."

Well, a couple of years ago, partly as a joke, partly to pay for a holiday in Italy, I wrote one single paper-back detective story called *The Long Day.* It was in a way a parody of the "whodunit," but there was no more sex in it than in Conan Doyle.

". . . a number of semi-pornographic novels. . . ." The first time I read that sentence I laughed, but now I felt it was all part of a plan. Whoever had compiled my dossier had involved himself in the stupidest contradictions in an endeavor to defame me. The last page, I thought, and I felt my face turning red.

I turned again to the last page and reread the last three lines: *"Probable reason why he never married may be connected with the strong suspicion that Edmonton is a homosexual."*

Probable . . . may be . . . suspicion. This time the author of the report made no direct accusation, but had contrived to give his statement a deceptive sense of objectivity.

How easy it would have been to look up my marriage or divorce record at Somerset House, I thought. Probably the man had done so and deliberately suppressed the fact. If taxed, he would doubtless say: "Well, so many homosexuals do marry. In any case, he was divorced, wasn't he?"

There was no doubt about it; the object of the man who had compiled this dossier had been to blacken me in every conceivable way. What frightened me at first was the deadly accuracy of his statement about my financial affairs and the fact that he had discovered that over twenty years ago as a student I had attended Communist meetings at Oxford. As a matter of fact, I could not be positive now whether I did actually *join* the Communist Party as such at the age of nineteen. Probably my name had been on some membership list.

There were two other statements which, again, were partly based on fact. I did publish a novel under a *nom de plume* and I did work, even though for a very short time, for the Plaistow people. But since he had managed to dig out things which were comparatively difficult to disinter, why were all his statements of other facts, which were more easily verifiable, so false?

Persecution mania comes fairly easy to a lonely and sensitive man, but this was not something I was imagining. Clearly, the compiler of this dossier was seeking to discredit me and, now that I had recovered from the first series of shocks, I suddenly guessed the probable reason at least for the existence of the dossier.

Some two months earlier I had applied to a Government department, called the T.F.O., for a propaganda job, which had been advertised in *The Times*. At their request I sent them a detailed life story. Arthur Waterton, with whom I had worked in the M.O.I. during the latter half of the war, signed a recommendation. Then about a month later I was interviewed.

It was in an office near Piccadilly, and there was the usual set-up: a group of three people, one from the department I was trying to enter, one from Personnel and one, I presume, a psychologist. I vaguely remembered having seen the fellow from the propaganda department somewhere. He was a red-haired man of about thirty-five; I had probably come across him in some ministry during the war. It was he who did most of the talking during the interview. He said he had read my books, and the way he said it implied that he had read them with interest and appreciation. He mentioned my work for the M.O.I., and I thought that was possibly where I had seen him, but I could not be sure. Then he began to talk about my future salary—almost apologising about its size—and I concluded that the interview was a success.

As I came out of the room into the corridor I stumbled into Mrs. Gold. She had been Moynihan's secretary at the M.O.I. I told her I was applying for a Government post and was there for an interview.

The next day she telephoned, saying I must keep it under my hat, but my interview had been a success. "You won't hear from us for quite a time," she confided. "You'll get a letter in due course. But for God's sake don't let on that I've told you."

I was now pretty sure that the folder and its contents were connected with my application to the T.F.O. There must have been a check-up. Though the folder contained a large number of blank sheets, it seemed complete. It could not, in fact, have been much more so. But, of course, one never knew. It may very well have been that the compiler had intended to take it home in order to work on it, and I began to wonder what other damaging lies he would have added. Again, it may have been that the folder was being shown to someone, and had been, as the saying goes, "lost in transit." If that was the case, was it lost *after* it was shown or before?

But who had compiled it? I remembered bitterly that I had wanted to be a private detective when I was a child and that later I had entered a profession which was part fulfilment of the childhood ambition. But it was very difficult to guess at my detractor's personality from the scanty

10

clues at my disposal. The Piraeus was not a famous restaurant, but it was fairly expensive and quite smart. The canvas bag was almost as impersonal, classless and nondescript as a pack of cigarettes. It could have belonged to almost anybody. Nor was there any clue in the marshmallows or the flute. The trouble was, I could not even laugh at them.

The report itself was typewritten with the exception of one pencilled line in the margin at the foot of the last page. This was another lie—I was not a "friend" of Eric Fontanet, although I had known him years before, and seen him on and off since. The handwriting was small and round—it could even have been feminine—but in any case it was a "spiteful" handwriting. It went quite well with marshmallow, I decided. Then I tried to control my anger.

There were some obvious conclusions to be drawn from the style, or at least from the phrasing, of the sentences. One might reasonably assume that for such a job of snooping they would not engage a university don; certainly not when it came to a person as unimportant as a writer applying for a minor propaganda post. The phrasing was certainly inferior and pretentious. It had a stilted, ambitious preference for pompous long words as opposed to concise, smart, short ones. Grammar school or some cheap public school, I thought bitterly, and I could already hear the accent: Concealed Cockney or Concealed Provincial. There was a moustache, I felt, a signet ring with a crest and a seedy attempt to cut a dash; possibly a dilapidated racing car, and a quiet, illiterate blonde who seldom washed her hair.

Could it be just stupidity or was it really deliberate malice? I tried hard to be objective, but the second motive seemed more likely. There appeared to be a definite consistency in the argument, in the presentation. The man seemed to have taken great pains to denigrate me. He had used two main arguments, both basically false, but there

11

was no doubt that the first—Communism—was enough¯ to have killed my chances of employment.

He was certainly concentrating on the Communist angle, but in trying to make out a case against me he had brought in practically everything derogatory he could imagine. It was amazing how much he knew, but equally amazing how much he seemed not to know. But . . . was it really ignorance? I was now inclining to believe that he had found out more than he had revealed. For example, he must have known, I felt, that I had been married and divorced, but he knew that the suggestion of homosexuality would be more damaging.

Did the man know me personally? I had wondered about this as I read through the document. In that case he was an "enemy." "Any enemies?" That is the usual police question put to the victim on whom an attack had been made by some "unknown" person. But I had no enemies, for all I knew. I was not important, influential or successful enough to be seriously disliked by people. Certainly not to make such a bitter, venomous enemy as this.

It was then that the idea suddenly came to me that the worm who had pencilled the reference to Fontanet on the margin of the last page, might deliberately have introduced him in order to supply a kind of link between the two false accusations. Fontanet—at one time at least—had been a Communist, among other things, and he certainly was a homosexual.

As for the statement about my friendship with Fontanet, there was, I realised on reflection, a tiny element of truth. At one time I had known Fontanet and for a brief while he might have been described as a friend of mine, but that was many years ago—probably twenty. I began to feel that the author of the dossier must have known us in our Oxford days.

My association with Fontanet did not make me a homosexual any more than my adolescent flirting with Commu-

12

nism made me a Communist. I supposed if one wanted to make out a case against a person, certainly someone like myself, it was not difficult. After all, I was a writer, and it was not surprising that I should know casually, or even semi-intimately, a whole crowd of people of different sorts and sizes—other writers, publishers, critics, painters, actors, journalists, for example.

If the man who had prepared the dossier had bothered, he could have strengthened his case by saying that Emley, one of the characters in *Bombay Duck* (who later on appeared as Fitzalan in *The Man in the Moon*) was a homosexual. But if one was going to argue on that sort of basis, practically anything could be made to suit any opinion. The same set of facts could tell Senator McCarthy I was a Communist and the *Daily Worker* I was a Fascist.

The truth, I realised, was probably that as a type of man I was peculiarly well placed, by my contacts and experience, to understand both homosexuality and Communism; and it was for this reason that I was so vulnerable to many of the half-truths stated in the dossier.

I was accused, either directly or by implication, of being both a Communist and a homosexual. Neither was true. I was never one to be strongly anything. That was my tragedy. It accounted, I thought, for my comparative lack of success. Reflecting once again about the dossier, I concluded that all even the most biased person could truthfully say, about me, where Communism and homosexuality were concerned, was that at one time I may have been a fellow traveller.

Then I suddenly realised the horrible political implications of the word!

3

By noon I felt so upset that I had to take a stiff brandy, although I hated the idea of drinking before the evening.

I tried to think clearly, but it was impossible. I was applying for a job which paid £700 a year. My unearned income—about £150 a year—was just about enough to pay my rent. Lately I had been unable to make more out of my pen than another £300 or £400. Even £550 was barely enough to live on, and this had been very much in my thoughts for the past two or three years.

And the T.F.O. position was a plum job. The red-haired man at the interview had asked me whether I would go on writing my books, and when I hesitated, thinking it was a trap, he had volunteered the information that the likelihood of overtime was very slight, and that I would be free after five every day. He was, in fact, recommending the job, trying to rope me in. A job on the B.B.C. or reviewing would have been far more exacting and probably less well paid.

To lose the job now would be something of a disaster. My last novel had just earned its £250 advance and did not look as if it were going into a second impression. I had my notes and an outline for a new novel, but I felt this was a book I ought to take time over. It was, it seemed to me, just the type of book to write in my time left free by the T.F.O. job; I could finish it during the summer holidays. (Four weeks, they had said, or was it six?) In the last few years I had done a lot of hurried work. Now I must change my tempo, and, having carried the idea of this new book for more than ten years in my mind, I wanted to do it justice.

It was true I might have persuaded Hackwood to advance me another £100, or even £200. I had about £100 in the bank and I could count on a further £150 from various royalties during the year. That would have been enough for eight or nine months. I had given considerable thought to the possibility of carrying on on that basis, but had decided against it.

The truth was, perhaps, that I was waiting for a particular type of inspiration, not for the plot and characters, nor for the way of telling the thing, for all that had been more or less decided. A steady job meant that I need not rush into the book before I was really ready.

I was trying to do something new and more or less untried. An experiment, perhaps, but I felt I had to do it. For the past few years there had been a slump on the fiction market, and I was sure it was intimately connected with the crisis in our civilisation rather than the result of economic circumstances. My own belief was that "decadence" played no part in our time; nothing was getting smaller and nothing was withering. In fact, the very cause of the trouble was that everything was getting bigger. We were witnessing the birth of a new world, and the arts had got into a crisis, partly at least because at best they were merely indicating the change, the transformation, instead of interpreting it. I was not worried about the novel as an art-form. I felt it would survive, but I was sure that the type of novel I and my contemporaries had been writing would not last ten years.

The prospect of a job that was decently paid and was not too arduous seemed a godsend. It promised to act as a breathing space, almost a holiday, a period for limbering up. And I would be working alongside other people. That was a good thing. In the last few months I had been feeling desperately lonely for the first time in my life.

What could I do? I asked myself this question over and over again. It would have been risky to go to the T.F.O., even though I had reason to feel that the red-haired interviewer was keen on me, and even if Mrs. Gold could have found out his name for me.

There was, of course, Waterton, who had recommended me. I knew he liked me. But what would happen if I showed him the dossier? He did not know me well enough not to believe some, at least, of the malicious lies. He was, I thought, a man of limited imagination and the "no

15

smoke without fire" principle was one in which he would doubtless believe, even though he might have entertained some doubts about the intelligence or integrity of the department which had compiled the dossier.

Then what about my friends? The four or five I thought of immediately were not really in a position to help me. None of them had the necessary influence or connections in any case.

Then what about the people I knew who had influence, but who were no more than acquaintances? There was Hackwood, my publisher. Ex–Horse Guards, a peer, he had a certain amount of money, a brother in the Admiralty, and his wife was related to Royalty. He was always very helpful about my contracts; he used to take me to lunch at the Garrick, but he was remote in spite of his charm, and vague, and he would in the end most charmingly do nothing to help me.

Those of my contemporaries at Oxford who had succeeded in life, none of whom I knew well, included Tim Gilpin, who was now a junior Minister, John Brinton, already an Air Vice-Marshal, and Alan Lockheed, one of the most promising of the younger set in the Foreign Office. I felt sure all of them would remember me. Lockheed, in fact, would at once ask me to lunch at his club. They would all listen sympathetically, say a "few kind words," and in the end do nothing. Perhaps if I were in a police cell, innocently accused of murder or some other felony, they might at least try to help me. But I was not in a police cell yet.

Fontanet. I thought of him once more, and now no longer brushed aside the idea. His was the only single name mentioned in my dossier, and it was, thinking back on it, odd that there was no further explanation about him. I looked at the folder again. In the margin, right at the foot of the page, I read: *"A friend of E. Fontanet."* Just like that. Was he so well known that no explanation seemed necessary or was the reference an afterthought to be developed later? Fontanet was a diplomat. I knew that he had been employed recently at the Embassy in Washington. He had been for a time on *The Morning Mail*, then on the B.B.C., and he had had some "important job" during the war, but he was certainly not a man of "national importance." A possible explanation was that whoever had scribbled his name on the page, or the people for whom the dossier was compiled, must have known Fontanet well.

Suddenly I felt slightly relieved. Disastrous though everything seemed, I was after all not completely alone. Fontanet seemed to be involved too. And even though Fontanet was not a figure of national importance, he was ten times more important than I.

But. . . . And I began to feel anxious again. How much did they know about Fontanet, and what sort of things? People talked about him; indeed, he had quite a "reputation," and I felt sure that this was deserved. It was, in fact, always a source of surprise to me—and perhaps to other people as well—that Fontanet had never got into trouble, but perhaps I knew too little about the official attitude towards people like him. I had, as a matter of fact, heard rumors about him during the war, and I had reason to believe some of them. Since then I had lost sight of him. Perhaps he had quieted down a little.

I wondered what he was like now. He had always struck me as the "dashing" masculine type of homosexual—for he made no secret of his emotional life. He was hard working, hard drinking, a chain-smoker, a man with tremendous ambition, and as ruthless as they come.

At eighteen or nineteen, fresh from Eton, when I first met him at Oxford, he was already the aggressive careerist and the accomplished poseur, but that was not obvious to me then. Charm you could not deny him, nor intelligence, and in his Oxford days he was certainly good looking, with

17

a clear skin, curly fair hair and an almost un-English round face.

What would happen if I contacted Eric Fontanet and showed him the dossier? I seemed to recall having met him for a few moments about two years earlier, but I had not seen him since. I had heard, however, that he had returned from Washington, because only a week or ten days earlier I remembered someone saying that he had seen Eric in Oxford Street "in a dirty camel-hair overcoat." Maybe he was on leave or waiting for a more important post.

Yes, I suddenly remembered, it was quite two years ago, and I had seen him at a party given by my publisher at Claridge's. He was very charming as he came up to me, but then I was talking to an important writer, whom he did not know personally.

What would happen if I telephoned him? It would depend, I felt, very largely on the mood in which he found himself at the time. Like so many people of his emotional make-up, Fontanet could be overwhelmingly charming or very casual or even very rude. This was a risk I had to take.

But there was less risk than I feared, I reflected a moment later. The fact that his name was on my dossier provided a very good excuse for me to contact him. He might become furious, but not necessarily with me. In fact, he might try to find out who was responsible for my dossier. Now, come to think of it, I vaguely remembered that during the war Fontanet had been engaged on Secret Service work. Or had he merely been trying to give that impression? The chances, however, were that he was the man who could find out something.

A diplomat, especially of the type of Fontanet, was essentially a man who had the necessary contacts. Wasn't his brother . . . ? No, I thought; that must have been somebody else's brother. Fontanet, as far as I remembered, was an only child. I must have been thinking of his father, yes

—and I suddenly recollected the extremely good looking man with silver hair in a wheel chair at some Oxford function. I had no reference book, but I recalled vaguely that his father had been a Court official, a Royal secretary or Comptroller or something, who had to retire on account of illness.

I rang the Foreign Office, and the girl at the switchboard put me through to Fontanet's division, but the man who answered said Fontanet was on leave.

"It's a personal call," I said and told him my name. "I'd like to get in touch with him."

"Why don't you try his flat?" the man said peevishly, "The number is in the telephone directory."

It was, however, not in the book, or, rather, not in my out-of-date copy. But Information gave it to me. It was a Paddington number, so presumably we lived near each other. But his number was engaged.

It was now half-past one. He was unlikely to lunch out, so I could try to ring him later. But in the meantime I felt I ought to eat something—a cheese sandwich with coffee, perhaps.

As I got up to go to the kitchen, I knocked the dossier onto the floor. I bent down and picked the sheets up and tried to put them together. It was then that I noticed that the sheets that followed those concerning me were not all blank. There was one at least that I had not so far noticed. It was marked *"Page 46"* on top and there were only a few lines on it:

"-quent visitor to the Pig'n Whistle and the Decatur."

Not unnaturally, I assumed that the first word was meant to be "frequent."

"Last December he was reported by Sir Evelyn Pollock, the Conservative M.P., for anti-British views.

"In March this year the Concord affair (See p. 37.)

"Dreisverner

"C. A. McIver

"P. Frame"

That was all. I read the handwritten lines again; now, it seemed to me that the first of the three names mentioned was probably *Dreisoerner,* but even so it was as meaningless as the other two, or for that matter the whole page. It was written in ink; a scratchy, ill-tempered handwriting. The page was apparently from somebody else's dossier. If there were some forty-six pages on him, he must have been somebody far more important than I, or more suspect. The names seemed unfamiliar, except for the M.P. and the word "Concord." Perhaps it was meant to be "Concorde," the Place de la Concorde in Paris.

As I looked again at the sheet of paper against the orange-colored back of the folder, I saw the watermark. I picked up the page and held it against the light. Yes, the watermark consisted of the letters S.O. and the Imperial crown above them. I knew that watermark very well from my work during the war. The letters, of course, meant "Stationery Office." So, it was official paper as supplied to Government departments.

After I had eaten and drunk a cup of coffee I tried Fontanet's number again. This time he answered.

"This is James Edmonton," I said.

"Impossible," he roared into the telephone, and there came a peal of Regency laughter. "How did you know I was back? . . . Oh, about a month ago. . . . Then we're neighbors." He seemed obviously in his "port-winey Duke of Wellington" mood.

"Eric," I said after a while, "would you mind very much if I came round to see you?" I added almost without thinking: "If possible, at once. . . ."

"Well. . . ."

"It's something really important. . . . I don't want to discuss it on the telephone. That is. . . ."

"Then don't," he shouted. "It's all right if you can

come straight away. Take a taxi. . . . But I'm expecting someone else later."

There was no need for a taxi. I hurried down the stairs, cut through the side streets and in less than a quarter of an hour I was ringing Fontanet's doorbell in Gloucester Terrace.

It was decidedly not a diplomatic neighborhood, I thought. The architecture, like so much of Paddington's, was good, and the houses large and well-proportioned in the early Victorian classical tradition. There was an unmistakably warm atmosphere around them, exciting; sinister even. But this part of the district, which had been English "Stranded Gentry" before the war, was now largely Irish "Manual Labor." The houses and the miniature gardens at the back were unkempt and a little derelict, and the leprous façades in the warm, leaden, late spring afternoon somehow looked foreign.

2

"HE marshmallow and the flute certainly make a good beginning," Fontanet said with a slow grin, and the telephone rang. He reached over from the armchair to lift the receiver. "Speaking," he said. "How are you? Certainly. It'll save trouble. I'll wait. . . ." He closed his eyes.

I was not annoyed by the interruption which had come almost as soon as I had started to tell him what had happened. Ever since I had spoken to him half an hour earlier I had felt relief, and now I was interested in the details of his place. It was a shabby converted flat on the ground floor of a shabby house; there was a hall, two rooms, and

21

presumably a bathroom and kitchen. We were now in the living room. Over the soiled and worn beige carpet, which must once have been expensive, there stood two large, dilapidated armchairs and a settee with dirty tweed covers, a yellow hickory sideboard and a refectory table covered with books, pamphlets, newspapers, bottles and glasses. There were three table lamps, their parchment shades askew or torn. Against the window a large bookshelf, tottering under the weight of the books, faced us.

The picture over the mantelpiece was a somewhat messy composition of three young wrestlers, with over-sized, orange chests and shoulders, sitting on the beach. It gave the impression that the painter had decided to do a pornographic picture, but had changed his mind halfway. It was a strange room for a man of some taste whose salary alone was surely well over a thousand a year. The only worthwhile thing in it was the large, dusty glass chandelier hanging from the ceiling. It was beautiful, probably English and quite valuable.

Now I suddenly heard the muffled voice from the other end of the telephone in Fontanet's hand. "That's good of you," Fontanet said. "Hundred and three and a half. Very nice. You advise me not to sell yet. All right. I'll leave it to you, then. . . . No; I'm not going away till—well, I suppose August. . . . Probably Italy. . . . Not since the war. And you? . . . I say, that's important. Glad you reminded me. . . . I'd better look it up. Will you hold on? . . ."

Fontanet put the receiver on the table, got up and crossed over to the sideboard. He pulled out a drawer.

I looked at him closely for the first time in two years. He seemed less fat than before, but he somehow still gave the impression of a cherub—an aging cherub, perhaps. But—and this was something that had occurred to me about him earlier—things which once he had got away with when he was young—his untidy appearance, for example, his nicotine-stained and dirty hands, his crumpled collars and torn shirts, his unshaven chin—could no longer be excused now that he was approaching middle age. I dare say if his get-up had been less formal, his untidiness would have mattered less. If, instead of the iron-grey pinstripe suit, cream shirt and silver tie, he had been wearing a turtle-neck pullover, flannel pants and sandals, the contrast would have been less startling. The sun was playing on the back of his head, and I felt that, like the chandelier in his room, his hair was the only impressive and attractive thing about him. It was a rich and luxurious gold—the hair of a young man.

He pushed back the drawer almost angrily, and picked up the receiver again. "Sorry, I can't lay my hands on it. Can you look it up for me? . . . Imperial Tobacco and the Bloemfontein. . . . Thank you. . . . Yes; I'd love to. Today week at the St. James's. One o'clock. Thank you. Good-bye. . . ."

He replaced the receiver and got up. "What will you have? A whisky?"

"Very little, thanks," I said.

"But do go on about the marshmallow."

I waited till he had brought my drink over.

"In the same bag," I said, "there was a kind of dossier with my name on it, and inside the dossier the most malicious and damaging report about me that could possibly have been invented. That I was a Communist, a homosexual and what you will. . . ." The memory of the thing angered me so much that I could not see the reaction to my words on Fontanet's face.

"A lot of screening's going on and a lot of tittle-tattle is being collected," he said. "But do go on."

"The only reason I came to see you," I said somewhat peevishly, because I felt he was a little bored by my story, "is that your name is mentioned."

This time I saw his face. I was deliberately watching it,

in fact. It reflected a mixture of surprise and anger. "In your dossier?" he shouted. He put down his glass.

"In pencil. It says that I am a friend of yours. . . . I didn't consider it an insult. In fact, it was probably the only nice thing they said about me. . . ."

But he had obviously not heard the compliment, if compliment it was. He was now looking at me almost accusingly.

"Are you sure it's my name?"

"Unless there's another E. Fontanet."

"Where is the thing?" he asked.

"In my flat. Why?"

"Where do you live?" he asked instead of replying. Then he must have remembered about our being practically neighbors, because he looked at his watch. "I must see it at once," he said.

"Right," I said. "I'll go home and bring it over to you."

"No," he said, standing up. "I'd better come with you. I have an appointment later." He went to the telephone and rang for a taxi. Then he lighted a new cigarette from the stub of the one he had been smoking without offering me one. I was wondering if his sudden change of mood was anxiety, casualness or just self-dramatisation. I decided it was probably all three.

He quickly scribbled a note on a pad, then tore it off. We heard a taxi draw up outside.

"Let's go," he said.

But as I got up from the armchair the doorbell rang.

Eric looked at his watch. "A friend of mine," he said angrily and hurried into the hall.

"David," I heard his voice a second later. "You're half an hour too early. I must go out at once, but I'll be back in less than an hour. It's absolutely urgent. But come in and wait."

I saw a tall young man of about twenty-five. I wondered later why it was that he immediately gave me the impression that he was an actor, because the younger stage people today usually look to me more like superior shop assistants, junior Service officers or engineers. Perhaps it was his entry: stage-managed public school and a dubious self-confidence, partly supported by his height and the suit he wore, which somehow looked like his only good suit. He was masculine, good looking and, I thought, hard as nails.

"This is James," Eric said. He added as an afterthought: "Edmonton . . . David . . . field." He slurred the first syllable. It could have been "Wingfield."

The young man gave me a little, stagey bow and tried to sum me up on the spot, like a dealer arriving at the last minute at the auction room with the porter already holding up the article and the auctioneer looking for bids. I saw that my name was unfamiliar to him, but why should it not be? I realised that he was the sort of person who, in these particular surroundings, wanted to know two things: was I one of Eric's homosexual friends and was I important? I was flattered that he decided instantly that I was probably important, because he flashed at me the sort of smile which young men on the make keep in readiness for someone who may be of use to them. Eric, I remembered, was always keen on good teeth.

"The drinks are here," Eric said, waving a hand towards the sideboard; "and you'll find some cigarettes there, and the papers. . . . So sorry about this." The way he spoke the last four words, tenderly, charmingly, and the way he put his hand on the young man's shoulder suggested that David must have been Eric's boy friend.

2

Eric seemed less worried after he had read the dossier. I noticed that he was examining my room, as I had recently studied his. The last time he had been to my flat was before the war.

"How did they get hold of my bank account?" I asked. "All those figures on the first page are absolutely correct."

"Oh, don't be a country bumpkin," he snarled, his expression becoming professional. "There's no privacy in England any more. You'll have to forget such old, liberal ideas as bank secrecy. For one thing, the income tax people have their contacts."

"They can't go to your bank," I said.

"Not directly; but they don't need to. There are hundreds of ways and means." He shrugged a shoulder. "But the Inland Revenue are your least worry." He remained silent and for a moment looked at the white mandarin sitting in his pew above my mantelpiece. Eric had once told me it was a masterpiece, but I never believed him.

"You mean M.I.5?" I said.

"How do I know?" he replied, and looked me straight in the eye. "There are no fewer than six secret services in England at present, all busy screening you, following you, steaming your letters open, listening into your telephone calls, looking into your wastepaper basket. If you can get into the racket, you've got one of the best jobs going. You get well paid for very little work. There's no income tax."

"Why?"

"Because, for one thing, the Inland Revenue people mustn't know that a nominal captain or a nominal Civil Servant is earning a much higher salary than the normal six or seven hundred a year plus expenses. And nobody's ever allowed to look into the question of *expenses*. You *can* ask questions in the House, if you defy the Chief Whip, but instead of an answer you get a polite rebuke from the Minister in writing—or verbally in the corridor. There are six departments, and they don't share their information with each other. Half of them are twerps, in any case, who collect tittle-tattle or invent. . . ."

"But somebody surely controls them?" I said.

"Oh, some elderly admiral or young general tries to see

26

that they don't use too much public money, that they don't loaf around too much and that they're not enemy agents."

"But why pick on me?"

"You made an application for a T.F.O. job, so they screened you as a routine matter."

"Are they malicious or just stupid?"

"Neither. They're just drunk with power or afraid of losing it."

"I wonder who the other victim is," I said, more to make conversation than anything else. I did not quite know in what words I could ask Eric to help me. His attitude was not too promising. I suddenly decided to say straight out: "What's your advice?"

"What other victim?" he said, ignoring my question.

"The Mystery Page," I said, looking up. "Oh, you haven't seen it." I got up from the chair, took the file from the mantelpiece, where Fontanet had put it, and opened it. Apparently I must have replaced the inconsequent page where I had originally found it, behind the blank sheets. "Here," I said. "I can't make head nor tail of it. But you can see from the watermark that it's Government paper. . . ."

I went to the cupboard, intending to offer Eric a glass of sherry. I picked up a glass and saw that it was clean. Then, as I turned to ask him if he would like a drink, I was somewhat startled by his extraordinary change of expression. There was an amazed look in his eyes. "Why didn't you show me this first?" he asked, as if accusing me of some nasty betrayal.

"What do you mean?" I said. I must have looked stupid with the bottle and glass in my hand. His glare, his tone of voice, the question itself, took me by surprise. "I forgot all about it," I heard myself saying weakly. "I just put it back where I found it, at the end. It doesn't refer to me. But why . . . ?"

27

"Oh, it doesn't matter," he said after a time, graciously, forgiving me, the way he might have let off a manservant at his club. These sudden changes of mood were so typical of him. He cast a brief glance at the bottle in my hand. "Have you got any brandy?"

"I think I may have a little," I said. I decided I might as well bring out the half-bottle of Martell from the top shelf of the linen cupboard in my bedroom, where I normally hid spirits from the charwoman. It was only when I returned to the room that I began to wonder why the Mystery Page could possibly have upset him.

"Do you know the man?" I said, handing him a glass of brandy which he drank in one gulp.

"No," he said. He took a fresh cigarette from his pack and lit it. I saw that his hands were trembling. Eric was a chain-smoker.

"Those names," I said, but he did not seem to hear. The drink apparently had had a strange effect on him. I seemed to remember from the old days that he reacted oddly to drink. He no longer looked angry, but rather instead absent-minded.

"The man must have an extensive dossier," I went on, "if this is Page 46. . . ."

"Oh, shut up," he said, and it was then I noticed how pale he was; the veins in his trembling right hand stood out like whipcords.

"Look," I said, "there's no connection between us, and there's no reason why your name should appear at all in my dossier. The whole thing's a bundle of lies, in any case. All we've got to do is to prove it is. Under normal circumstances, that would be impossible, but we actually have the dossier, and we can produce it to refute its own claims." This, I thought, was the best line to get Eric's co-operation.

"What good will that do?" he said with his eyes closed.

"Look. What I'd like you to do is to help me trace the

man who lost the dossier, or the man who wrote it; it's probably the same person in any case. You've got sufficient influence to find out. Then, if we find the man, we can discover why your name was pencilled in," I added as an inducement.

He opened his eyes and stared at me. "What exactly will you do if you find him?" he said, but I was too carried away by my emotions to watch the expression on his face.

"Oh, I'll offer to supply him with the correct information, if he must have a dossier about me. But, seriously, I'd like to ask him a few questions. How he came to write what he did about me, and so on."

"You're being childish."

"I often am. But why in this particular instance?"

"Because you don't know their power."

"You mean M.I.5?"

"I don't know," he almost screamed.

"For God's sake, Eric," I said. "I admit I've been selfish considering myself first, but my position . . ."

"Now look," he interrupted, dropping his cigarette ash on the carpet. I saw that he was now trying to be patient with me. "I'll do what I can. But don't do anything till you hear from me. How many people have you told about this?"

"None. I only found the thing this morning." He got up. I said: "D'you want to take the dossier with you?"

He hesitated for a brief moment. "No," he said, "but I strongly advise you to hide it in some safe place in your own interest."

"Where?"

"Really, James, do I have to wet-nurse you?" He shook his head. "Certainly not at your bank, in any case. D'you belong to a club with a safe deposit or a locker? . . . The cloakroom at Victoria Station . . . anywhere."

The cloakroom at Victoria Station! It was now amusement I felt instead of anger or surprise. So his whole attitude was one big act. But on reflection, was it perhaps that he was trying to hide a genuine concern or embarrassment behind a dramatic pose? I did not remember him well enough to be certain, but I seemed to recall that this was one of his parts: the Phillips Oppenheim part. There were, of course, many others.

The important thing, however, was that he had promised to do something, and, unreliable though he might be, I fancied that this time he would keep to his word.

"Where's your telephone?" he asked.

"If it's a taxi you want, it's much quicker to walk to the rank. I'll come with you."

As we got out into the street, I felt I had to speak. "You're doing me a great favor," I said. "You must let me pay you back later in some form or another. I mean it, Eric."

He practically stopped. He looked at me as if surprised. For a second he could apparently find no words. Then suddenly he said: "That's nice of you, James."

His voice was warm and intimate. I hardly recognised it.

3

It was in my second year at Oxford that I first met Eric Fontanet. He was then a freshman, but there was nothing of the first-year student about him. I had seen him once or twice, at the O.U.D.S., at the Union, walking with friends in the High, at the Randolph; fair, good looking, independent, slightly older than his years. Grey Dustwick, who already at nineteen sounded like the personal column he was later to write for the *Standard* before he got killed, called Eric the most promising person of his year. He had had a distinguished career at Eton, was in "Pop" and was now reading history. "He'll probably be asked to stay on as a tutor," Grey said. "But he's not likely to be satisfied with that for long. I'm sure he's got a brilliant future before him." Later, I heard the same thing from a research fellow at All Souls', in longer sentences, weightier words and a more pompous tone.

Then one day, as I was browsing through books at Blackwell's, Fontanet approached me with casualness which was then new and attractive to me. "I must congratulate you on your story in *Isis*," he said in his slow voice. "I wanted to write to you, but I knew I'd bump into you one day."

It gave me a marvellous feeling that someone of whom I had heard so much should have come up to me like that and said flattering things about my writing. And that he should have known who I was. I thought nobody knew me at Oxford outside about two dozen undergraduates and a couple of tutors.

"One of the things I meant to say in my letter," he went on, looking at me with a very friendly expression, "was that I wanted to see some more of your work. I hope I shall. Are you busy now? Will you come and have tea with me?"

We went to his room at Merton and he talked a great deal about my story. "I presume," he said, "that you'll later expand it into a novel," and I looked up, for that indeed had been my intention.

"You write about India as if Kipling had never written a word about it. It's a pity he did, of course." He smiled for a second. "Your completely fresh outlook struck me as remarkable. . . ."

Then he changed the subject temporarily and talked about literature in general, about Oxford and art and politics. He was about a year younger than me, but I was swept off my feet by his amazing maturity and worldliness. The modern Alcibiades, I reflected later, so rare in our age of specialisation. A perfect balance between the philosopher and the man of the world; charming, good look-ing with an effortless intellectual superiority. Probably a good athlete too.

I later sent him my other story—the first that ever got published—and a couple of manuscripts, and his enthu-siasm was something for which I had never dared to hope. It must have been at our fourth or fifth meeting that I told him that I planned to use the Christmas vacation to work on my first novel, *Bombay Duck,* based on the story he liked, and that I wanted to dedicate it to him.

One gloomy January afternoon he embarrassed me by suddenly appearing unannounced at my parents' flat in London. At that time we lived at Nevern Square in a maisonette that filled me with depression. When I was around twenty, although I loved my parents, I was at times ashamed of them, not perhaps entirely without justifica-tion.

But Eric seemed not to notice the helplessness, the self-pity, the undertones of hysteria, the unnecessary shabbi-ness of my home atmosphere, from which Oxford was a marvellous refuge. His geniality, worldliness and charm hypnotised my mother, and she at once lost her irritating and agonising shyness of strangers.

"Your mother's attractive," Eric said after tea and the statement was relieving because it seemed convincing. Then, to my further surprise—I had hardly got over the shock of his unexpected visit—Eric proposed taking me in his car to attend a Communist meeting at Dalston.

"You probably know," he explained in the most casual manner as we came to the Brompton Road, "that I'm a Communist."

I didn't know, and the revelation was a shock, but a pleasant one. This was a further example of his inde-pendence and daring. Fontanet seemed the type of youth who got away with things because of his personality, charm, good looks. At that time it was not envy I felt for him, but admiration.

Until I met Eric I knew surprisingly little about Communism, apart from my father's semi-hysterical opposition, which I already suspected was a cover for his confusion. I realise now that my father hated Communism for the wrong reasons. At Oxford, until then, I had known few Communists: the fashion, the epidemic of Communism, came a year later.

The contrast between Eric's appearance and personality and Communism was a further source of fascination. I already guessed, in spite of my ignorance, that Communism was a religion, and Eric was very worldly. The one single thing that might have given a tiny hint was that, though expensively dressed, he was not smart. But even that was probably without significance. The Age of Elegance, young bucks and dandies in fancy evening coats attending champagne parties, was over and was little more than a legend by the time my generation got to Oxford. The intellectual hedonist still lingered on, but only just. The Age of Purposefulness, the period of the Young Man on the Make, was already drawing near.

4

Eric began to show me around. "You say you've never met Gallen," he said one day, and he wetted his lower lip. "You ought to. He thinks very highly of you."

I became very excited. C. C. Gallen, the novelist, was then at the height of his fame and, like so many young writers, I admired his style and—in my understandable bitterness—his philosophy and attitude to life. Eric said he had sent my stories to him, and that he was expecting us at his flat the following afternoon.

Gallen divided his year equally between his villa in the

Pyrenees, his house in Paris and his Edwardian bachelor's chambers in Jermyn Street. He was trying to be nice to me, but my first sight of him gave me a shock all the same. A tiny man with dyed hair and moustache, close-set eyes and a lecherous smile, he talked at a great length about my stories, asked me about my plans for the future and said I must come to see him again soon.

A few weeks later Eric took me to Arthur Beaufort's house in Brompton Square. He was what was called a man of influence in literary circles. A tall, thin, sickly-looking man, Beaufort had been secretary to a Liberal Prime Minister, and towards the end of the First War had been attached to the Embassy in Paris; he had known Proust and Anatole France. Now and again he edited somebody's letters, translated a French book or organised an exhibition of "Narrative Pictures of the Eighteenth Century." He was a talented and successful literary dilettante with faint Socialist leanings. He had inherited money from a rich wife who had died two years after their marriage.

I thought that I had made a good impression on Beaufort, as I had on Gallen; but both men made me uneasy. There was something sinister about them in spite of their charm, wisdom and culture, and I felt somehow I was too young to be fascinated by it all, and too sensitive to laugh at their desperate efforts to look youthful. I had already had a hint from Grey Dustwick that Eric was "wicked," but I was desperately slow and inexperienced. The revelation came weeks later.

"It was very obvious from your story," Eric confided one Sunday morning in my room, and I felt devastated by multiple emotions of which embarrassment was the strongest. "Charlie Gallen said the same."

Perhaps Eric saw my embarrassment, perhaps not, but he dropped the subject. But a few days later he brought it up again. "You probably sensed it about me the way I sensed it about you. After all, you're an artist."

34

This was an open confession and it left me even more limp. In fact, it plunged me into a crisis. I was lonely and timid and poor. I had no friends and, in the circumstances, Eric was a godsend. He had singled me out, given me his friendship, introduced me to important people. He not only took an interest in my writing, but became my builder-up, a kind of amateur—but extremely efficient—publicity agent. I also felt that his interest in me was genuine. However, I was no longer happy about my association with him, and I was worried about where it might lead. I felt caddish and mean, but after a series of sleepless nights I decided I must be honest and tell him that our friendship must end.

As it turned out, however, it was not actually necessary for me to say anything. Eric must have sensed what was in my mind because his attitude towards me gradually changed, and although we always remained on good terms, he more or less dropped me.

Years later I had the feeling that my incapacity fully to return his sentiments had had little to do with the fact that, after a time, he left me and transferred his interests to someone else. The process, for one thing, was gradual and by that time—my third year at Oxford—I was getting on quite well with the leftish intellectual circles, and one or two of my stories were coming out in *Outlook* and the *London Mercury*.

The man who supplanted me in Eric's interest was Alan Lockheed. Even then I was sufficiently objective to realise that Alan was a more interesting and important person than I, although it still filled me with some bitterness to think that I had been cut off from access to Eric's useful circle, however unpleasant I found them. Alan was the son of a Conservative Cabinet minister, who, had he not died suddenly and fairly young, would have been in line for highest executive office. James Lockheed, the grandson of a Scottish crofter, was universally respected—even by

35

high Tories and ardent Socialists. He was a very liberal Conservative who had married into a wealthy industrial family.

After I left Oxford, I got on to the staff of *Outlook,* first as a reviewer, then as an editorial assistant, and when Rudge took over I went for a year to Paris as their correspondent. I saw Eric from time to time in the cafés of Montparnasse and St. Germain; then I heard that he had visited Russia. Later he got on to an evening newspaper. His articles were a disappointment. They conveyed nothing of his interesting personality and little of his occasional conversational brilliance. I heard later that he had wanted to become a history don at his former Oxford college, but there was some disagreement or scandal. Then I lost track of him for some time, only to learn that he had a fairly important job on the B.B.C.

This was during the time of the Spanish War. To me, and indeed to most people who had known him earlier, it seemed that Eric's great promise had somehow not been fulfilled. Perhaps it was that we had overestimated him, or that, like so many people who had talents in more than one direction, he could not find his true métier. Or was it his emotional life that had become a stumbling block? That was possible. It was once easy for the homosexual to climb to the top in almost any sphere—as a politician, a diplomat, a soldier, even a scientist. But those days are over, and today it is becoming increasingly more difficult for him to conquer or shine in any field except the artistic —literature, painting, music, the stage; and Eric had no artistic talent, whatever he may have thought.

During the war, while I was in the Air Force, I heard that Eric had a very important position in one of the Service ministries; a liaison job. Then I saw him once or twice when I worked for the M.O.I., and noticed the change in him. He was unconventional in his appearance, almost shabby, but full of self-importance. For a long time

I had regarded him as a careerist. He had always exploited his family and school connections, not to speak of his influential friends, but before the war this had been less obvious, or else the opportunities had been fewer. Now, however, he gave the impression of ruthlessness. Then one day, towards the end of the war, he suddenly landed a wonderful job in the Foreign Office. How he managed this was never made clear, but it was rumored that Arthur Beaufort had more than a little to do with it.

"They talk about no favoritism," my informant said. "Should any candidate try to approach a member of the Selection Board he will be immediately disqualified"— and he laughed bitterly. "All that Beaufort had to do was to go up and talk to someone at his club. And once you're in the Foreign Office, you stay in."

I had no idea how true all this was, but a couple of years after the war I learnt that Eric had been taken on the permanent staff of the Foreign Office.

After that I hardly saw him. Following my divorce, I was isolated from most of the people I had known before or during the war. My second novel was a bestseller, but the third and the fourth were comparative failures.

5

There was no doubt, I thought while having dinner at a little Italian café in Westbourne Grove, that Eric's great anxiety was genuine, but dramatised and intensified, and that it was connected with some impropriety. In common with other people, I had heard a number of stories about Eric since he had been in the Foreign Office; he had not been too discreet and was even reputed only narrowly to have avoided a scandal. It was true that things had changed a good deal in England since the war, and the old rigorous standards of conduct no longer seemed to operate, but Eric, I felt, must certainly have caused some comment. For a diplomat to live in a sordid flat in a doubtful neighborhood, to look shabby, to drink heavily, to frequent pubs which were watched by the police, to be grossly indiscreet, was enough to arouse comment even in these "democratic" or apathetic days. Nevertheless, Eric, I had always felt, was the sort of person who could get away with things. He was important enough for a scandal in his case to be hushed up; or, to be more exact, his patrons and protectors were important, and that was what mattered.

"Importance," I thought bitterly, was a very relative matter. Real power now was not in the hands of those with whom the average citizen usually associated it. The few well-known people who were prosecuted nowadays were not really important, although the action against them was first-rate window-dressing for the man in the street, who thought them important and was thereby persuaded that even people in "high places" are not invulnerable.

The rain started again when I left the café, so I decided to go into the little repertory cinema next door. I had missed the film they were showing when it first came out, and had long wanted to see it. It was the screen version of a novel I had read, and the scenario was written by a man I knew.

After the first half-hour or so I began to feel that the two and threepence I had paid for my seat was wasted. The man had thrown away two really good dramatic scenes, and what he himself had put in was conventional and uninteresting. The dialogue was stilted and bookish. Towards the end I could not restrain my feelings that not only could I have made a better job of it, but that I had already *done* so in the past.

As I hurried home I suddenly felt a desire to go back to my novel. This was important, since it indicated to me that I was no longer as worried about my discovery of the dossier as I had been. Now that Eric was helping me, whether he wanted to or not, my situation was not as desperate as I had at first thought. If I got the job, I could always slow down on my writing, but in any case I had a fortnight or a month ahead of me during which time I could work uninterruptedly. And I could make a number of important notes. I took the book on canonical law, which I had forgotten to return to the Library, and began to search for references.

3

AS I was drying myself in the bathroom the following day I thought it was, in a way, a pity that the sun was shining so brightly, because I had decided to spend most of the day indoors, rereading my notes and trying to get some blue-printing done if possible.

I had found one or two useful references in the book I had looked at the previous day, and I felt that at a later stage I should discuss them with Father Jablonsky. He was a youngish American, a Catholic priest, who was exceptionally broad-minded towards Protestants. He knew, I thought, that a religious compromise was foolish, because the likelihood was that both sides would sacrifice what was most valuable in their beliefs. His idea was more of a passionate fusion of faith from which a new hope might emerge. As I went into the kitchen to put on the kettle, I decided the best idea was to ask him to dinner—probably at a quiet Soho restaurant that was not too expensive. It was then that my front doorbell rang.

It was just around eight-thirty, so it was probably the milkman with the bill I had not paid the previous week.

I went to the bedroom, looked for some money in my trouser pocket and put on my dressing-gown.

But it was Eric who was standing outside. My surprise was so great that all I could say was "Good morning." Then I stood aside and let him in. "I'll give you breakfast," I said.

"I've already had it," he said, but by then we were already in the living room and I could see in the bright light of the morning that his face was unshaven and that presumably he had not slept much during the night.

He said nothing, and I noticed a heavy sullenness about him which all of a sudden made me feel angry. In all probability he had got drunk instead of trying to find out about the dossier for me. "You don't mind a cup of coffee?" I said. "It's practically ready." I took my pack of cigarettes from the mantelpiece and led him to the kitchen.

He followed me without a word and his silence gave me another thought, which suddenly changed my near-annoyance to near-anxiety. The unexpected call at such an early hour was perhaps not just a piece of unconventionality on Eric's part. And the thought flashed through my mind that while in all probability he was dramatising things, his visit might nevertheless have been provoked by something unpleasant or frightening.

"Well now," I said, offering him a cigarette from the pack, "what is it?"

"What?" he snapped with something like an annoyed reprimand in his voice. It was as if I had woken him up from his sleep. He did not notice the open pack of cigarettes in my hand.

"What did you find out?" I said. I must be calm and patient, I thought.

"Oh," he said and looked away from me, his eyes narrow, his forehead taut. There was a longish pause. ". . . One of the Service departments . . ." He broke off abruptly. His voice sounded sullen, reluctant, secretive.

"Have you been in touch?" I heard myself saying. It was a stupid question to ask, but I had not seen Eric in this sort of state for some time, and I had forgotten how best to deal with him in such a mood.

I heard him say an impatient "Yes," but that seemed to be a reasonable answer to an unnecessary question, and he said no more. The electric kettle began to simmer.

"All right," I said. "I won't ask you whom you contacted." This was probably my best line. I turned away from him and began to lay the kitchen table. Sooner or later he would talk, but first it was important for him to work up the "suspense element." Very important. Having given him a cue, I for my part must not do or say anything further now, apart from maintaining "tense interest." But, I felt, he *had* discovered something. I had been so right in thinking he would try to help me, because he seemed himself to be involved in some way. The only surprising thing was that he had been so prompt about it; but, of course, I remembered he was on leave from the Foreign Office.

He spoke now and his voice sounded remote: "In any case, you've nothing to fear. You'll either get the job straight away or not." Then his voice assumed the tone of the friendly adviser. "If you don't you can always try to blackmail them with the dossier."

"How?" I said, a coffee cup in my hand. So, he apparently could not or would not do anything to help me. He was not even acting; he was hamming. All he had said was bogus. I doubted whether he had contacted anybody; he was probably inventing the whole thing.

"By threatening to have questions asked in Parliament, or that you'll persuade a newspaper to print the story," he said.

"Threatening whom?" I felt my voice was rather sharp.

"You'll see. One day, soon, they'll come here to ask for the dossier. You've hidden it, of course?"

I decided not to tell him I had not. I said, "And if they don't come for it?"

"Then you must tell someone in authority about it. Your former C.O. in the Air Force, your M.P. Anybody who knows you. I mean, you have your friends. But don't forget to have photostatic copies made of the sheets, and hold on to the original, whatever you do. . . ."

He came to a stop. I looked at him. His expression seemed calm, and it was difficult for me to keep back my bitterness. "You mean you can't help me any other way?"

"What other way?" he said slowly, as if pretending to be stupid.

"By telling them it was a brutal, stupid mistake. That an innocent man is being falsely and maliciously accused —I mean, you yourself told me that they were incompetent . . . drunk with power. . . ." I thought angrily how typical it was of Eric to wash his hands of me with a piece of "good advice." It was just on the tip of my tongue to say, "What about you?"

"Sorry," Eric said as if reading my thoughts. "I can't help you. I haven't the contacts. I must leave the country at once. . . ."

Had I not already placed the cup on the table, I might have dropped it. "You?"

I searched his face, but all I detected was a suggestion of sadness around his lower lip and uncertainty about his eyes.

"Yes," he said, then he came a little nearer and the kettle began to buzz. I had no time to reflect further.

"James," he said. It was strange to hear him address me once again in the same friendly tone he had used twenty years earlier, and now the voice was deeper and quite uncertain. I saw him feeling in his inside pocket. "I'd like to ask you a favor. A very small thing, but it's important. Could you please book two return tickets for me to Paris? Any class for tonight if possible. There's a train at eight from Victoria. If they're all taken," he said, and I saw a white envelope in his hand, "tomorrow will do. Here's the money." He put the envelope on the kitchen table.

". . . Yes, of course," I said, after what might have seemed to him a long pause. Then I repeated, "Yes, of course," as if I did not remember having said that before. My bitter mood had evaporated with such dramatic suddenness that I found it hard to hide the fact that it had now changed into a fresh emotion.

"I've no right to ask any questions," I heard myself say, and I also seemed to hear how untrue and insincere I sounded. "Is it as serious as all that?"

There was a pause, and like lightning I switched off the kettle, anxious not to miss even a word.

"It may be," he said to my back. "I can't take a chance."

"I wish I could help you a little more," I said. I was half-facing him now. How could I ask him, what could I say to induce him to tell me, what it was all about? Curiosity was gnawing like teeth at my heart. But I spoke automatically, exuberantly, knowingly: "Is it boys?" I said.

"Of course," he said, slowly, but with hardly any hesitation.

"It's none of my business," I said in the generosity of my triumph. Then I became bold. "Are you leaving with What's-his-name?"

"David?"

I could not avoid looking at him closely. I always hate myself for it, but curiosity is in my nature, and my profession is a feeble and secondary excuse for it. His eyes gave the answer before he could speak:

"For God's sake, avoid him. He's most dangerous." He almost shouted the words, then he suddenly began to whisper. "A police spy. I'm sure he's the cause of all the trouble. . . ."

"You mean, my dossier . . . ?"

He brushed aside my question. His expression suggested "Who cares about *your* bloody dossier?" but what he said was: "There's no need for you to worry. My name got in to your dossier by mistake. You're completely in the clear. I'll tell you about it later."

"You mean you're coming back," I said, "when the trouble's over?"

"Oh, of course." His face was impatient again. "Will you be in by half-past one?"

2

I rang up Cook's after breakfast. I was feeling as elated as seldom since my childhood. Adventure, even the unusual and unexpected, was so rare in the life of people like me, who had apparently been reduced by Fate to be always spectators. Once in a blue moon, I suppose, people of my type are called on to play a small part in the drama of life; the secretary who takes the fatal telephone message, the manservant who overhears the quarrel. But the sense of being left out of things is probably far worse for the writer, because he usually has such a vivid conception as to what "things" are and what he is missing.

I was told that all seats on the Continental trains were booked for the next two days, but there was a cancellation of two separate seats that night—one first-class—and would I pick them up at once?

"It's a miracle," the man said, because even though it was only May, people seemed to have been going abroad earlier than ever, possibly because the currency allowance had just been increased. "Of course, you can always take the ordinary train at six o'clock, but you'll have to queue up."

From Cook's I went to a stationer in Oxford Street, bought a large manila envelope and placed the orange folder inside. Then I took the bus to High Holborn. I

44

decided it was best to take the dossier to my solicitor, but I did not like the idea of photostatic copies—they cost money, for one thing. Now I no longer felt that Eric had been play-acting. Perhaps it was angry exasperation with me that had made him suggest the cloakroom at Victoria; a bitter, sarcastic joke. The canvas bag with the marshmallow and flute inside could remain in my flat, in case anybody ever claimed them, but the dossier had to be safeguarded.

As I got off the bus I decided to tell Prentice that there were family letters in the envelope.

But he was away and the young clerk wished to prove to me that he knew all the formalities. He put enormous seals on the envelope, made me sign my name four times under them and typed out a long receipt. I went to the Oxford Street Corner House and had an early lunch, before the crowds arrived.

3

It was towards seven in the evening now, and I found I could work no longer. Eric had arrived soon after I returned home. He looked relieved when I told him I had the tickets; he took them, patted me on the shoulder and left at once. I made myself a cup of strong coffee, went to the living room and took up my notes. The sense of elation I had felt in the morning was gone and I clenched my teeth mentally as I prepared to work. The disinclination to sit down and concentrate on the book was now almost overpowering, but I thought here was an opportunity to practise self-discipline. My trouble—I felt—was really laziness masquerading under various disguises, some impressive, others mere nonsense. That was the real cause of my failure. How often had I told myself that when I did take a chance, I nearly always succeeded?

Now, when the desire to reflect about the happenings

of the past twenty-four hours was so strong, here was a really splendid opportunity for self-discipline. I could think about the dossier in the evening after dinner. That would be much cheaper than the cinema and more satisfying. Now I must work.

I read the notes I had recently made and tried to think of the ideas I had wanted to put down that morning, when Eric had interrupted me. I closed the window and soon found myself sweating, but I knew that something was coming. I shut my eyes and began to concentrate on the second half of the book. This was, I remembered, a good idea; I had done it with my last book. First plan the line of action in the second half, and work out approximately how many words it could yield. Then adapt the first half to it. That way I may have less to cut later on.

Towards six I had a kind of blue-print of the plot provisionally divided into chapters. There were eleven of them. That meant roughly forty-five or fifty thousand words; all clear, relevant matter. Then I hurriedly picked up another sheet of paper and began to jot down an idea I had for a dialogue between Norman and the trainer of a weight-lifting club. It was something I had thought of early that morning, and which I wanted to discuss with Father Jablonsky.

But after I began jotting it down in my own shorthand, I decided to write it in full. It was stilted, "dummy dialogue," of course, for my own private use. It would have to be translated into colloquialism and perhaps a few author's comments inserted. In the past I had used little of these and tried to convey the particular character's emotions by the arrangement of the words.

This dialogue took up some four pages, roughly eleven hundred words or so. I read what I had just written. It was quite promising, but the really important thing was that I had actually recorded it. The idea was on paper, and I was unlikely to forget it now. It could always be changed or rewritten later. I made a note in the margin, then I began to feel genuine exhaustion.

It was seven o'clock. I opened the window and saw a pink and smoky sun setting towards Kensal Green. In about an hour's time Eric and his friend would be leaving England.

The same thought struck me again, but by that time the effect of the mental anaesthetic which I had administered to myself when Eric dashed away had completely worn off. They would be leaving England . . . and I was assisting two men to escape from the law.

This was the first time I had thought about that frightening cliché, but I immediately felt it was nonsense. In the first place, it was not in the least likely that anybody would ever find out that it was I who had booked the tickets, and even if he did, my alibi, my explanation, was perfect. Eric was someone I had known for twenty years. He had dropped in that morning and asked me to do him a favor. We were practically neighbors, and I was passing Cook's that morning, in any case. . . . "But why are you asking me this?" I was already rehearsing the scene. "You're not suggesting that a prominent British diplomat is wanted by the police, are you? I think I'd like to see your identity card. . . . Thank you. . . . Well, Inspector, in that case I must believe your story, but—now this is strictly between ourselves—I think there must have been a slip-up. . . . Oh, not on your part, Inspector." After that I would look at my watch and say with the friendliness of a busy author, "If there's any way I can help you, do call again. But please ring up before. . . ."

These were then the lines of my defence, if it came to that, but the chances were that it would not. If the police let Eric slip through their fingers, they would hush the thing up, especially considering the nature of the charge.

But what was the real "nature" of the charge? The police suspected him, and the young man, David, was a police spy, Eric had told me. Perhaps he had been checking up on Eric. This was, of course, a new departure, to put up a decoy pretending to be an invert. Or perhaps it was no pretence.

Some years ago there was a comment in a left-wing political weekly that the police employed *agents provocateurs* at certain places in the West End, actually trying to involve people in a charge of importuning. There was even the rather amusing, if pathetic, case of the clergyman at a railway station who had mistakenly accosted a plain-clothes policeman.

If this was true—and lately one had come to believe strange things about the authorities in general—it was as loathsome a policy as the technique of the yellow Press which Sunday after Sunday dished up sexual filth, because the editors knew that filth sold, but in order to cover themselves up and plead justification to dabble in filth, they expressed hypocritical shock and insisted on punishment and a clean-up of the vice which was their news material. They were safe, knowing full well it could not be cleared up.

I put on my jacket and decided to go out. After work, I usually took a stroll in Kensington Gardens or walked through Westbourne Grove, which towards the week-end quite often gave the impression of a street in a mythical foreign town: nondescript northern architecture and southern faces and gestures, gaudy but vital shops and a sweet pulsation of life.

I was not hungry and I decided to walk in the Park, then to eat at a little place at Marble Arch. But as I reached the end of Queensway I suddenly knew I had no real intention of entering the Park. Thinking about this later, I did not find my change of decision strange. The strangeness was rather in the fact that I had not thought of it before. But this reflection came only when I was already on the bus on my way to Victoria to see who Eric's fellow traveller was.

It was, in a way, so like me to think of this only at the last moment. I had not pressed Eric to tell me who the other person was, partly out of a reluctant sense of discretion and partly because his decision to leave had taken me so by surprise.

It was obvious that whoever was leaving with him might perhaps provide further clues as to the cause of the departure. I wondered whether it might be someone under age, which would explain the suddenness of his leaving. But I had never heard such a suggestion about Eric, and what little I knew about him led me to doubt this. Who was it then who got him in trouble so serious that he was forced to leave England? I knew Eric was not very selective in his friendships. I had seen him in the company of many different types of people, of all shapes and sizes. There were two wartime stories about him: one that he had beaten up a shop assistant who had tried to blackmail him, the other that he had himself been beaten up by a Canadian soldier. Eric belonged to the most unfortunate group of inverts, who could never settle down, but who were on the hunt all the time, basically because they were unable to love anybody but themselves.

As I changed at Marble Arch I decided to hide myself from the two men; if, however, they saw me, I would say I had come to see them off. There was an element of danger in this, of course, because if Eric were detained—and this was possible—I might get into trouble. "Something," in fact, told me it was unwise to go. But, I thought, I was involved in any case, the element of danger acted as an additional inducement, and the defence I had concocted before leaving my flat still seemed good to me.

I did not have to wait for the second bus, and it travelled fast, during the brief lull between two rush-hours. It took less than ten minutes to get to Victoria and the train was not yet in. Gramophone music—bits of a Sousa waltz —came over the loudspeakers as I walked slowly through that shabby, gaudy, intimate, oversized hothouse. There was a tiny knot of early passengers in front of the Continental gate, a group of earnest young men in blazers, busy giving themselves the airs of expensive schools; not too successfully. Then a rugger team arrived with a prewar boisterousness. Eric was nowhere.

I walked away towards the booking office. Then I became conscious of a youngish man, whom I had seen when I came in and who was pretending too hard to be a bona fide traveller waiting for a train. A detective, I instinctively wondered? But I changed my mind equally fast. No; the post-war plain-clothesman looked very different from his predecessors, but no policeman could possibly look quite so emaciated or have such a starved intensity. Nor would he dress with that anxious simplicity. This was a man whose own activities were more likely to attract the attention of the station detective.

I went to the buffet and had a sandwich and a cup of tea. I took my time and did not come out until a quarter to eight. The train was in and I bought a platform ticket and went through the gate. It was a long train and I walked as far as the end, then slowly back, looking into each compartment, at first a little nervously, then, as my impatience grew, with open curiosity. Soon I reached the last few coaches. The men were not there. Was it possible that I had missed them somewhere near the engine? A man on the run is not anxious to call attention to himself by arriving at the last moment.

Almost angrily I looked into the remaining coaches and compartments, and I had the strong impulse to push aside a fat man who was blocking my view. They were, however, not behind him.

But people were still coming through the barrier; a few time-snobs who refused on principle to arrive before 7:55, which was the time now, and a few breathless mothers with oversized daughters. There were a couple of clergymen behind the ticket collector, so I decided to take up my stand beside the railings, watching the gate. But there was no sign of Eric and his fellow passenger, and I felt sure I had missed them; they must have been in the front part of the train, which I had examined less carefully. Of course, it was possible they were not taking this train, after all. Or. . . . Well, in any case I could telephone Eric's flat—naturally, not from my place, but from one of the public telephones at the station. I looked at the clock. It was two minutes to eight and I heard a few doors being slammed with authoritative finality. I might as well stay on till the bitter end.

I was now sure I had missed them; that they must have arrived early and taken their seats in one of the front coaches. But the thought suddenly came to me that most of these seats were unreserved, and I had bought reserved seats. . . . I wished I could have remembered the numbers. I was a fool not to have made a note of them; I could then have walked in leisurely comfort to the exact place without all this idiotic searching. A bloody fool, I thought; that's what I was, and I saw a man hurrying towards the gate in an ugly, but brand new, white mackintosh, a cheap fibre suitcase in hand; a man I knew. But it was only when he came to the gate that my heart missed a beat, because I saw that Eric was behind him; and as they passed through the barrier Eric had the tickets in his hand.

They were together. I no longer cared if they saw me or not—in fact, I wanted to run towards them, to speak to them, only I was too limp. For the first time in my life I felt that the old saying about knocking someone down with a feather was no grotesque, unconscious verbal surrealism. The man in the white mackintosh was Alan Lockheed.

4

$\mathcal{S}$OME moments you remember all your life: the grit in the air, the smoke in the lungs, the low-toned whirl of the trolleys, the posters that advertise Bourne-mouth and Bovril, the shabby warmth and familiarity of a railway station. You remember the way your heart stops and the way you suddenly become deaf and blind. . . .

When I came to myself the train was already gathering speed, but I still stood there at the end of the platfrom by the entrance gate like a child gazing in the wake of a shooting star which he alone has seen.

I know that after a time I walked home. I presume I went by way of Grosvenor Place and cut through the Park, but I did not remember, nor did I remember my thoughts; the excitement was too much and too sudden. This had surely been the greatest surprise of my life.

It was only when I reached Bayswater that I tried to sort out my thoughts, and even then it was difficult. I still did not know where to begin, what was most important, most significant, most shattering. The desire to sort things out was typical, I suppose, of a writer. The rest of human-ity, which includes many people with far tidier minds than mine, is not as a rule interested in this particular pursuit. People guess, I think correctly, that a story has neither beginning nor end and that the writer fancifully picks out one given moment or episode with which to open, and another with which to close.

It was, I remembered, a melancholy afternoon, late in October—melancholy, but beautiful with sharp air to brace the senses. In the college gardens they were burning the dry leaves and the grey warm smoke joined the cold mists of the Cherwell, the Isis and the Thames. This was to be my last year at Oxford, I thought again and again, and a bell chimed somewhere at Merton or Balliol.

As I walked across Wellington Square on my way to my rooms, I suddenly saw the gowned figure of Eric Fontanet against the magic curtain of the mists.

"James," he announced, "I've just met someone from your college. His name's Alan Lockheed."

"I think," I said, "he actually has my old rooms or the ones next door. . . ."

"A really first-class brain and only eighteen." Eric's tone sounded wistful and middle-aged, but enthusiastic. "You must meet him."

I did. It was at dinner with Eric at the Clarendon, and we talked of Hitler, who had recently risen to full power. Lockheed said that Hitler's success may have looked like a last desperate attempt to put the clock back and save capitalism, but it was far more likely that his "counter-revolution" was an alternative to Lenin's revolution and a definite veering away from capitalism.

Just as in Eric's case a year earlier, I was impressed by Lockheed's maturity. He had none of Eric's verbal fireworks, nor his restless brilliance, but a far deeper seriousness and wisdom. My first impression was that Lockheed had the mentality of a very mature adult and an almost amazing sense of balance; his intellect somehow shone through his features. He had dark hair, grey eyes and a Scottish handsomeness marred only by a small chin. There was also a perceptible graveness about his movements which might have been ridiculous had he not been good looking and had his brains not capitvated all with whom he came into contact.

Later, Eric having said that my interests were literary, Lockheed began politely to discuss Balzac and Stendhal, whom he admired in spite of the fact that both of them were "reactionaries." Then Eric mentioned Gide's *The Counterfeiters* deliberately, it seemed obvious, to test Lockheed's reaction. Carefully, I watched Lockheed as he formulated his reply. He looked for a moment at the tablecloth. Then he said: "I read it recently. It's a very fine piece of work, but it has one very serious fault. The characters all behave as if society wholeheartedly approved of their private morals."

This was a very sharp and very mature comment, but was it also, by implication, a polite reproof to Eric? But Eric did not take it as such, for he agreed, and I saw that Lockheed's opinion had served only to impress him further. Next they talked about Malraux, who was then only a name to me, and Lockheed said he was reading one of his novels. "A style like the rattle of machine guns."

"Heard from the distance," Eric added.

As I walked home I felt it was such a pity that there was a barrier between Lockheed and myself, and I felt somehow that it was the sort of barrier that could never be knocked down. Later, I began to think about this, and further meetings only confirmed my vague first impression that Lockheed, so to speak, "saw through me" and found me not perhaps "inferior," but immature—possibly shallow and unserious.

I had no doubt, from the first meeting on, that Eric would take his new friend under his wing, almost certainly at my expense. His enthusiasm, and the thrill over his "discovery" were unmistakable. It may be, of course, that I had prepared myself for being dropped by Eric so successfully that my preparation in fact provoked it.

I realised, further, that Lockheed had many advantages that I lacked. I had enough sense to see that he promised to be a far greater attraction for Eric than I could ever be. For one thing, in spite of Lockheed's youthful gravity, Eric could probably dominate him much more easily than he could me. For another, Lockheed's mind was undoubtedly more interesting than mine; I was still at the stage when I used to talk about the "quality of my despair." On the other hand, I was already rehearsing for one of the most lonely professions in the world. Finally, Lockheed's social background was really important. His father had been a member of the Cabinet, and Eric at that time was already what one might describe as a power snob. At a period when most snobs, at Oxford or elsewhere, were still largely preoccupied with titles, or—less often—with artistic fame, Eric's passion was for those who came from the magic circle of power: sons of prominent politicians, industrialists, newspaper proprietors, top-grade civil servants.

A few more meetings followed, always in the company of Eric. He gave Lockheed my stories to read—by that time some had already appeared in the *Criterion* and the *Mercury*—and the draft of my first novel. Lockheed's opinion, tactfully conveyed, was that they showed considerable talent, but were "evasive."

That word was new then, not yet hackneyed, and, looking back on *Bombay Duck* a couple of years later, I felt that he had been right, but at the time it was most upsetting to hear the criticism from someone a couple of years younger than I.

And my bitter feeling was rendered only more concrete and painful when I found that practically everybody who counted in my estimation at Oxford had the highest opinion of Alan Lockheed, who was easily the most promising undergraduate of his first year.

It was hard for me to see why he conquered so easily. He did not seem to have to be "nice" to people, to cajole, flatter, go out of his way. He took everything in an effort-less, easy stride. I tried to comfort myself with the belief that it was partly snobbishness in the case of most people, or at least a desperate "traditionalism." They would have been satisfied with much less from the son of a prominent man, and were pleasantly surprised to find him mature and intelligent.

Then, early during the Hilary Term, his father suddenly died, and Eric seemed to spend much of his time in Lockheed's company. "It was a dreadful shock to Alan," Eric said, but I found this difficult to believe, because earlier Eric had told me that Lockheed disliked his father, and for that matter his three sisters; but he was passionately devoted to his mother.

Then during the Trinity Term, my last at Oxford, I saw Lockheed at Communist meetings. I felt that this must have been Eric's influence, but then the fact that Alan had "lost" his father, possibly long before Sir James had actually died, may have had something to do with it. A religion is always a parent-substitute, among other things.

Lockheed was a great success among Oxford Communists too—a great gain undoubtedly—but the fact that we both of us now belonged to the same movement did not bring us any closer together. The last time I saw him at Oxford he said he longed to be a worker: a dock laborer, a miner, a truck driver.

I knew this was typical of the romantic guilt feeling of some young men of the "Oppressor Class." I was only too conscious that I was not a member of that class and my guilt feeling was small.

3

Then three years passed, maybe four, during which I lost sight of Lockheed, only to see him unexpectedly again at a dinner party at Southwick Crescent.

The place had a brown stucco colonnade, not as austere as the work of the brothers Adam; warmer, more friendly, nostalgic, mid-Victorian. It is no longer there and the street itself is now a different place. At the time I considered it the loveliest part of Bayswater—but then I was in love with Selina.

Lockheed now seemed a little taller and broader and less grave than at Oxford. I had heard that he was in the Foreign Office, and I noticed that his vocation had already left some marks on him. He looked and behaved like a young diplomat, but again the whole thing was effortless; one had always felt that he was going to be a man of consequence, and it was a welcome surprise to find him also so pleasant. And never for a moment did he become the caricature of a diplomat like so many of his contemporaries.

He was at the end of the table talking to Selina, and I began to feel the old jealousy. How loathsome was that splendid integration of his, that good balance and elasticity of mind. It was clear that he had left the Communists; he had "grown out of them." His brief political flirtation had been part of his development, an obvious and essential stage. His interests were now with the anti-Communists, the ruling class, but presumably he would always treat his former comrades with "magnanimity" and feel indulgent towards their errors.

In my own case, Communism had proved a bitter disappointment. The last chain in the link had been Eric, but it was, I think, largely loneliness that had driven me to them, although a faith seldom derives from reasoning. Then I had lost my Communist faith without finding a substitute, and I was lonely again but for my one single friend—Selina.

I had met her a year earlier at a dinner party given by Lady Barbrook, my sister's godmother. I was "too old" for the social round, but it was a duty to go about with my sister, who was then plain, gawky and unattractive, to various dances and dinner parties.

"I'm putting you next to the Hampden girl," Lady Barbrook gasped; she was very asthmatic. "Her father's in Parliament, rather a dull man, but the mother is very cultured and charming . . . speaks absolutely perfect English . . . you'd never know she was a Bostonian."

Shall I ever forget Selina as I saw her that night in pale blue lace with that magnificent ash-blond air, those hollow cheeks and all that sweetness and grace? There was something of the early nineteenth century about her; an ever so faint hint of tragedy. Was it just merely loneliness? Like me, she was too old for the social round, and she seemed out of her depth with the hard, boisterous, unfeeling or vampish debutantes. Ours was the meeting of two outsiders.

She knew I was a writer. Lady Barbrook must have told her between two gasps. At that time two of my novels were already out, and I sent her one. A couple of days later Selina telephoned and told me she was so impressed that she had bought the second one, and would I like to visit her family?

We talked of writing, and she showed me her books, and little by little she told me about herself. How perfectly she fitted into the atmosphere of Southwick Crescent, an old mezzotint in soft colors I had seen so often in my childhood dreams; tender and melancholy during the day and silvery during the night, and not far away, somewhere in the background, a canal with waters shiny and motionless like green linoleum. She would die young, I thought. Then, before I knew where I was, I was in love with her.

The first symptom was that I gave up Lucienne, a nice, serious girl, the secretary of a politician. The second was that I did not regard Selina as a girl with whom I wanted to have an affair. I wanted so much more from her.

We had long conversations and walks together. It was a seemingly innocent affair, but it was selfish just the same, as love always is. I knew she could change me, and I wanted desperately to be diverted from my former life, from my frustration, poverty, isolation, loneliness. I felt that otherwise loneliness would stunt me, twist me, embitter me. I told her everything about myself and I told her that life, outside my work, of course, now had a new meaning for me.

When Lockheed suddenly made his appearance at Southwick Crescent, I was frightened. My meetings with Selina continued, but I soon began to sense a certain strain.

Then one day, not long afterwards, Selina said she was going to Paris to stay with her mother's relations, and I suddenly felt this was the end, but I did nothing. The obvious thing would have been to run after her and try to blackmail her through her enormous sense of pity. I knew at the time this was no afterthought; and yet I did nothing. What was it that paralysed me? Pride? Inferiority complex? Timidity? Masochism? I shall never know. *The Man in the Moon,* which I wrote many years afterwards, suggests a strange but dusty answer: that for a certain type of man suffering is essential, and in the last resort he must even provoke it. I believed that when I was writing the book; but that was before the Flood.

When the announcement of their engagement appeared in *The Times,* the blow had already fallen, and by that time I had already half explained things to my satisfaction. Although Selina was not the sort of a girl to have insisted on what is known as an eligible young man, with good looks and splendid prospects, she had chosen Lockheed because he was far steadier than I. And security was a thing most women valued. But all this, of course, did not explain love.

It was, I think, the war that helped me to get over it.

The war caused many personal tragedies, but it also solved some. Soon enough I was called up, and while on leave I met Ann at the house of a woman playwright who liked my books. In retrospect, I realise it was Selina I saw in Ann. There was certainly a resemblance in the appearance and also in the voice. There were the hollow cheeks, the thick eyebrows, the bony hands which looked almost old. But times were different now, and so were we. We spent the remainder of my leave together; later we had an affair; and five months after we first met I married her.

4

I lost sight of the Lockheeds almost completely for several years. For one thing they were abroad most of the time. I had a Christmas card every year from Selina: British Embassy, Paris, Washington, Cairo, Teheran; then finally an address in Trevor Square.

I saw them perhaps three times after the war. Selina looked a little more conventionally contemporary now, but the old natural sweetness was still there, and she asked me to come to see them. And Alan was very correct, going out of his way to be nice to me. How I hated it all, his generosity towards his defeated rival, his success. One day at a literary function, I casually mentioned to an elderly diplomat with literary ambitions that I knew Alan Lockheed. He looked up and began to examine my face and my clothes with undisguised and anxious curiosity. I could see quite clearly that he disbelieved me. How could a man like me know someone so important?

But now I began to think that the elderly diplomat might have been right, after all; for the wrong reason, of course.

What now was the new connection between Eric and Alan? The idea that Alan may have shared Eric's sexual inclinations had naturally occurred to me at Oxford. Soon

60

after our first meeting I had an idea that Alan's reserve, or perhaps disapproval of me, might have been due to an unconscious feeling of guilt. He may have thought I would see through him if he were not on his guard. I had a talk with Eric about it just before I left Oxford, but to my surprise Eric denied emphatically that Alan was "queer," and said, moreover, that their friendship was nearing its end.

But now, it seemed, my early thoughts must have been correct, and Alan must already have been an invert, in theory at least, at Oxford. The bisexual variety is a recognised pattern, and in the same way that he had come to terms over his political views he had probably come to terms over his emotions too—the problem is not quite the same, of course, but has facets of remarkable similarity. His natural inclinations may have been towards Communism and inversion, but his interests—and in the end maybe even his loyalties—were definitely his career and a career-marriage.

What on earth had happened? There was no doubt, it seemed to me, that the flight of the two men had resulted from a very serious scandal of a sexual nature. Had I been told that disaster would one day overcome Eric, I would not have been entirely surprised. But that Alan should be involved took me aback. He was by all accounts one of the most prominent younger diplomats in England, and was internationally known as head of an important American section of the Foreign Office. He was distinguished, serious, through his wife well-to-do, happily married with one or two children, a man about whom one had never heard a breath of scandal. This was—even if I separated it from my own private emotions—one of the sensations of the century.

Eric and Alan were both diplomats, and presumably both inverts, but was there another link between them? I dare say their Oxford friendship had continued, even though Eric at the time had said it was coming to an end and even though I had never once seen them together since coming down. But then I was, of course, out of their lives.

Were they both involved with the same person, and had they perhaps been warned or threatened?

And how was this all connected with me? Only through that single reference to Eric in my dossier? What else? A lever had been released, a button had been pressed, perhaps accidentally. A few years back I might have felt some satisfaction about it and would have remembered the mills of God, but now all I felt was an overwhelming sense of surprise.

Book Two

5

$\mathcal{I}$T IS amazing how an untoward happening, an unusual adventure or experience, occasionally even personal crises, as often as not fail to distract me or to prevent me from continuing a given job of work. Sometimes, on the contrary, they even act as an inspiration. I remember only too well, for example, how stimulating I found the first days of September, 1939. The previous night I had been overwhelmed by what had happened to me at the Continental platform at Victoria. I could neither eat nor drink, and I had no idea how soon I fell asleep. But the next morning, while I was having breakfast in the kitchen, I felt curiously elated and excited. There was no need now for remorse and self-discipline; I was aching to work.

Around me was the beautiful death of Bayswater on a Sunday morning and, as if nothing had happened the night before, I began to think of Norman and June, the two main characters of my new novel. I did so spontaneously, as if inspired, without any sense of duty. Yesterday afternoon I had forced myself to work; today work looked like being a pleasure.

Norman was twenty-one. Yesterday he had been rather unsubstantial, but today his personality was taking a more promising shape. I saw his high-cheekboned, friendly, good-natured face, the rebellious hair, the grotesquely broad shoulders, the square fingers. Norman was a furniture polisher by trade, a nice, pleasant, serious Cockney boy who practised body-building three times a week at his club in Stoke Newington and was in love with June. This morning, it seemed, I really saw him, heard him; perhaps I might manage really to get under his skin, and this was absolutely vital, for it was Norman himself who would be telling the story. And as I lighted my first cigarette the idea of making him tell it in the first person singular did not seem quite as fantastic or as formidably difficult as it had only the day before. For the story, though as old as Genesis, was an extremely difficult one to tell, even in the words of a highly trained Jesuit priest or a non-believing professor of psychology, to say nothing of a furniture polisher of twenty-one from Stoke Newington.

It was the story of a miracle. Soon after the book opened, in the second or third chapter, June was to die in a street accident and strange things were to begin happening to people she had known, but not to Norman, at least not till the end. Norman and June were neither Catholics nor agnostics; both were sweetly and innocently ignorant of religion.

The attitude towards the ancient idea was something new, something that had been haunting me for years, but would I get away with it? Norman would not become converted at the end; he would remain as muddled as ever. The book was to be more than a Protestant, or at least non-Catholic or even universalist and ecumenical, view of miracles. The main thing was that at the end nothing whatever was to happen, except that the genuineness of the miracle was to be established.

Norman's diction and vocabulary presented no problem. For painfully good reasons, all readable "working-class" novels in England were written by people of my background, and I was completely at home with their dialect. My main difficulty was that whereas a working-class character is usually chatty and repetitive, Norman had to tell the story with the economy of the professional who knows that "less is often more."

It was, of course, essential to make Norman a sympathetic character for one thing; for another, he had to be someone with whom the reader could easily identify himself. What I had to avoid at all cost was to make him too like myself.

My plan that morning was to continue the blue-printing of the second half of the novel; then after lunch I might go out to Stoke Newington and refresh my memory about the atmosphere. I knew the place pretty well for an outsider. One winter morning I'd discovered Arcola Street under the mild undulations of the Hackney Downs, and, with some excitement, the mid-Victorian gardens off Shacklewell Lane. It was a London off the literary map, a private London of my own, and in order to become really well acquainted with the area, I accompanied a door-to-door insurance salesman for a couple of weeks who had once been with me in the Air Force.

I went into the living room, made a few fresh notes, then looked at the pages I had done the afternoon before. No, I felt, the dialogue bit was unreal and childish even as drafts went. I should have to redo the whole thing. I was again pleased, however, to think that the project had at least been recorded, and I started another version based on the original outline. I was in a mind to take the notes with me in the afternoon and reread them. The idea of reading what I had written in its own background was something that had worked once or twice in the past, although the trick had its dangers; descriptions tended to become photographic.

It was then that the bell rang, and I realised with a little spurt of annoyance that I was not displeased by the interruption. But who could it be, I reflected, neither angry, nor alarmed, but curious, because it was Sunday and a quarter to eleven.

As I opened the door I saw a shortish young man in a flashy suit, a shiny blue damask shirt and no tie.

"Mr. Edmonton?" he said, and his lips parted in a

friendly smile, two large, gold teeth flashed at me right in the centre of his mouth.

"Yes?" I said. His curly, shiny black hair and dark complexion suggested the Eastern Mediterranean, but the hairstyle was strictly North Atlantic. He saw my surprise, but seemed to guess that it was not perhaps an unpleasant one.

"I am Nikki," he said simply, like some Renaissance painter scorning the use of his surname. Then he added earnestly, "From the Piraeus Restaurant."

A button had been pressed, and now I felt like an automaton, inspired by forces outside my control. "Oh, yes," I said, and how warm my voice must have sounded. I reached out to clasp his small dark hand. "You brought back my bag." There was apparently no need for rehearsal; I spoke as if I had rehearsed this scene in a previous existence. The automaton knew precisely what it was doing. It had already inserted the possessive pronoun "my" so as to decide the rest of the conversation.

I saw the naïve surprise on his face as I stood aside to let him in. "Is it yours, sir?" he said.

"Yes; of course," I replied, surprised at my own capacity to lie so easily and convincingly. Like so many people whose livelihood depended partly on their skill in inventing plausible and, if possible, exciting lies, I had thought I was a poor liar in my private life. But this time I managed to bring my professional experience into play. "Yes, of course. There are a lot of bags like it, but I know my own. Come in, will you?" I said, and led him into the living room. "Just a minute."

I went into the kitchen to fetch the bag from the cupboard where I had put it, next to my broken-down coffee percolator and the clean dusters and dish clothes.

"Here you are," I said now to the young man's back. He had been looking at my bookshelves and turned slowly towards me, so unlike an English boy, who would have

68

looked guilty as if he had been caught in an act of impropriety.

"I'm a writer," I said in my friendliest manner, and he looked impressed, like most people who never read books. "Well, this is the bag." I put it on the sofa table and pulled the zip, then pulled it quickly back for fear he might notice that the marshmallow and the flute were still inside. "Here," I said. I pointed at a piece of sticky paper, which might have been part of a cloakroom ticket or hotel label, seeking in this way to establish my ownership, but this was stupid and my supporting evidence was quite unnecessary. I was surprised by my own appalling fluency: "It was clever of you to find my address on the file . . . that orange-colored cover inside. You'd make a good detective. . . ." Nikki showed his gold teeth again. "But what made you think it wasn't my bag?" I asked. What indeed I thought, and I felt my pulse.

"Because you came in last night for it. . . ." Nikki smiled gently, trying to remind me in a half-deferential, half-chummy manner that I must have had a bad memory. "I was off duty, you see. But this morning, Milti said—" He interrupted himself. "That's my friend. We share the room where I live. . . . Milti said the gentleman came last night and he said he left it under the table on Thursday. That's why I came now. I thought maybe you haven't been here lately and wouldn't know I brought it back for you. Milti said the man would come back to see me tonight after eight."

"Which man?" I said and I felt my heart in my throat.

"You," Nikki said. "That's what Milti said."

He suddenly burst out laughing, "Milti said you had a moustache."

"Did he?" I heard myself saying, then I made a feeble attempt to laugh. My heart was thumping. So the man would be going to the Piraeus that evening after eight.

"You see, Milti told the boss I found the bag, but he didn't know I brought it to you."

"Some stupid misunderstanding," I said. This was not a good line, but a second later I already had an idea. "Look," I said, "did you see the papers inside the cover?" This was a near-rhetorical question, for I felt sure he had not. And even if he had he had probably not understood a word, in any case.

"I didn't," he said simply. There was no profession of innocence on his face, no consternation, no apology. It was the direct statement of a child; a child with an adult body. "What was it?" he said politely.

"A story I'm writing, but"—I raised my forefinger across my mouth and winked at him—"not a word to anyone." I took my wallet from my trouser pocket and gave him a pound. "D'you know what happened?" I said.

"Thank you, very much, sir," he said in a loud voice, then immediately after, in a soft one, "What?"

"I asked a friend of mine to bring it back as soon as I remembered where I'd left it. And he didn't go to your place till last night! . . . He is *okniros.*" I hoped I had remembered the word correctly, but Nikki apparently understood it. I saw him smile. "D'you speak Greek?" he asked excitedly.

"I learnt it at school. A different Greek from yours. I just tried it on you, to find if they still use the same word in Greece."

"I come from Cyprus," he said.

"Well, now, Nikki, listen. I shall come to the restaurant at eight tonight, but I want to play a little *theatron* on my friend. You mustn't tell the boss I'm the one."

"He isn't coming tonight. Sunday," Nikki explained with some relief.

"That's splendid." It was indeed. This was, I supposed, what was known as a lucky break. "And Milti?" I said anxiously.

70

"He may be in tonight, but I'll tell him not to speak."

"Thank you. Well, now, when the gentleman comes, just bring him to my table."

"I shall, sir," he said. He was entering wholeheartedly into a boyish lark. I offered him a cigarette, but he pulled out a pack of Americans. "Like to try one of these?" he said. "Poll Moll."

I took one. "When did Milti tell you?"

"This morning. I went to the Lyceum last night. Very good." He suddenly pointed towards the table. "You play jazz?"

"I wish I could. Why?"

"You've got a . . . *salpinx*." This time he pointed towards the bag, and I realised I had been a little slow. "Oh, you mean the flute. I only play opera," I said uneasily, but Nikki had already changed the subject.

"We have a waiter, Leo," he said, "he has the accordion."

2

Towards half-past seven I took a bus to go to the Piraeus. Now that the time was drawing near to put the plan into practise, my scheme did not seem such a good one. Nikki was a pal, wholeheartedly on my side, but I could surely have made some less chancy arrangement. What would happen, for example, if the man came in earlier tonight and I missed him? It was worrying.

To have asked Nikki to find out the man's address would have been too complicated, even had I thought it possible to tell him the truth. Despite Nikki's friendliness, he might have refused to co-operate, and I could hardly have blamed him. He would have understood some of the implications, for he was not a stupid lad. We had talked before he left me about Cyprus and England and women, about films, the Lyceum and women, about his job and

71

women. He had a nice, warm, Mediterranean simplicity, and a vitality which the London air had not yet washed out of him.

After he had left me I had gone back to my desk, trying to look at my notes, but it was no use. This time the excitement was too personal, I was too directly involved. In order to calm myself, I read a couple of Sunday papers, and in the afternoon I did go to Stoke Newington, on location, but the notes I then made were newspaperish and commonplace. After tea I was completely unable to concentrate on the book, and I began to wonder, for the nth time, whether I was after all to meet the man who had left the dossier at the Piraeus. Had he himself written it, or was he just using it, adding to it? In any case, he was Power; part of the anonymous "They," powerful, precisely because he was anonymous. To meet him would be a really glorious occasion for me. He would face a man, a representative of "Us," who was not afraid of him, who would match him. He would find himself in the ridiculous situation of the policeman hiding in the cupboard, only to discover that the man he had been watching was not the suspect, but his solicitor, who, to make matters worse, would knock on the cupboard door and say, "Do come out, Constable. You'll get varicose veins if you stay there much longer."

And I wondered again what sort of man I might expect to meet. I was right in any case in thinking he would have a moustache. In my bitterness, I had been inclined to agree with Eric about the formidable power of the authorities or organisation responsible for compiling my dossier, their appetite for privileges, their ruthlessness and their corruption. I had felt this even more strongly after the circumstances of Eric's departure. But now that it seemed probable that I might meet my detractor in person, I was less inclined to take a view that, on reflection, was based

72

on the hysterical fear and impotent anger of a guilty person. I was not guilty. I had been involved as the result of a stupid blunder. As I got off the bus and walked towards the Piraeus in Dean Street, I felt that Eric had, in a way, paid the authorities a compliment by running away. It seemed just a case of hysteria now. But did they know he was running away and that Lockheed was with him?

As I entered the restaurant, I decided I had probably arrived too early, because it was more or less empty. My recollections had been correct. It was here that Hackwood had given me lunch some eighteen months earlier when my last book had been launched. In order to reach the cocktail lounge, you had to go through the dining room, which was the smaller of the two rooms—a stupid waste of space.

There was a woman sitting at one of the tables with two younger men, one of whom had a black square beard. I remembered vaguely that she was an industrialist's widow who always had a menagerie of artists and writers around her. At another table there sat an elderly couple, remarkably alike down to their pince-nez.

I walked through the dining room and reached the cocktail lounge, which was empty. When I sat down on a divan by the wall facing the entrance, I saw Nikki coming towards me.

He looked much taller in the black and white get-up. He smiled at me. "The gentleman hasn't come yet," he whispered. I ordered a glass of sherry and decided to wait a little before going in to dinner. It was five minutes to eight and the man might be delayed. I saw a crumpled Sunday paper on the settee and picked it up.

I heard the door open soon after I had skimmed through the front page and I looked up to see the fat man in the dinner jacket, who I decided was the manager, greet a tall young man and a lanky girl. They made an unconscion-

73

ably slow entry, then took their seats at a table as if arriving at a funeral supper. Maybe it was.

Then Nikki brought my drink and the menu, and I decided to give my order. I was too excited and impatient to want anything, but I had to pay just the same, and it was obvious the dinner could not come to less than thirty shillings without drinks.

So I ordered a shrimp cocktail and chicken to follow and took the paper with me to the table to which Nikki led me. The whole place was so small that every one of the twelve tables was in a strategic position.

There was nothing else for me to read except the gossip column; a tremendous energy and journalistic skill wasted in an attempt to produce interesting reading matter out of totally uninteresting personalities. Then Nikki began to serve me, and I went through the motions of eating. The portions of food were so generous that I decided he must have put in a good word for me with the chef. I heard the door open again and a giantess of a woman came in with a tiny, bald-headed man; they looked like a variety turn and were shown to a table next to mine.

Soon after, I finished playing with the chicken and chose a pastry and I said yes, I would have coffee. What a waste of time, nervous energy, money. I lit a cigarette. It was now nearly nine o'clock and the man had not arrived. The only thing to do was to wait till Nikki came to me with the bill and ask him to try to get the man's address when he next saw him. But would that work? Unless I could think of some good reason for Nikki to ask him, the man would probably refuse his address or cause a fuss, in which case my deception would become apparent. No doubt I could always explain things afterwards to Nikki. But that was not the point, I knew, and I felt angry.

What time would the restaurant close? It was five minutes past nine. How long could I reasonably stay at my table? Perhaps, I thought, I should order another coffee. There were still five vacant tables and nobody seemed to notice that I had finished my meal. For that matter, nobody seemed to notice my presence at all.

I decided to do the cross-word puzzle, something I had not attempted for years. I looked at the horizontals first. Greedy heart, four letters. Wrinkles come with it, three letters; that was too easy. On with it for the monster, seven letters. Clumsy thing to do on a canal, five letters. . . . It was then that I heard the door open. I looked up half-heartedly, because I had vaguely noticed that the industrialist's widow and her two young men had earlier risen from their table. But the party of three must already have gone, because I saw instead a man coming in. Another typical Piraeus customer, I thought.

He looked round, then, seeing that the manager was not there, came into the dining room, apparently looking for a table. His face was bored, infinitely bored; he was tallish, around thirty-five and dressed in a striped suit. A businessman, I thought, who had doubtless had an Army commission during the war and had not somehow recovered from it. There was the regimental tie, the narrow shoulders, the close-fitting coat, the clipped moustache. He reached the table next to mine and lingered about, apparently waiting for the manager, then abruptly he changed his mind and turned back towards the entrance. What a tired lot the customers of the Piraeus seemed to be, I reflected, as I watched his slow, measured steps. Then the manager suddenly appeared from the service door and flashed a smile at the man, who said something to him and, in spite of some apparently exasperated protest, opened the door and walked out.

It was the manager's face that told me the story, the expression of confusion, the way he looked at the back of the man making his way out, and I began to curse myself

75

for my own calm stupidity. No doubt the man had seen me after he had entered the room and it was my presence that had made him beat a quick retreat. What a fool I had been, trying to guess his profession, making pompous, idiotic, deductions from his clothes and bearing. His moustache should have given me the hint. I suddenly got up, but I was too late, I knew, and sat down again, hot with impotent rage. Then I saw the service door opening again and Nikki came out with a pile of napkins in his hands. The manager turned to him, said something in Greek, shook his head and smiled.

The look on Nikki's face provided the last link in the chain. It was quite unnecessary for him to have come up to me and, without knowing it, to have rubbed salt in my wound. "The gentleman's just been in," he told me, "but he said he forgot something and went out."

If only—but there was no if only, I thought bitterly. "It doesn't matter," I said to Nikki, not caring what emotion my face suggested or whether he noticed it. I told him to let me know if the man should come again, and gave him my telephone number, in case, but I knew it was useless. The man would never return. I asked for my bill.

If only the restaurant had been a little larger, if only I had arrived when the man was already seated at a table, if only I had gone to use the telephone, or to the lavatory, at the time he had entered. If . . . if . . . if.

The man would never come back to the Piraeus. He had seen me and he must have known that my presence there was no coincidence. Apart from anything else, he knew enough about me to have been aware that I could not afford a place like the Piraeus. He must also have seen that I was not afraid of him, but was in fact challenging him. But there was another point, more important. Here was a man who knew me, recognised me, without my knowing anything about him, except that he was about five foot ten, around thirty-five, probably bought his suits from Simp-

76

son's, wore a moustache and had probably been in the Army.

The bill came to one pound six shillings without the tip.

6

$\mathcal{I}$ DID not sleep much that night, partly perhaps because of the strong coffee I had drunk at the Piraeus. But that was just an afterthought. I felt so depressed as I woke up that the mere idea of my appointment with the dentist quite cheered me.

Hogan first talked a little about cine-biology, about a remarkable old character in County Mayo, then again about his fish. He was interrupted by the house-telephone announcing the arrival of a patient, and as he replaced the receiver he waved me towards the chair.

There was no pain as he touched the tooth and there was no need to drill much. "I don't think I need see you again for a couple of weeks," he finally said. "The temporary filling will last until then. What I'd like to do is to put a white-gold cap on that back molar. . . ."

I immediately thought of Nikki, and of what happened the night before. As if I needed to be reminded. I had asked Nikki to ring me up in case anything further happened, but I knew in advance that nothing would occur. The man with the moustache was obviously not a complete fool. He had summed up the situation at a glance and would no doubt let the matter drop. My dossier would be replaced by another. If he had forgotten the details, he could always invent other damaging lies. But my job at the T.F.O. was out; that was certain.

I boarded the bus on my way home at Oxford Street. There was nothing to be done until I received the official notification that, much to their regret, they could not offer me employment.

It had been a waste of time and money to go to the Piraeus. Now I must return to the novel. It would be another day of forced labor, but I had to make use of the time between then and the day when the brief note of rejection would arrive from the T.F.O. Then I might perhaps start a little campaign.

As I walked up my stairs I saw two men coming down with toolbags. One was whistling. Why should he not be, I thought? Must everybody feel miserable because I was in a fix?

I decided to make a cup of coffee, but as I went into the kitchen, I was startled to see on the floor the bag that had held the dossier. It was wide open, but the flute and marshmallow were still inside. I looked round. This was not one of Mrs. Graham's days to clean the flat. The remains of my breakfast were still on the table where I had left them, but the cupboard door was open. Then I looked into the larder, into the waste-bin. It was obvious that somebody had been to my flat while I was out, and I immediately thought that the place had been searched. I ran into the living room.

At first blush there was hardly any evidence of anybody having moved things. *The Times* and the *Express* were still on the armchair, but the books on the shelves looked as if somebody had dusted them.

I tried the drawers of the writing desk. They had not been forced open. My habit was to lock up most of my papers and letters and manuscripts, because of Mrs. Graham. She was a perfectly honest woman, but I knew this from her other employers—she could not resist pulling out all open drawers and reading all letters and papers. In my case, this meant spending half the time for which

78

I paid her for charing at a study of the new material of what I hope can be called literature.

I unlocked the drawers. It was their too-perfect tidiness that gave away the game. They had doubtless been opened with skeleton keys and their contents searched; everything had been put back in an orderly fashion, but not always where it had come from. There was an old envelope, for example, containing six pounds spare cash. I knew it had always been at the bottom. Now it was somewhere in the middle.

It was obvious that an examination had been made behind the books on the bookshelves. I ran into the bedroom. Again there was the same apparent lack of change. The bed was unmade, as I had left it, but it had been searched; that was agonisingly clear. I had left the flat in the usual mild disorder, and even if whoever had searched it had had time to put the canvas bag back in the kitchen cupboard, between my broken-down coffee percolator and the dusting sheets, I should have known that something was strange, unusual, wrong. I would have made matters far easier for them had I left things tidy. It was, I realised, impossible exactly to reproduce disorder. There is a certain method in disorder; there are personal touches which are a law unto themselves. I saw that someone had searched under the bedroom carpet even; the one in the living room had been spared only because it was close-fitted and nailed down.

I had been out for about two hours. That was more than enough for someone thoroughly to search a small flat like mine.

I went downstairs and looked for Mrs. Graham in the basement.

"The telephone repairmen are up in your flat," she said before I could speak. She apparently thought I had just come in.

"Oh, yes," I said, and looked away to hide my confusion.

I was glad that there was now no danger of my having to tell her what had happened. "I came to ask you if you knew of a reliable carpenter," I said.

"Carpenter?"

"I'm thinking of a new bookcase." That was true, for I had been thinking about it for six months at least, but I knew it would cost more money than I wanted to spend at the time, however cheaply I could have one made.

"Do you know Keedick's in Moscow Road?"

"No. I'll try them. Keedick's. Thank you, Mrs. G."

It was clear how the men had carried out this search. They had employed the technique of burglars. One no doubt had kept watch while the other had searched, and my return must have disturbed them. But that they had got the co-operation of the telephone division of the Post Office! Surely this was something new. . . . But why the hell should it be new? Telephones had been tapped ever since the telephone had been invented. The only contemporary note was that today it was not a living snooper listening in, but a tape machine automatically recording all the suspected person's calls. Perhaps, however, the men had only been dressed as telephone repairmen to allay suspicion. They may have had no connection with the Post Office. But some Government agency was responsible. So Eric had been right, after all. It was not just dramatics on his part to warn me to hide the dossier. He had thought I might find the document useful. But how could I use it, at least until my application was rejected? To go to the police was useless. Private detectives would either not touch the case or would squeeze such money out of me as they could, and in the end doubtless tell me that I must have been suffering from persecution mania, or that the dossier was the prank of one of my friends.

I wondered to whom I could go for help. I had already decided that it was useless to approach the one or two influential friends I knew.

80

There were, of course, Eric's friends. I knew some of them and disliked most of them, or was it the other way round? They knew me for exactly what I was; an unsuccessful writer, poor company, no connections, no money and probably a bore or a bright bore, whichever was worse. There was Fowler-Hesketh the historian, who looked like a nice frog and talked as if he were carrying on a telephone conversation with a poet from Nepal. There was Hatry, the energetic don, whom I remembered well from my Oxford days. There were Robb, Poole, Morgan, all successful, all charming. And there was, of course, Beaufort, the great patron, who had helped Eric in the past. It would be fun to go to him and tell him the story, and to hear his reactions to Eric's exit, if he were not too preoccupied with licking his own wounds; he had tried to marry another rich woman and had been rejected, and this was followed by the flop of his lecture tour in America.

These were old friends who had known Eric as long as I had, and far more intimately, but who were the new ones?

Of Alan's friends I knew none, except perhaps the Lavingtons at whose party I had last seen him and Selina. Selina . . . and a moment later I was already on to Long Distance to find out her number.

It was a Denham number, but after waiting three minutes the operator told me there was no reply. I decided to try later. But what should I tell her, and how much did she know?

It was later, towards lunchtime, that I thought of Keith. He was a painter whom I used to see frequently in Soho pubs during the war. He had known Eric well. Keith was a little fat man, who drank a lot, but never got drunk. He was amusing and he had more or less the same opinions about Eric as I. I remembered discussing Eric with him only about a year before.

I rang him up and arranged to call on him straight away for a few minutes.

He was having a show at Gimpels in a few weeks' time and I was now in his Holland Park studio, looking at his work. Keith was a primitivist, so called, I suppose, because he painted as if he were the first man who had ever painted a tree in Kew, a fountain in Stockholm, or the Plaza Mayor in Madrid. If one did not know him for the man he was, the trick came off beautifully, though lately there had been too many would-be Academicians painting like him.

He had a large and attractive collection of drawings, mostly eighteenth-century, and among them a Blake angel with a fishing hat. But there was no time for that now.

"You know," I said, "I saw Eric Fontanet the other day in the street. He's back from America. . . ."

"You bet he is," Keith said. He was putting a frame together. "You haven't heard the story?"

"What story?" I said. I looked up. Was it possible that Keith already knew of Eric's escape?

"His exit from Washington."

"What happened?"

"He was sent back. Quite recently. I heard about it from Don Tripley, who's on leave from Washington. He knew Eric quite well. Apparently Eric didn't like Washington at all. I'm not surprised, knowing him. Probably his style got cramped."

Keith paused. Impatiently waiting for him to continue, I looked at the Chantrey bust he had picked up for a pound some years before in Fulham. We had loved it.

"Well, Washington's a small place," he finally said. "It's not like New York, and if you're queer you're in a difficult position, even if you're not a foreign diplomat or Government employee. There are parties, of course, and a few queer bars, but that isn't much, and you've got to be careful. Things would have been better if Eric could have settled down with someone, but he isn't the type. . . . I mean, you know . . . he must have his new boy friend every month or every week."

A Siamese cat got up from the settee and began to look at me with glassy blue eyes.

"Of course, if one's rich or in with the queer set, things are easier, but for some reason Eric always kept to himself. He probably thought the smart set snobbish or stuffy. I know them only too well. But, anyway, Americans are much more violent against queers than we are, perhaps because they've got so many of them, so the American queer is more reserved. Back home at least. In fact, they nearly all seem to get married. Don says Eric was pretty well thrown on his own resources in Washington, and that's not much, I can tell you. You've never been there?"

I shook my head.

"Well, there are bars which are frightfully dark, and someone plays the piano. There was one, I remember, called the Windup, then they changed the name to Pig'n Whistle."

The penny dropped so loudly that I almost heard a thud. The Pig'n Whistle. So, the Mystery Page referred to Eric, beyond doubt. I had had my strong suspicion when Eric's mood had changed while reading the page from mild amusement to bewilderment and anger.

". . . went to them regularly," I heard Keith continue. "Then he took off every available week-end and went to New York. The usual places," Keith smiled, "Central Park around the East Seventies, Riverside Drive, the pubs in the Village, Times Square after midnight. . . ."

Keith was now apparently full of his own past, but I said nothing.

After a time he returned to Eric's story. "Well, around Christmas last year, or earlier this year, I don't know, he bought a car and began to tour the countryside around

Washington. Not for the beauties of Maryland and Virginia, but for picking up likely people. Now, that's a particularly dangerous thing to do in the States, where hitchhikers are quite likely to rob you if they find you're queer, or perhaps even murder you. One week-end Eric picked someone up—I don't know where—and they spent the night at a hotel. Apparently nothing went wrong. Don said the young man was quite charming. But the next morning, as they were near Concord—it's a tiny place in Virginia: I know it—the young man wanted to take over the wheel and Eric let him. He had an accident and traffic cops came along and it came out that the boy had no driving licence, was driving dangerously, had done time, or was on probation, or for all I know may have escaped from a reformatory. So you can imagine the situation. There was the 'C.D.' plate on Eric's car, so the story was kept out of the papers, but, of course, the police informed the State Department and they informed the Embassy. . . ."

"That's why he was sent back to England," I said.

"Yes; but they may also have wanted to get rid of him just because he was queer. They think queers are unreliable. Bad security risks! I suppose the idea is that they may give away State secrets. You know yourself that they've been sacking civil servants just because of that."

I was interested in Keith's story while it lasted. I felt sure it was true. It was perfectly in line with Eric's character, and the Mystery Page slipped into my dossier confirmed it. But I soon saw that it gave no immediate explanation as to why Eric should have run away from London.

Just before I left I asked Keith if he knew Alan Lockheed, but he said not.

I HAD no idea why I left Keith in such an indecent hurry, because I had absolutely nothing to do. Work, for one thing, was quite out of the question. He had told me a number of interesting things, but they were irrelevant, irrelevant at least to my own problem, which was that my chances of getting a Government job were negligible as a result of the dossier, which was considered sufficiently important to cause a search of my flat. I was being thrown inevitably back on my reserves as a writer. And now I was not even in a mood to write, to put it mildly.

As I walked from Holland Park towards Bayswater, I thought, not for the first time, that working for a wage in an office had certain advantages. Hours would have to be kept, discipline was imposed from above, there was a pay envelope at the end of the week or a cheque at the end of the month. For that matter, I had managed inter- mittently to train myself to keep office hours at home— certainly between nine and one. It is so easy when one is not forced to work to a régime to succumb to laziness, but I had usually succeeded in conquering minor ailments, in- dispositions and even my morbid tendency to melancholia —or was it just self-pity? Last Saturday afternoon had been one of my triumphs, but today was different. The fate of my job was the worst item undoubtedly, but there were others. There was the nervous hysterical speed of a whole chain of events during the last forty-eight hours, the sense of impotence against heavy-footed stupidity, if not in- trigue, and perhaps the feeling that I myself had been

involved, no matter how mildly and—yes, I had to face it—
the fact that the story into which I had become entangled
seemed more interesting than the novel I was trying to
write.

I was shocked the moment the idea crystallised in my
mind. For a writer this was a painful confession to make.
I immediately thought—or rather forced myself to think
—of the anecdote about Balzac. When a friend burst into
his room to report, out of breath, some world-shaking political news, Balzac interrupted: "Let's return to reality.
Who's going to marry Eugénie Grandet?"

Yes, who? But that was in 1833, and Balzac had far
greater will-power than I, and a much richer life than
mine; a good deal had happened to him and he was well
used to unusual happenings. Besides, the world-shaking
political news in question was not to affect his life immediately, directly and intimately. And, finally, if I was right,
he had already worked himself thoroughly into *Eugénie
Grandet* when he made that statement.

I was not at Notting Hill Gate. If I went home I knew
exactly what would happen, and I dreaded that prospect.
That Selina was out when I had telephoned was an added
frustration. I thought, under the circumstances, it might
not be a bad thing to visit her unannounced and await her
return if she were still out. Of course, even if I found her
at home she was unlikely to be able to help me with my
own problem, but I had to clutch at any straw. I knew
there was a telephone booth in a Post Office by Notting
Hill Gate, and now I was hurrying towards it. Perhaps
she would be in this time.

It did not take long to get her number. A minute later
I heard what I thought was her voice.

"Is that you, Selina?" I asked, and, without waiting for
her reply, "This is James Edmonton," I said.

There was the briefest pause. It was on the tip of my
tongue to say, "Is that Mrs. Lockheed?" when a voice,

which sounded strangely unlike her, said quickly, and out of breath, "James. . . . I don't know. . . ."

The voice suddenly trailed off and I missed a couple of words that followed. Then, she said: "Are you there? . . . A dreadful thing has happened, James. Alan's disappeared."

It was lucky, I thought, that she could not see my face and did not apparently attribute any particular significance, except the obvious one, to my long silence after she had spoken.

2

I took the four-fifty train to Denham. I did not know Kingsclere at all, but Selina had explained on the telephone how to get there.

There were two soldiers in the compartment, who fell asleep promptly, like children, as the train moved off. I had time to think.

Selina's reaction was something on which I had not counted, but I soon realised that I counted on nothing. When I telephoned her, I had no plan as to what I would say. All I had was an impulse, an angry, desperate, semi-hopeless impulse, to talk to her. For all I knew I might have blurted out the whole story, if she had hesitated, if she had kept calm, but the surprise of hearing from me was too much for her and she had spoken first. Now I must think. Would it be a wise thing to tell her what I knew, and what I had done? Would it help her and would it help me if she knew?

Under her present circumstances I would not have minded telling her, and damn the consequences to myself, if any, if I were certain it would help her, but I was unsure. This was a problem which I could resolve only when I saw her. And I had a first-rate excuse: "I didn't want to say anything on the telephone, you know."

I had last seen Selina at a party some months previously. It was a gathering of young marrieds, and I had felt a little out of place. It was Selina who came up to me; she always did. "We shall always remain friends, James; and I mean it. . . ." I remembered her words with bitterness, albeit a bitterness that had faded with the years. On that last occasion she said she had ordered a book of mine; that Alan had been ill in Cairo, I think it was, that he had had to come home, but had soon recovered and been made head of some department or other. Then she had said, "Why don't you come and see us? We've taken a house in Bucks. In Metroland." She smiled, giving away her age with the period phrase. "But the country around it is really lovely."

Yes, it must have been almost exactly a year ago, for she had said something about strawberries ripening and had made an oblique reference to the fact that I used to be fond of strawberry ice cream if made of real strawberries. I might have accepted her invitation there and then, had Alan not joined us two minutes later, quoting a review in the *Spectator* of my last book and being so effortlessly charming to me and inviting me himself. I knew then that I would not go. Then I thought, how I would have jumped at the invitation had I been writing about a peevish, envious, grudging, semi-failure of a man, and how such a man must feel when his successful rival was killing him with deliberate or unconscious kindness—which was it? I felt I could easily have got under the skin of such a character; perhaps I was ignoring my true and proper subject. Then I remember drinking three dry Martinis in quick succession, and I forgot all about it.

But now the situation was entirely different. Some years ago I would decidedly have felt, if not exactly pleased, at least greatly relieved that the man who had scored off me had now come to such a sensationally sticky end. Today even the mere thought of such emotions filled me with shame.

Selina was a different proposition. Her rejection of me was a brutal, savage blow at the time, yet I had never for a moment hated her. In fact, I still went on loving her, I suppose; but it was so difficult to assess how I had felt.

Now I was going to see her, primarily for selfish reasons, curiosity and a chance for distraction, but I began to tell myself I might have gone just the same if I had had absolutely nothing to do with Alan's disappearance. Of this I was now feeling certain. And one of the soldiers woke up and said excitedly, with saliva on his lips: "Have we passed High Wycombe?"

3

She waved to me from the window as she saw me coming up the drive, so I did not have to ring the bell, and as we met in the doorway she kissed me. This was the first time she had ever done so. It had always been I who had kissed her. "Oh, James, I am so miserable," she whispered, a sentence which in the past would have sounded unbelievable from her lips.

She wore a black housecoat, as if she were already mourning for Alan. It was the first thing I had noticed about her from the window, but now I suddenly realised the probable reason for it. She must have been expecting a child.

All this was too much, too much for me. I would have stood there in the doorway, in the dark hall, just gaping, like a fool, utterly removed from the present and unable to speak, but she was too full of her own anxiety and noticed nothing, and I allowed her to lead me by the hand as if we were children. She took me through a dimly-lit hall into a large drawing room gay with chintz and pearl-grey Wilton and a number of pictures.

"It was so very good of you, James," she said and shook her head. "I must get you a drink." For a second she looked at the bell by the fireplace; then she muttered something I was unable to catch and went out.

The room was large, a sort of "happy" room in a "happy home" of the higher income brackets. It was part of a landscape. One knew there was wealth behind it and a certain amount of good, personal taste. It had so obviously been arranged by Selina, who would have expected from an interior decorator something too smart and cold and impersonal. A decorator would probably have suggested a shiny apple-green for the walls, would never have tolerated the Sèvres dishes on the mantelpiece and would have chosen a more severe pattern in chintzes. There was the Naysmith landscape over the mantelpiece, the only thing I remembered from Selina's past. It had once hung in the dining room at Southwick Crescent. No decorator would have permitted the placing next to it of that French post-Impress. I got up to look at it. It *was* a Léger.

I wandered over to the third picture. What an orgy of color, unrest, social protest, more like a revolutionary poster than a painting. Some Latin-American. I wondered how it had got there. It was not her taste. But was it his? How did it get into this "happy home" with its chintzes and flowers? And Selina came in with the decanter and the sherry glasses in her hand.

"You ought not to have bothered," I said, but I filled the glasses and emptied mine in almost one gulp. I noticed that she did not touch hers. She never used to drink. "I've just had a letter from Mother in Boston," she said. "She's quite well now, but I can't bring myself to tell her about Alan. But Margaret's coming over tomorrow." Margaret was a cousin, I seemed to remember. "She'll look after me while I'm expecting my baby. . . . Oh, there's no need to worry. The doctor's been here today." She gave me a faint smile. Suddenly I felt here was the old Selina again, graceful, well-disciplined, but sweet and intimate. Even her voice became calmer, and now I saw with some astonishment, and for the first time, that she was beautiful. In the past I had seen many other things in her, but I had always thought that one of the most remarkable things about her was that she was not beautiful. So, this was *not* the old Selina, after all. But all the same. . . .

". . . too tragically sudden." I had missed the first part of her sentence, but her voice cut short my reminiscing.

"On Friday evening Alan telephoned and said he had some important work to do," she said, "so he wouldn't come home, but would spend the night in London. Then he telephoned again after lunch the next day, to say he'd been working at the office and that he'd be back for tea with a friend. Well, they came all right and we had tea in the garden; the first time this year. Then Alan said they had to go and see someone in the country who was in trouble, and that they'd probably have to spend the night with him at Andover."

"Who was it who came here with Alan?" I asked.

"A man called Constable. I'd never met him before."

I held my breath. I had taken for granted that the friend was Eric. "It all sounded rather strange," Selina now continued, "but the man was there, so I said nothing. I asked Alan what time he'd be back, and he said definitely before lunch. Then he ran upstairs to pack a few overnight things into a little grip he had. . . ."

A little grip. I recalled the cheap, new fibre suitcase in his hand at Victoria.

"So he didn't take any clothes with him, apart from pyjamas and so on?" I asked. "What about a raincoat?"

"No. He left both his coat and raincoat here."

So the white mackintosh had been bought in London. I saw a worried look around her lips. "What is it, Selina?" I said.

"He took the boy's photograph with him from his bedroom." She looked at me speechless for a moment. Then she said simply, "You see," leaving me to guess her meaning. There may also have been a photograph of Selina in his bedroom, I thought, and he had probably left that behind. But this was something I could not possibly ask her.

"Did you ask the name of the man they were going to see in Andover?"

"No," she said. "I couldn't very well."

"Why not?"

She shook her head slowly, and there was a little pause.

"For one thing I didn't like the man—Constable, and I suppose I didn't at the time expect anything to happen. Alan had gone off like that before."

I tried not to look up. Who on earth was Constable? I had automatically assumed that the friend was Eric, and now here was this added complication.

"What did Alan's friend look like?" I asked.

"Oh, he was about Alan's height or just under, possibly a journalist." How well I could feel from these commonplace words that she disliked the man. "He was untidy, a chain-smoker . . . nicotine-stained fingers. I think he was wearing the Eton tie, but I'm not sure. He had a sort of slow grin and rather a loud voice. The sort of person I don't like."

That was Eric all right, I thought with some excitement and confusion. But why the false name. Automatically, I said, "What didn't you like about him?"

"I don't know," she said. "I'm probably quite wrong. His appearance, I suppose; I so often find that appearance goes with something deeper. I think he was about forty, but he looked younger. I don't know how to explain it. . . ." She almost smiled now. "The first impression he gave was that he was under thirty, then on second thought one could see that he was much older. Perhaps it was the haircut. He wore his hair very long; it was a dirty golden color."

Of course it was Eric, I thought. But how odd that Selina had never met him. Or was it?

"Then what happened?"

"Saturday night we had an invitation to go over to some people in the village. I went on my own and apologised for Alan. He didn't come home for lunch the next day, and I felt worried. I rang the place where he had a room in London, but he wasn't there. Then I rang the Foreign Office. It was Sunday, and there was no one there who could help me. I thought perhaps they'd caught him there at the last minute on official business; it had happened once before on a Sunday. I didn't say anything to the Resident Clerk who answered the phone because Alan had done unexpected things once or twice before, and there was usually an explanation. But when I heard that he hadn't even been at the office on Saturday, I was really worried, because this meant he'd lied to me."

I said, "What did you do?"

"I spoke to Geoffrey Staples. He's Alan's Under-Secretary. He said he'd make enquiries and I wasn't to worry, and that there was no need to contact the police or the hospitals, or anything like that. He promised to ring me back. Well, he rang me later in the afternoon, and I got a little frightened."

"Why?"

"It was the way he talked. He said he was very surprised, but I could feel that he must have known about it all the time and I wondered if Alan were on some official business —something secret. But Geoffrey kept asking me for details, how Alan had left, with whom, and so on." Gently she looked at me. "What worries me, James, is that Alan isn't too well."

"What do you mean?"

"I suppose you know he was very ill some time ago? Then he got better. . . ."

"You told me last year."

She nodded. "Yes; I remember now. I think when I last saw you he had just gone back to the office. After six months' sick leave. He had a nervous breakdown."

"I didn't realise that."

"No. We were away at the time in Egypt." She looked at me, hesitated momentarily, studying me with a serious expression, then slowly said, "I'd better tell you the whole story. About two years ago, soon after we returned from Washington, Alan was appointed to the Embassy in Cairo. It was a big job, everybody thought; he was young, and Cairo's an important post. Everyone, from the Ambassador down, thought the world of him—at least I think so—and Alan worked very hard. Then he became ill. I thought it was overwork and the climate. Well, it may have been partly. I don't know. . . ." She paused for a moment. "I have to tell you this, James. By then we'd been married ten years, but there were times when I felt I didn't know him. He had fits of depression, he cried and he drank far more than was good for him. In the end it was suggested he should go home and have treatment."

"He always seemed so steady to me."

"Well, that was the general impression. But I knew. . . . And I'm sure—" She shook her head. "Well, lots of people found out about it. All his friends. . . ."

"Who were his friends?"

"Oh, he had all sorts. They weren't all diplomats. There were painters, writers, journalists and so on. I don't quite know what happened to him; it was probably strain, too much responsibility. It's happened to a lot of people in the service, you know; especially in America. But in the Foreign Office too. They have to work very hard sometimes."

94

This was the moment, I thought, to introduce Eric's name. I said: "Do you know Eric Fontanet?"

Selina shook her head. "Who's he?"

"He used to be at the Embassy in Washington, but I'm pretty sure not in Alan's time; he's only recently come back."

So he really was unknown to her. Then why the false name? I said, "You told me Alan occasionally drank more than was good for him."

"Yes. . . ."

"And that he sometimes went away for a few days without telling you?"

"Once or twice, but not like this; and he always rang up or sent me a wire."

"What reason did he give?"

"That he was feeling tired and wanted to be on his own. It was since we came back from Egypt." She was silent now, and I felt that she must have had to put up with more than she was willing to reveal to me. Suddenly she spoke again.

"You're staying for dinner, James, I hope."

"That's very nice of you. . . . If I may. . . ."

She got up and went out of the room, obviously to give instructions. It was nearly seven.

I "filed" the information she had given me surprisingly quickly. This may have been because something else had now begun to interest me. Was Selina still in love with Alan? It was puzzling. Once or twice during the conversation I had thought about the wisdom of telling her what I knew, but I had checked myself. It was risky. I did not mind particularly what she might think of me for telling her; by now I could hardly have cared less. But if she were still in love with Alan my story would break her heart. She might, of course, find out from someone else; and probably would, for that matter. But then I began to wonder whether perhaps she was not holding out on me as much as I was on her, but for a different reason. They had been married for over ten years. In that time a woman of Selina's intelligence and intuition might well have discovered almost everything. In that case, did she accept Alan for what he was and love him in spite of everything? That was the real question.

I found something of an answer, or so I thought, when she returned a few minutes later.

"Don't get up," she said quietly. "Everything's settled." Then she crossed over to the mantelpiece and drank her sherry.

"I never see you now, James," she said, and I looked up. I was wondering if it were pain which was making her talk as though our break had been a matter of a few weeks, instead of a decade. It was now that I realised that this was a Selina I had never known before. It is a characteristic of mine—probably of most of us—that I cannot help thinking about people I have known in the past, how they have developed, how they have stood up to life. I had thought about Selina probably more than about anyone else, but this situation I could never have visualised. And I suddenly remembered my first thought of her: she would die young.

We were both silent now. The original reason for my visit was forgotten. She was in pain, but I was still not certain whether it was the pain of the scandal or the pain of unrequited love. I decided to tell her what I knew.

"Selina," I said, but before I could begin we heard a car coming up the drive, her face went white and she ran to the window.

"Good Lord!" she said, and I heard the tone of bitter disappointment in her voice. "Someone's coming to dinner. An Egyptian doctor. Alan asked him and I forgot to put him off. Thank God you're here. I'll go to the kitchen and help Mrs. Murray. You talk to him, will you? But

96

please not a word about Alan. Just say he's away on official business. I'll explain to him later if I have to."

The doorbell rang and the maid led in a young man of about twenty-eight or thirty. He introduced himself as Dr. Eldin. With his large, dark eyes and fine, chiselled features, he had the good looks of ancient Egyptian paintings. He refused a glass of sherry, and we talked. He told me he was doing psychiatric research at St. Gabriel's Hospital. "In my country people are too poor and primitive to suffer much from psychiatric ailments," he said. His facial expression gave me no clue as to whether this was meant to be a plain statement of fact or a joke. But I guessed there was an affectionate nature and an intelligence underneath the almost too correct manners, the carefully tailored light-blue gaberdine suit, the surgically clean collar and shirt, the manicured fingernails and the gold identity bracelet.

4

Eldin gave me a lift to town, and on the way back we talked for a time about literature. Like so many psychiatrists, he was a novel-reader. Then, just as we were approaching Uxbridge, he suddenly said:

"Do you know Mr. Lockheed well?"

"He was at Oxford with me, so I've known him a long time, but not intimately. Why do you ask?" I said with some curiosity.

"I don't know. . . . I'm not sure about Mr. Lockheed."

I had not expected this remark, although once during dinner I had a fleeting impression that Eldin must have suspected that something was wrong. Did the man know something? I said, "How d'you mean, 'not sure'?"

"Oh," he laughed. "I mean it kindly. Excuse my English. What I mean is that I'm worried about him. You see, I knew him very well. In Egypt. Mr. Lockheed met me through a friend of mine. Another doctor. But, you see, I ought to tell you more in the beginning. Mr. Lockheed was an exception. I mean the English diplomat in Egypt, even if he's serious, you see, meets only the upper class. The diplomat goes to parties, plays sports with them. Mr. Lockheed told my friend he was not interested in parties, in the upper class. His interests . . . sympathy was with the young reformers, like my friend, journalists, economists, writers, scientists." Eldin's voice suddenly became warm. "Do you know that he learnt Arabic?"

"No; but I suppose many diplomats do."

"Well, he took lessons from a friend of mine, a schoolmaster, and he spent nearly all his free time with us. We had long discussions, and he likes us. I think, if it comes to what you call a show-down, we can count on him." I could hear the inverted commas round the word "show-down." "And it is coming—all over the world, all over the East. . . . Do you know that Mr. Lockheed's illness was connected with Egyptian problems? I am sure!" Eldin's voice suddenly rose.

"Well, no. How do you mean?"

"It may sound what you call . . . far-fetched, but the last bit was the poverty in Egypt, which gave him a nervous breakdown. It *can* happen." Eldin added intransigently. "He took it too much to his heart. He felt too much responsibility. But, of course, it was deeper; yes, yes. It started earlier, long before he came out to us. I have a theory. . . . You would not feel offended, please. . . . It's serious. . . . The English and Western people in general, but especially the English, are not very healthy mentally, or not healthy in the modern period. Physically they are strong, yes, tall, well-built and resistant, but not mentally. I always knew that mental illness . . . lunacy is very frequent in England, but there is something else. We don't know why. It's new—I mean recent. Probably because they left the soil. I am really sure that industrial civilisa-

98

tion has some very bad effects on people, which we must find and try to cure, because we can't go back to the soil. But also there's something wrong with the whole social structure. Morals. If I want to flatter you, I would say your illness is caused by responsibility for power, but the truth really, I think, is *maintaining* power. And that problem is full of strain now."

"How does that connect with Lockheed?" I said.

"A case of a neurotic. You can say it would have happened, might have happened, sooner or later anywhere. Maybe you would be right. It's a difficult question."

"But what actually did happen?"

"I was just going to tell you. He was very nice and full of energy as he came out. I met him a month after he arrived, you see. Then after a time he began to behave strangely. I realised he was taking to drinking. Many English people do, but not for the same reason as Mr. Lockheed. Mr. Lockheed was not bored in Egypt. He told me he was drinking because it was a release. I understand that. I don't drink myself, partly because I'm a Moslem, but I think I understand the psychology of the man who drinks. It *is* a release, but a very bad one. And Mr. Lockheed became angry when he was drinking—violent."

"You mean knocking people down?" I said this more or less as a joke, but Eldin replied, "Yes," and my impatience vanished.

"You see, the great reason why he had to come home to England is that he beat up an American diplomat and broke up his furniture. I know you wouldn't go on repeating this story to anybody, but it's true. It was kept out of our newspapers. It happened one evening, when he got drunk. . . ." Eldin became silent now, and my first reaction to his statement was surprise and my second doubt. Alan did not seem to me the sort of man who would beat up people and break up furniture; in fact, the very opposite. The story seemed fantastic. However, I was beginning to wonder, and I tried to think how Eldin's version of Alan's behavior fitted in with what Selina had told me.

"What happened afterwards?" I said.

"The Ambassador said to him he should go on sick leave, and Mr. and Mrs. Lockheed came back to England. That was last year. I got my research scholarship and came to England six months ago. I wrote Mr. Lockheed a letter to ask how he was, and he asked me to dinner. Because I am a doctor, he told me a few things about himself. It was a pity, you see, I came to England so late."

"Why?"

"Because, you see, I would have asked Dr. Weblen to see him. He is one of the greatest English psychiatrists. I'm studying under him at St. Gabriel's. The problem is this—but please don't mention it to Mrs. Lockheed—Mr. Lockheed's doctor sent him to a psychiatrist, who has been treating him, but I don't like it. I'm wondering if he's really cured. The doctor did what we call a short-cut analysis, which sometimes is good, sometimes not enough. Of course, I'm only guessing. I took Mr. Lockheed to the Egyptian Club to lunch a month ago and he seemed all right, but one never knows. Probably I'm wrong. Please don't mention it to Mrs. Lockheed."

Since Bayswater was on his way, I asked Eldin up to the flat and gave him a soft drink. We discussed Alan for some time. I managed to get him to talk about homosexuality in the East as compared with the West, but while he talked very intelligently, he did not connect Alan with inversion.

I shrugged my shoulders. Perhaps Eldin had not known Alan as well as he thought, although the things he had told me were certainly new and surprising.

Then I thought about Selina. As we were saying good-bye she had asked me twice to go back to see her soon.

8

I OPENED the door.

"Mr. Edmonton?" said the caller. He was about my height, and around thirty-five; he wore a blue pin-stripe suit and carried a soft brown hat in his hand.

"Yes," I said, feeling just a little self-conscious in my tattered dressing-gown at ten in the morning. Mrs. Graham had said something about a surveyor coming to look at the flats. But if indeed he was a surveyor, why had he not telephoned?

"May I have a word with you?" the man said, and it was clear at once that he was trying hard to be polite against his own inner convictions. This was no surveyor.

"Come in," I said, and in a flash I knew who he was. For the past four days I had been praying for a chance to meet him, and I had rehearsed my lines over and over again.

We were in my study and he looked round with a certain amount of uneasiness, as if his self-confidence had suffered a sudden eclipse after crossing my threshold. I saw him look at the bookshelves, the white mandarin and the carpet, but he pretended not to notice them. He looked at the front of my dressing-gown. His voice was slow.

"I'm sorry to trouble you, but I understand that through the mistake of a waiter you were handed a canvas bag which is not your property. . . ." Here he paused as if trying to make out what effect the "line" was having on me. Under the circumstances it was easy for me to decide on my own "line" at once.

101

"That's quite correct," I said. "I owe you an apology, Mr. . . ." I raised my right hand expectantly, socially.

He probably missed the catch, but all the same he hesitated for a second. "It's Read," he said.

I nodded, "I take it it's your property, Mr. Read?"

"Oh, yes," he said. It was all very amiable and social. Here was the chance for which I had been waiting.

"I'll go and fetch it. Do take a seat. You'll find cigarettes on the mantelpiece."

But when I came back from the kitchen with the bag, I found him standing exactly where I had left him, his back to the window, facing the door as if overcome by his unexpectedly easy success.

"Here you are, Mr. Read."

He was now, I thought, trying to be brusque in order to hide his excitement at his triumph. I guessed that at the back of his mind was the idea that he would gently let me off with a caution. He pulled the zip so fast that I thought the word "lightning," which is the French equivalent for zip, was perhaps the more apt term for it.

His eyes were now facing me. They were a mixture of childish peevishness and court-martial severity. "There were some papers in the bag?"

"Oh, yes. Wouldn't you like to sit down."

"Where are the papers?" he demanded. He was now apparently talking to one of his underlings.

"Where they should be, Mr. Read. Among my personal effects."

He blinked. "Could I have them back, please?"

"I should like to keep them, Mr. Read."

"I'm afraid you can't." He shook his head, politely. He had a little more elasticity than I had credited him with.

"Well now," I said. "I should like to make you an offer. The dossier you're looking for contains four pages about me. I'm sorry to say they are grossly inaccurate in every way, except when it comes to my income. Now my offer is

102

this: that I shall type out four pages containing the true facts about myself. Or, if you like, more than four. In fact, to make it really satisfactory, I suggest you ask me the questions and I'd give you the correct answers. Furthermore, I can get other people, highly reliable and respectable people, in important positions, to testify that everything I tell you is. . . ."

"I haven't got much time." He closed his eyes.

"I'm very sorry to detain a hard-working public official. I can send you the stuff by post. May I have your address?"

"You're not going to side-track me."

"I don't intend to. Incidentally, was it you who collected all that information about me?"

"That's beside the point."

"I suppose it is." My timing was getting better. I was now looking at his shoes as if I were interested. "If you prepare a dossier about me, it's your affair and beside the point, but it you fill it with inaccurate rubbish, that's mine. Very much mine. Incidentally, what department do you represent?"

"It's not for you to ask questions." His voice rose now. "You've got hold of some important Government papers."

"I couldn't agree with you more. I'm not sure whether they're important, but we needn't quibble about that. All you have to do is go and tell the police."

"That's where you're wrong." He tried to smile "sarcastically"; I had always known it was difficult. "We don't have to. We have other means of dealing with you."

"For example, forcing an entry into this flat on false pretences, and *failing* to find the papers. Then coming here and threatening me—not exactly successfully."

"You can be locked up for this."

"I don't believe it, Mr. Read. That would be difficult even in wartime."

"Oh, yes, you can. Official secrets . . ."

"Interesting secrets. You *secretly* collect rubbishy tittle-

103

tattle about people. At public expense, too. I'm not surprised you have to keep it secret. Incidentally, do they pay you by the word or by the hour?"

"I don't want any insolence from you, Edmonton. I'm warning you. Unless you hand over the papers you'll get into real trouble. We know exactly how to deal with people like you."

"You mean writers?" I asked with a smile.

"No; I don't mean writers."

"Then what do you mean?"

"I'll tell you." He put the bag on the floor and looked me straight in the eye. "There are two very good grounds on which I could get you into serious trouble. And I mean sent to prison."

"You seem to forget that you can't have secret trials easily nowadays. It's a tricky business."

He snorted, forcing a smile on his face. "Why should there be a secret trial? It would be so public that you'd never forget it. People like you should be careful."

"What about you?"

This time he lost his temper. "I'm not a homosexual like you."

"Oh, I see. So you and your department have decided I'm a homosexual. You've *certified* me. That's a new one."

"You could have been arrested any time during the last twenty years. You haven't got a leg to stand on."

"On the contrary, I've read all that rubbish in my dossier. I thought at first it was just a mistake or sheer stupidity, but now I see you quite firmly believe it, and actually think you have something on me. It's a very good line, if it works. I dare say some poor bastards are easy to frighten, but I'm not one of them, and I can't be frightened."

"You're not trying to deny it."

"Not *trying?* I *am* denying it."

"Your friends, your contacts . . ." He smiled again. "Don't try to fool me."

104

"What about *your* friends and *your* contacts?"

"You're not married," he jeered.

"Now I can see you're a bigger fool than I expected. I suppose you think because a person's married, he can't be a homosexual. In my case, anyway, you've made a complete idiot of yourself. It says in the dossier that I've never been married. If only you'd taken the trouble to go to Somerset House . . ."

"You're contradicting yourself, but that's beside the point. If you want to fight, we're ready. We've gone into the matter very thoroughly. We know that you frequent certain clubs and bars."

"I'm a writer," I said.

He laughed; this time his laughter sounded natural. "Don't try that line; it won't wash any more. Your name was once taken by the police in a raid."

"If it was—and I don't recall it—so was everybody's. You were probably there yourself."

He looked at me angrily, but said nothing. He glared at my shoes, then, as if they gave him some inspiration, he suddenly raised his head and his voice was triumphant.

"But even if you say you're not a homosexual, though, there's every evidence you're a Communist. You can't deny that."

"Your information about that is just as incorrect as your information about my emotional life. I'm not a Communist. You managed to find out that I joined the Communist Party nearly twenty years ago, but you most conveniently omitted the fact that I left it very soon after."

"All your friends and most of your contacts are Communists. And you wrote a Communist book under a false name."

I laughed aloud. It was, I admit, my intention to laugh, but I did not realise it would come off so well, nor that I should laugh so heartily. He looked annoyed, but his voice was triumphant. "You admit that you published it under a false name? Would you like to say why."

"I certainly will. Have you read it?"

"That's beside the point."

"Everything's beside the point that you find inconvenient to answer. Well, that's one question you don't have to bother about; I already know the answer. You've never read a book, and now you're trying to brush me off because you've made a fool of yourself again. Now, I'll tell you why it wasn't under my own name. It was a penny-dreadful detective story, which I wrote only to make money, and I'd have been ashamed to have put my name to it. You, however, ought to read it. The detective in my book seems to know his job better than you do yours. But perhaps I'm not fair. In real life it must be difficult to do these things, especially in a democratic country like England. What can you do now? You've threatened me with bogus evidence; I've broken it down, laughed at you, and you'll go home, I suppose, and try to invent something else equally stupid."

His face was very red now, but his voice was quite calm. "We're not prepared to discuss this any further. You must hand over the papers."

"I can let you have a copy and a few comments on your statements. I couldn't be fairer than that."

He moved. He was now almost stiff. "The joke's over. You've been warned, but you've paid no attention. You'll have to face the consequences."

"You've spent the last ten minutes here threatening me. You don't realise that the consequences can be quite unpleasant for you too."

He looked at me for a moment, then he smiled. "How?"

"There are one or two M.P.s who might be interested, not to speak of newspaper editors. And I happen to know a few."

106

Now he was uneasy. I could see it. His pretence at equanimity was unsuccessful. "You can't prove anything," he said.

"Don't be a fool. I can prove that you claimed the bag at the restaurant, I can prove that one of your men came for it again last Sunday and bolted when he saw me. My housekeeper will say that two men came here pretending to be telephone repairmen, and the Post Office will say that they've never sent anybody here. I can guarantee one thing, however," I said slowly. "There won't be any questions in Parliament about this case. I owe that to my country. The dirty linen won't be washed in public, but, by God, it will be washed in private. . . ." I bowed, ironically. "Over to you. . . ."

He smiled, he shook his head. "I know you're a wit," he said. It had become obvious while I had been talking that he was changing his tune. Suddenly a look of sadness crossed his face and his voice became correspondingly quiet. "But all you say, your whole attitude is so very typical of you talented writers, not to have a shred of patriotism. Jeering, snarling at your country, making fun of the Services. . . . I'm sorry I lost my temper with you, but you must admit you were very provocative, weren't you?"

"I was," I admitted. I decided to act repentance. "What do you suggest then?" I enquired.

"If mistakes have been made and you say there's been a slip-up, I can assure you I'll do my best to make amends. We're all human, you know. Mistakes can be made. . . ."

"I accept what you say. Then what do you propose to do?"

"I'll do my best to reopen your case and give you a fair deal. But the essential condition is that I must have the dossier."

"You mean because, in order to make corrections, you must have the pages first?"

107

"Precisely." The triumph was unmistakable.

"Right you are. Let me have your address, and I'll send you a copy at once."

"Why do you want to keep the original? Isn't my word good enough for you?" He was trying hard to sound reasonable. I became a trifle angry. He was taking me for a fool.

"Well, I'm afraid I can't have too much trust in a man who comes here and tries to threaten me, and then finds it won't work and changes his tune. . . ."

"And you say you're not a Communist," he said. He smiled lopsidedly.

"No, old boy. If this were Russia I might give you the dossier. You'd be a commissar and could probably torture me if you wanted, to obtain the customary public confession of a crime I'd never committed. Sorry, we're not in Russia. But since you question my patriotism, I'll prove to you exactly how patriotic I am."

"How?"

"By exposing you. You're spending public money like water and you're inefficient. You let atom spies slip away and pick on perfectly innocent people like me on no evidence at all. You commit blunders, then try to cover them up by other blunders."

"You don't know anything about these matters. I'd advise you to keep your opinions to yourself."

"Thank you for your advice. I shall make my opinions public."

"You can't do anything with those wretched papers," he smiled. It was now a hideous smile. He was showing his lower front teeth.

"Who says I can't?" I said quietly.

"Nobody'd believe your story. A scribbler . . ."

"Two minutes ago you called me a talented writer. How quickly you change your opinions. But you yourself told me that people *would* believe my story."

"I said nothing of the sort."

"You're virtually saying it now. You'd do anything to get the papers back. Would you like to tell me why?"

He looked at me with contempt; but apparently no insult, no repartee came to his mind. He was completely speechless, but I saw the rage.

"I can tell you why," I said. "We still manage to maintain democracy in this country, Read, with a free Press and public opinion, and what you're afraid of is that some M.P. or newspaper editor will get hold of this story."

"I'd lose my job," he said ironically.

"I don't think you would. Full employment in a free society, you know. . . . You won't have to resign your commission in the Air Force, but—"

He tossed up his head like a horse. "Who said anything about the Air Force?"

"Wrong question, Read." I shook my head sadly. "The correct question is: How do you know? Well, how do I know? I knew it the moment you came in the room. You must have seen from my dossier that I was in the Air Force myself, and it isn't difficult to pick out a regular airman. . . ." I wanted to add three more words: "especially ground staff," but I thought he had had enough.

"All that," he said wearily, "is beside the point. Tell me what *do* you want?" He shook his head.

"I want to talk to the man who actually wrote my dossier—if it wasn't you—and find out how he made so many appalling blunders."

My words seemed to have revived him. "Is that all?" he said. He managed to bring a little irony into the words.

"The rest doesn't have to concern you."

"You have your connections, no doubt." He was still ironical. I felt rather angry again.

"No doubt," I said.

"Who, for example?" he was smiling broadly, tauntingly.

"Anything to oblige. Aneurin Bevan for one." This was a bow at venture.

"You know him?" His sarcasm was thin now, but it was still there.

"You'll find out," I said. I bowed.

9

$\mathcal{I}$ WAS afraid he would, indeed, try to find out and that was worrying because I certainly did not know Aneurin Bevan.

The really alarming thing, of course, was that Read, or whatever his real name was, actually believed that I did. I had been too convincing. Read had clearly regarded me as a left-wing writer, and it was reasonable for him to assume, therefore, that I might have known one of the most famous left-wing politicians, who, furthermore, had once edited a political weekly.

It seemed fairly obvious to me from the beginning of the interview why Read had been so anxious to retrieve the file. He, himself, was personally involved. Losing official documents, even if they were of minor importance, was a serious matter, but how much more so when the documents fell into the hands of the man whom they intimately concerned.

Read's more than ordinary anxiety may perhaps have been due to the fact that his superiors were not yet aware that the file had been lost—I did not regard the man who had called at the Piraeus as his superior—and there was the danger now that I would spill the whole story. And what substance there might indeed have been to my threats had I really known Aneurin Bevan?

If my surmise was correct, and I felt it was, then Read's next move was probably to go to his superiors and make a clean breast of the story.

I paused for a moment to think whether he would then report what I had said to him. He would probably not admit that I had made mincemeat of him. Why should he? But would he, for example, say that I had asserted that the information in the dossier was false?

But a moment later I realised that this was unimportant. The really relevant thing seemed to be that Read's chief would almost certainly be told that I claimed Bevan's acquaintance and had threatened to tell Bevan all about it.

What then would happen? There was no reason why Read's boss should not believe that I knew Bevan, or at least that I had an entrée to him; so that first thing he might do would be to contact Bevan, before any real damage could be done to his department. And the chances were that—unlike me—the man in question really knew Bevan. The head of a Security or Intelligence or whatever department it was, was likely to have personal contacts with prominent politicians of all persuasions: right-wing, left-wing, centre. In that case, it was quite clear that I had prejudiced—if not killed outright—what had hitherto struck me as a good case. The trouble was that I had shown the weakness of my hand; by actually mentioning Bevan's name, I had thrown away my trump card.

What could I do now? The idea of approaching Broadwood suddenly came to me. When I had gone through the list of possible contacts, I had not considered him. It was thinking about Bevan that had brought him to mind. Broadwood was a "Bevanite" M.P. and a part-time literary critic. If I contacted him right away, he might be willing to report my version of the story before it reached Bevan from a source unfavorable to me. But that would not look well. In any case, Broadwood might be offended. "Why go to Nye?" he would probably say. "Don't you think I'm good enough to ask a question about it in the House?"

But the affair had further complications. Read had not once referred to Eric. Did he know that I had not only contacted him, but actually assisted him to run away in the company of Alan Lockheed? The Mystery Page clearly referred to Eric, and Read must surely have known it was in the dossier.

This was a serious matter. I would have to admit it to Broadwood, or to anybody I tried to contact. If only Broadwood knew me better. If only somebody knew me better. If only I knew somebody important. And my loneliness struck back at me like a blunt knife.

I thought again of Selina. Twice she had asked me to return to see her soon. Her pain had turned me into a friend. But now it was I who needed her, needed someone. And there seemed to be nobody else. I crossed over to the telephone.

2

I found Selina in the garden, knitting under a tree. She got up and led me by the arm to the house. "How sweet of you to come back," she said. "We couldn't talk yesterday," and the world made me feel guilty. I had come to see her under false pretences. I saw deep shadows under her eyes, which yesterday I had not noticed. "Have some sherry," she said. "My cousin John's coming to an early dinner. Do you remember him?"

"John Twining," I said uneasily, for this was about the first time that Selina had made a reference to what had been our past.

"So you do remember him," she nodded. "Rather a sad story. His wife went mad. She's been in a home for some time. . . . But there's so much to tell you." She took a tiny sip from her sherry and put the glass on the mantelpiece. "We couldn't talk yesterday. I don't think you knew Alan very well. . . ." She looked at me, and again she nodded as a much bolder woman might have done. I had noticed this same characteristic when I had last seen her.

"Did I tell you about our holiday in the French Alps?" she finally said. "Well, it was about two years ago. Before Alan was sent to Cairo. We went to the Alps with John Booker, the painter, and his wife and another married couple. From the Treasury. It was rather fun. I thought Alan was enjoying himself, but one evening he said he wanted to go and spend a couple of days on his own in the next village."

"Just like that?" I asked.

"Yes. He said he was rather tired and wanted to be on his own. I thought perhaps the people with us were getting on his nerves, so I suggested going together, but he said he wanted to be alone. Well, it was difficult to explain to the others. That was the only thing. I could put up with it myself. People get into moods like that."

Yes, they do, I thought and I felt a pang of envy for her understanding. And what had Alan done in the next village? Had Selina tried to find out? And did she know now?

"Anyhow," she continued, "two days later Alan came back. I didn't ask him a question and pretended that nothing had happened."

"Didn't the others ask you?"

"As a matter of fact, they hardly noticed. I invented a story about Alan being invited by an old friend." She shook her head, "You see, that time there was an explanation. He said he was tired and wanted to be completely alone, even from me, for a couple of days. But this time there's the deception. He pretended he had to go to the office on Saturday, which wasn't true, then the story about a friend in trouble. And this time a lot of people must know about it."

"You were," I said, "married for over ten years, and

nothing which you'd call strange happened till that summer two years ago. Is that it?"

"Well, Alan's highly strung, but so are many people . . . but we got on."

This was evasion, I thought, almost angrily. I said: "You're still in love with him."

But at once I felt sorry for what I had just said. It was a jealous outburst, but fortunately she did not appear to have noticed it.

"It's difficult to define love," she said, and her face almost reflected apology for not being able to answer yes or no straight away. "Mother calls it 'harmony.' I used to laugh at the word. It seemed such a prosperous New England expression, rather like 'gracious living,' but I think she's right. You see, in the last few years there was always something that stood between us, something I can't define, a kind of . . . withdrawal on Alan's part. It would have caused trouble to some people, but we were lucky. . . ."

"You never discussed it with Alan?" I said.

"Never. We had a kind of tacit understanding, and I felt Alan knew, and it worked. With a woman, of course, who has two children. . . ."

Yes, I thought, the old formula of the faithless husband. Give her children, tie her down, tie her round yourself through them, make divorce difficult. I was carried away by anger again and said: "You've never thought there may have been someone else. . . ."

"That's what Margaret said. Probably because her sister carries on with men—so I've always heard—but I don't know. With Alan, at least till he became ill, I always knew I came first and that he was in love with me. And that was always enough. But this time, I'm seriously worried. He's been gone four days now; not a letter, no explanation, nothing. He's absent without leave from the Office. I no longer believe it's a secret mission. But I think the Foreign Office knows something, and they won't tell me. That's what worries me. There's something quite serious. . . ."

"Some scandal, you mean?" I said.

Selina suddenly moved towards me on the sofa and took my hand. She was looking at me hard, as if she had been asked to identify a suspect.

"Why do you say that, James?" she said quietly in the end. "Have you heard something?" Her voice was quite strange now. I could hardly recognise it. She said with resignation: "There's no need to spare me. This time . . . I must know."

"Darling," I said and gripped her hand. "I *do* know something. I wanted to tell you yesterday, but I couldn't. Later, I'll tell you why I couldn't. . . ."

3

". . . After that," I said, "the man left in a huff and I was in half a mind to call him back and say, 'You've forgotten the marshmallow. . . .' "

She did not smile. I had not expected that she would, but it was amazing how calm she had been while I was telling her the story. When the idea of telling her first crossed my mind I had decided to leave out the reason Eric had given for his departure. If she asked, I had planned to shrug my shoulders, say something vague, and in the end ask her what she herself thought. But as I finished, she made no comment. Did she know?

"I must ask you again to forgive me," I said quickly, "for not telling you straight away. I thought it would upset you even more."

She took my hand again. Then she smiled, for no obvious reason. She bit her lower lip, and a moment later I saw a tear in her eye, and she soon began to cry. This was the first time I had seen her cry. I had been in love with her once, but we had never been as intimate before; her tears created a new bond between us.

I wondered what she was thinking now. While I was speaking, she had hardly ever interrupted and had asked only one or two unimportant questions, as if merely to indicate that she was listening. But now I suddenly felt that the questions were about to come. And I knew it would be as painful for me to answer them as for her to ask them.

She moved. I saw her hand rise, then stop halfway in the air. "May I have your handkerchief?" she said, and her voice sounded calm. I gave it to her and she wiped her eyes, then she looked at the handkerchief for a second.

"I'm sure it was Fontanet who came here Saturday afternoon and went away with Alan," she said. "Only I can't understand why he used a false name, why the lies. . . . Or perhaps it was all part of it. . . ." She turned away from me. This was a withdrawal, an unexpected break in our intimacy. Perhaps my original idea had been correct. What I had told her had obviously hurt her more than even I could realise. It was true that sooner or later she must have found out about Alan; somebody would surely have told her. But why did it have to be me? She had asked me, but I could have pretended I knew nothing. I felt as if I had hit her when she was down. She might easily think I had acted out of revenge, holding back my poisoned dagger for twelve years, waiting for my chance and then stabbing when it came along. Suddenly I felt like a cad. To get up and leave her now would have been a dreadful thing to do. To stay on was worse. I could not see her face, but there was no doubt she was going through a terrible crisis.

I am an impulsive man, but then I dared not speak to her. I longed for a drink, a cigarette, but I felt it would not be right to take one. In this particular situation nothing was right.

116

I do not know how long we sat there silently, Selina facing the mantelpiece and I gazing into the vacuum, seeing nothing and feeling like a cad.

Then I suddenly noticed she was looking at me. I saw her smile. Her eyes under their dark brows were dry. "I wonder how I can help you, James," she said.

The words were so unexpected that for a moment I could not speak, and how strange my own voice sounded to me when I said, "Help *me?*"

She nodded and now she was definitely smiling. "You may think I'm only worrying about you so as to take my mind away from—" She shook her head. "But now I can understand something I didn't seem to understand before."

I looked up. What on earth could she mean? Had she known all about Alan for some time? Or was what I had told her merely the last link in the chain? But before I could get any further she said, "Look, John's coming to dinner. I think he'll be able to advise you what to do. As a matter of fact, I rang him last night, told him all about everything and asked him to find out what he could for me. . . ." She shrugged a shoulder as if to say: "Nothing can surprise me any more. . . ."

"John's at the Admiralty," she continued. "He's got good connections. That's why I 'phoned him. He'll probably be able to help you as well."

"It's very good of you, Selina."

"It's the least I can do for you," she said and her expression for a moment seemed a little severe. "James," she said, "I'd like to ask you something very personal. . . ."

"Yes," I said. "Go on."

"You got married during the war."

"Yes," I said, rather surprised that she knew. I wondered what she was going to say.

"What went wrong?"

"Oh, it was chiefly my fault."

"In what way?"

"It was stupid of me to assume that she'd settle down to a life on a working-class income. . . ."

"You mean you didn't know her really well before you married her?"

"I'd say I was just bloody selfish. I married her because I was desperately hurt. . . ."

The sentence was out. It could not have been more out. I was looking at the Naysmith, or, rather, its frame, because I dared not look at Selina. This was about the nastiest, the most idiotic thing I could have said. "I don't know," I sighed, trying to undo the damage. This was even worse. I felt I was losing my temper. With myself, of course.

4

We were in the dining room.

"You have a very good case," Twining said after a while, looking at me like a barrister who had been briefed by a cousin on behalf of a poor acquaintance. Twining had changed a lot during the twelve years since I had last seen him. His hair looked green, at least by the illumination of the wall lights above the sideboard and over the mantelpiece. His face had become fatter and his left eye seemed to have slipped down about a third of an inch, giving the impression at times that it was artificial.

"Now I'll tell you exactly what we ought to do," he said. His voice was not that of a senior civil servant; it did not go with his dark suit and stiff collar, and with his membership of the Travellers' Club. It sounded more like a military command. "I have a very good friend," he said, studying me severely with his bad eye. "I won't mention his name, but I think he's the man who'll be able to help you."

He looked at his pocket. "Selina," he said, "do you mind

if I leave you two for a few minutes and use your telephone?"

"Certainly. It's in the drawing room."

As he rose and left the room, without closing the door behind him, Selina said: "I'm sure he's going to help you."

"It was very kind of you," I said. It was curious how in the last two hours she had talked more of me than of Alan.

Selina had heard the same story twice, and again I felt she had been very calm; in fact, once she had answered a question herself which Twining had put to me. And again I was conscious of something like a new intimacy between us. Or was this merely a piece of some strange, pathological wishful thinking on my part? Now that Twining was out of the room, I thought again of the things she and I had discussed just before his arrival. Why had she questioned me about my marriage? It was certainly not to make conversation. She must have known it was a painful subject to me. Then I forced myself away from the subject. For quite a time neither of us spoke. Then, "How little he found out from the Foreign Office," I said. This was perhaps selfish on my part and in a way an indication of doubt as to what Twining could do for me.

But before she could reply, we heard his footsteps, and he returned to the room. There was something dramatic in the way he walked through the doorway and resumed his seat. "I was lucky," he said. "I've just caught him. Selina, my dear, d'you mind if we go off soon? The point is that the man wants to see me tonight. . . ."

5

"I'm very grateful to you," I said to Twining as soon as we got out of the little turning that led into the main arterial road to London. "And very excited. Would it be too much to ask you what you said to the man?"

He was silent for a moment, as if concentrating on the steering wheel of the tiny car. Then he said, "Not if you promise to keep it to yourself."

"Certainly," I said.

"It was a chance coincidence," he said after a pause. "This morning I went to the Foreign Office to see a friend and take him out to lunch. I was trying to find out for Selina what I could about Alan. Well, my friend wasn't alone. I knew the other man in his room quite well though; and he knew I was Selina's cousin and why I'd come. When I said I'd be seeing Selina tonight, he asked me to ring him back immediately if there was any fresh development to report, such as a letter from Alan. Well, I thought your story was very much up his street. So when I rang him during dinner I told him I knew the fellow who'd bought the railway ticket for Alan, and he was on me at once. He was on the verge of going out, but now he wants to see me as soon as possible."

"He's a diplomat, of course . . ." I said.

"Now. That's all I'm going to tell you. But if anything happens, I'll let you know. By the way, are you in the telephone book?"

"I am."

"Right. . . ." He paused for a second, indicating that the subject was closed for the time being, then he said:

"Selina's taking it well. It's a very sad story. Much worse than I thought. Before I heard your version, I thought it was just a nervous fling. Alan was a bit of a problem child, you know. He hadn't been well recently and there was some talk of retirement. Now I'm not sure."

He suddenly said: "Did Fontanet tell you he'd been suspended from the F.O.?"

"No. We weren't really friends, you know."

"I realised that from what you told us. . . . So he didn't tell you?"

120

"Was that why Alan introduced him to Selina under a false name?" I said.

"I'm sure it was," Twining said.

10

*T*HE telephone must have been ringing for some time. Heavy with sleep I took the receiver. "Yes," I said.

"Mr. Edmonton." It was a woman's voice.

"Yes."

"Just a minute, please. I have a call for you."

"Who . . . ?" I said. But there came no answer, only a buzz, then the faint clicking of a typewriter somewhere far away. I waited and glared at my watch on the night table. It was half-past ten. It must have been nearly two o'clock in the morning when I had finally decided to take a sleeping pill.

There was the click of another switch on the telephone; then somebody said, "Is that you, Edmonton?"

"Yes," I replied. "Who is that?"

"John Twining—you remember we met yesterday."

"Oh, yes." I was now completely awake.

"I have some news for you. Are you busy this morning?"

"Well, no," I said. At least, that is probably what I said. By then I was too excited even to think coherently.

"Could you manage to go and see Miss Welgar?"—he spelled out the name—"at the Ministry of Education. Her office is in the new building in Malplaquet House, in Great College Street." He gave me her room number. "I'll have to ring her back to confirm it. Can you be there by twelve o'clock?"

"Yes," I said. I wanted to ask a question, but checked myself just in time.

"Splendid. I'll see you soon, I hope. Well, good luck." He rang off.

The porter at Malplaquet House apparently knew that I was expected, because when I was about to pull out my pen to fill in the usual form with name, address, name of official, object of visit and so on, he handed me a slip of paper which already had my particulars on it. For the third time, I wondered what sort of woman Miss Welgar would turn out to be. For some reason I expected a female don, seconded to Intelligence duties.

I felt disappointed when I was shown into a poky little room and saw two bespectacled, middle-aged women sitting at facing desks. Clerical grade, I thought, more in bitterness than snobbery. What next? One of them looked at me with an air of faint interest, then the other got up from behind her typewriter and came towards me. "This way, please," she said severely, and took me out of the room.

"It's Sir Paul Addyman who wants to see you," she whispered with the air of a professional *farceur*, after closing the door behind us. "Will you wait a minute, please?" And she darted off and knocked on a door at the end of the corridor, then went in.

I wondered why the hullabaloo, since she had told me the man's name; and immediately I heard the clicking of a machine from a room behind me. Mechanised Intelligence, I reflected frivolously; probably a thought-reading or a spying machine, which follows people's movements invisibly, but it ought to have been silent. Then the door opened and Miss Welgar said, "Will you come in, please?"

Considering that Malplaquet House was a brand new post-war building with automatic lifts and steel-framed windows, the room into which I was now shown was sur-

122

prisingly large and impressive. I just had time to notice that the furniture and pictures must have come from some old room in Whitehall. There were large engravings of Eminent Victorians on the walls with their edges slightly foxed. An enormous perpetual calendar in an oak frame stood on the mantelpiece.

Then I caught sight of someone standing against the wall; obviously Sir Paul Addyman—a tall, grey-haired, pink-faced man with bifocal glasses, in a dark grey cheviot suit. He looked like an Army doctor.

He leaned slightly sideways as we shook hands, said absolutely nothing, then waved me to a chair facing his desk.

"It was good of you to come at such a short notice," he said at last in a bedside voice. He sat down in a semicircular leather chair. "I know your name, of course," he nodded, and I saw him smile. Slowly he pulled out from his waistcoat pocket a concave, Edwardian cigarette case, which he held out to me.

I took a cigarette and offered him a light, which he waved away with his hand. Now I guessed why he treated his visitors to Turkish cigarettes of a brand which I thought had gone out around 1930. All this time I was conscious that he was looking at me carefully, as if trying to check someone else's diagnosis of me. Then he nodded.

"First of all," he said, and put both his hands on the table, "may I ask you to regard your visit and everything we discuss now as entirely private. You're a former Service officer," he smiled, "so I don't have to explain why. . . ."

"No, sir."

It was then that I saw that his hands were resting on an open file. Seeing me watch him, he looked at a piece of paper and quickly closed the file.

"I know all about that unfortunate affair with a man called Read."

I looked up. My first surprise was that Read was the man's real name and had not been invented on the spur of the moment for my benefit. It may, of course, have been his accepted code-name, but perhaps I was too suspicious. I said nothing. Addyman and I eyed each other for a moment or two, then he said, "Well, he made a mess of things. But that business of your dossier can wait. We'll discuss it later. Not today, if you don't mind, but certainly we'll discuss it, if you want to. That's a promise." He smiled briefly. "Someone would have contacted you about that in any case, but now there's something infinitely more urgent. I shall have to ask you a few questions. But before you answer them I'd like to assure you that you're in no way implicated. Right?" He looked at me then nodded again. "First, I'd like to know why you contacted Eric Fontanet when you did?"

"Because his name was in the dossier."

"Was that the only reason?"

"Well, yes. His was the only name mentioned. And I knew him personally. We were at Oxford together."

"But you weren't intimate friends?"

"No. We knew each other at Oxford, but I more or less lost track of him in later years. I only saw him occasionally."

"Would it be too personal perhaps to suggest that you disliked him?"

"Well," I said.

"Well," he smiled. "I think I have your answer. Now, tell me, how did Fontanet react to the dossier?"

"He became very agitated when he saw the extra page, and he came back the following day and said he had to leave the country."

"Did you ask why?"

"I did."

"What did he say?"

"That it was in connection with some sex scandal."

"Did he say that?"

"Yes."

124

"Then you bought him the railway tickets?"

The question made me uncomfortable, in spite of the man's assurances. Addyman noticed it. "Please understand," he said, "that what you did was perfectly innocent. Nobody's going to blame you for it. Tell me, did Fontanet seem grateful to you for showing him the dossier and getting him the tickets?"

I felt relieved. "In a way he did. Of course, he's a difficult person, very moody and rather unconventional. He's inclined to take things for granted. But he did thank me. . . . Now I remember distinctly, he *did*."

"Was he pleasant when you first contacted him?"

"Yes; definitely."

"And during the conversation?"

"Yes; again until I told him his name was in my dossier."

"I see." Addyman remained silent for a moment, removed his glasses, then looked at me again as if trying to search my mind. What on earth was he trying to find out?

"Now, let's assume that you met again today, do you think he'd be pleased to see you?" he said slowly.

"Well . . ." I could not quite see the point of the question. "So much would depend on the circumstances. You have to admit, sir, I don't exactly expect to meet him now."

"Quite so," he smiled. "But all things being equal, you think he'd be glad to see you again?"

"Oh, I think he would."

"By the way, did Fontanet tell you who his companion was?"

"No; he didn't. I didn't want to ask."

The second part of my answer was, of course, untrue, but Addyman apparently noticed nothing. "I see," he said. "So you only found out later. . . . Now, you're an old friend of Mrs. Lockheed?"

"Yes; I've known her a long time."

"And Lockheed himself?"

"He was at Oxford with me too."

"So he was," he nodded. "Were your relations friendly?"

"Again, he was a man I hadn't seen much since I came down—" I broke off abruptly. I knew Addyman was watching my face. I wondered if Twining knew that I had once been in love with Selina.

"You moved in different circles," Addyman said.

"Yes."

"I take it that he wasn't jealous of you?" He smiled.

"How could he be?" I broke out. So Addyman knew. I flushed with shame.

"You'll have to forgive me," he said. "It's all *very* relevant."

What on earth was he driving at? I asked myself again. Was he trying to implicate me? In spite of the fact that he looked and talked like a man I could trust, I was feeling uneasy now. He picked up his glasses, played with them for a second, then looked at me as if having come to a decision. His whole tone had changed. "Well, I've decided to take a chance." He replaced his glasses on the dossier. "You may not know it, Edmonton, and I can assure you nobody's going to blame you, but by a strange coincidence you tipped off and in fact assisted the escape of two men who may well have been traitors to their country."

The words were gently spoken, quite slowly and almost without emphasis. The shock, the terrible shock was not in the low-toned, medical voice, not in the glance which, devoid of the glasses, was friendly, almost avuncular, but in the words themselves. Perhaps it was the cold, legal cliché, the deadly finality of a stock phrase; as if he had said "premeditated murder."

Then I realised, with a sudden pang of guilt, that what I felt was not really shock, but a very intense and very violent excitement; an almost sadistic thrill. For a split second I could not decide whether it was a thrill over a

126

crime against power and authority or over the fact that two men who had scored off me in the past were now about to go to their doom.

I had been facing Addyman all the time, without really seeing him, and now I suddenly noticed him again. His expression had not changed, and I was back once more in his room. I was, or so I thought, conscious again, responsible, a citizen, a moral being capable, according to his own lights, of distinguishing between good and evil. And this time evil gave me no thrill, only disgust.

I now felt like a fool. I had automatically assumed there was some sex scandal. Looking back on it, in fact, I was not sure it had not been I who had put the idea in Fontanet's head. But the revelation that I had been on the wrong track only served to increase my bewilderment.

I had been tricked into helping two traitors to escape. But what had they done? Now that I was recovering from the shock, I somehow could not quite think of the two men—Lockheed in particular—in this light. Had I perhaps been caught up, like some character in a nightmare novel, in a huge and sinister bureaucratic joke? Were they perhaps as innocently accused as I had been in the orange-colored dossier?

But as I looked at Addyman, I felt—in fact, I knew—he had told me the truth. Now I saw the line of bitterness around his lips. "I didn't realise, sir," I said. I felt I had to say something.

"I know. How could you?" Addyman's calm, bedside voice gave me great relief. Among other things, he did not seem to be put off by that woolly, prep-school commonplace I had just uttered. "Incidentally," he said—he raised a forefinger slightly—"do you know a man called Barton?"

"A bank manager?" I said.

He shook his head. "How old?"

"Must be around sixty."

"Not the man. The Barton I have in mind is about forty

or so. His Christian name is Jan and he isn't an English-man. Actually, a journalist. . . ."

"I don't know him," I said.

He turned a page or two in the dossier and handed me a small passport photograph which he pulled from under a clip. "D'you know this chap?"

It was a man with prominent and outstanding ears and an air of infinite sadness. He wore horn-rimmed glasses. "No," I said.

"No." Addyman nodded and reached for the picture. "This is very important," he said, but he looked away from me and closed his eyes as if listening to something. But a moment later his eyes again were searching my face. This time the feeling was quite uncomfortable. I felt he was going to ask a question more embarrassing even than any-thing he had yet asked. At last he spoke.

"I should like to ask you this," he said. "Would you like to help me?"

"In what way, sir?"

"I'll tell you. Lockheed and Fontanet are in France. Would you be prepared to go over to Paris for us? I can tell you now that a good deal depends on you. You'll get the details later if you'll just say now you're prepared to go."

"Yes," I said. I wondered if I had spoken too soon, if I was betraying a childish eagerness.

I was right, because he blinked and said, "There's no danger about it, and you won't have to stay long, so I hope it won't interfere with your business. And, naturally, we'll pay all your expenses."

I was a little overwhelmed. I just sat there looking at him across the large Victorian desk. "What I've asked you to do is unusual, I know," he said. "Please think about it as some form of service to your country. Let's say you've been recalled to the Air Force. I hope," he continued and his voice was decisive, "you can be ready at short notice. We don't know yet, but you may have to leave tonight."

"I'm quite ready," I said.

"That's splendid." He looked at his watch; then lifted the receiver of one of his telephones and dialled one single digit. "Rayne," he said, "could you come over, please?"

"I'm sorry," he turned to me, "I can't ask you to lunch. I've got to go out, but Rayne will take you. I want him to tell you all about your job. He's a nice fellow. I hope you'll come to see me when you return from France. In the meantime, I'll take care of that business with your dossier. Perhaps we'll talk about it when you're back in London." He was now smiling.

A moment later there was a knock on the door. In came a tall, burly, red-haired man, who looked uncomfortable in the double-breasted flannel suit he was wearing. You could see at once that he would have been so much more at home in tweeds or in battledress.

"Rayne," Addyman said, "this is Mr. Edmonton." I rose in a hurry, and the man smiled. "He's very kindly said 'Yes' to our proposition." It was only when Rayne came near and reached out a freckled hand that I realised that he was much younger than I had first thought. Thirty maybe.

"Will you take him out to lunch and explain what you have to explain? I have an engagement. If you need me for anything, Miss Welgar will know where to find me."

2

"Sometimes," Rayne said quietly, "these things happen when you least expect them." A hundred small wrinkles seemed suddenly to have appeared around his eyes and lips. He was the type of man who looked much older when he smiled. I felt he must have been as excited as I and this

129

was a further link between us, though I had liked him from the first minute. He was the "reliable," "steady" type, broad-shouldered and hefty, but without the shyness which often goes with that sort of person. He looked like a really amiable bus conductor, but his voice was unexpectedly academic, with a faint suggestion of the senior common room about it.

We were having lunch near the Abbey, at a place that looked more like a luncheon club for M.P.s or civil servants than a restaurant. It was an all-male place where official England could for an hour or so shed its compulsory reserve. There was loud conversation and a hint of ribald jokes. The menu was masculine too—roast beef and lamb and plenty of sauce and apple pie and cheese.

"The trouble is," Rayne said now, "that there are several Intelligence Services and they more or less compete with one another. No information is ever shared. If your friend hadn't come along at the last minute, our job would have been twice as difficult."

"You may as well tell me all," I said. The noise was so great that it was not necessary to lower our voices, and in any case our table was so small that we were practically sitting on top of each other.

"I can't tell you the whole story, because there's no time, for one thing; but one of the two men had been suspected and had in fact been under actual observation. But it's so typical. . . ." His laugh had just a touch of contempt.

"So typical of what?" I said after a time.

"Incompetence. Of course, you played a part too. Quite unwittingly, I mean."

"I dare say. But who lost the dossier in the first place?"

Rayne snorted. "That's typical again. Luckily, our outfit had nothing to do with it. It was one of the rival firms."

"Would you like to see it?" I said.

"It would amuse me, but we haven't got time today." He looked at his watch. "We'd better leave as soon as we've finished lunch, because I'll be calling for you in a taxi at five. But before that I need your passport. I hope it's valid."

"It is. But surely we're going to France and there's no need for a visa?"

"No; but you'll need money, and your currency allowance must be entered. I'll send a messenger with you to bring it back to me." He looked at the table for a moment. "I'll call for you sharp at five, and we'll be leaving by air. I'll fill in the details for you on the journey if we get the chance. I don't know how long we'll be staying in France. Probably a week. So, bring whatever you think's necessary."

3

The aircraft was full and there was no chance to talk to Rayne, although I wanted desperately to talk to someone. The whole thing was incredible and improbable; a breath-taking transformation whereby from the hunted I was suddenly invited to join the pack of hunters. And this moment, high above the Channel, was my first opportunity for meditation. There was a comparative quiet and a bogus impression of slowness; we were flying high, and it seemed as though we were drifting along at about four miles an hour instead of two hundred.

After our lunch, I had taken a taxi in the company of an elderly passenger, to whom I had given my passport. Then I had packed. I had time enough, but I was not sure whether I had put in everything necessary for the journey. What was necessary for such a journey? Every now and again, looking round in the bedroom, I had stopped. I did not know which was the stronger, the excitement or the wish to talk to someone and communicate my sensations. I remember, in the middle of sorting out my socks—and I never had many—that I had got up, gone to the study

131

and taken the receiver off the telephone with the intention of telling Selina. It was only then I had heard the operator's "Toll number, please," that I had said, "Never mind," and replaced the receiver. It was the voice, the impersonal and anonymous voice of the State, that had reminded me that I must keep my news to myself. I had been asked not to breathe a word to anyone, and I did not doubt in any case that Selina's telephone was tapped; perhaps mine too. The thought suddenly made me feel important.

How much, I had wondered, did Twining know now, and how much would he tell Selina? Then I had thought that perhaps there was no harm in writing her a careful letter, which she would, in any case, not receive until the next day.

"A bread-and-butter letter," the sort one used to write to one's hostess after a dinner or a week-end, during the years before the war, I had thought. I had not written one for several years and was out of touch with conventional social forms. In the end I had written: *Just a note to thank you for the excellent dinner and for your sweet company. It was extremely kind of you to ask your cousin to help me. I am now going away for a few days, but I hope to give you good news on my return.*

A few days, I had thought then; a few days, I was thinking now. What would they bring? What had happened to me was not just one single sensational event, but a succession of events, full of feverish excitement and promise.

Nothing like this had ever happened to me before, nor had I even ever dreamt of such adventures. I am not that type of man. And having never dreamt about them, I had never written about them either. Everything, or nearly everything, that had ever happened to my characters had taken place in the mind. Ogilvy, it is true, in *The Man in the Moon,* contemplated murdering someone, but the idea came to nothing. Perhaps that was what was wrong with my books; I had been specialising on the mind and, once in a blue moon, on the heart. There was no action.

I was now thinking of the adventure stories of my childhood. While other boys at school had lapped them up, I had taken an almost instinctive dislike to them. Precocious child that I had been, I had thought them irritatingly unreal. They were, I suppose, crude, those Buchans and Sappers and Oppenheims, because the melodrama, the absurdity, the horror, were not humanised or given universal significance. But people read them eagerly, because they needed them. Living in a revolutionary age, people nevertheless failed to notice the revolution, and, finding life duller than ever, they were lonelier and more obscure than in any previous century.

I looked at Rayne. He was reading an evening paper. I was not sure if he was doing it to hide his excitement or to prevent me from talking.

After a time, he noticed me looking at him, and he said, "Another twenty minutes."

"This is the first time I've flown in a commercial aircraft," I said. How unreal my words sounded. I wondered if he thought so, or rather if he knew what self-discipline I was exerting just then to talk about commonplaces.

"Did you do much flying in the R.A.F.?" he asked, but he returned to his paper almost before I could reply.

On the way to the Waterloo air terminal in the taxi he had told me he was an Australian. So that was the explanation for his greater detachment, his broader vision, what seemed to me his more intelligent patriotism, and, above all, his appearance of classlessness which was there despite a certain conformity to Staff Officer standards. He was one of a new generation of Australians: no marked accent, no gold fillings in front teeth, no uncouth "colonialism." The older type of Australian was provincial: the pioneer who came to terms with lace curtain and aspidistra; Rayne's type is a near approach to the world citizen, who comes to terms with Toynbee and Russell. Compared with Rayne, we may perhaps appear rather insular.

Suddenly, I felt a slight suggestion in my stomach that we were fast losing height, and somebody behind me said, in a throaty French-cigarette voice *"Regardez, Félicien, la Seine."*

4

I was having dinner by myself under two Phoenix palms in the dining room of the hotel in the rue Arsène Houssaye. Rayne and I had talked a little on the way to the hotel. He had said there was plenty of time, and that he would brief me the following day, because he had to go out that evening after booking in at the hotel.

In the hotel room he had given me a thousand francs and said he was not sure what time he would be back. "I'm sorry I have to imprison you, but please don't leave the hotel tonight." His voice was social; the tone firm. "You're only supposed to be arriving tomorrow and you might by chance bump into someone who knows you."

He had presumably meant Fontanet and Lockheed. This was the first time I had thought about them since leaving Addyman's room. There had been so many personal, more or less insignificant things to think about that until now I had not bothered about the real thing, the root problem and Addyman's four dreadful, revealing words.

After my meal, I went up to my room and looked out of the window. The Arsène Houssaye is a narrow street, usually almost deserted save for the cars parked along the pavements, but as I leaned out of the window I could see into a part of the Champs-Elysées, and from the aura of light above the house on the corner I guessed that the Arch must have been illuminated. It was a warm, sweet evening, and I knew that men and women in improbable and unlikely shoes were hurrying with nervous Parisian speed up and down the Boulevards, and I could hear the rumble of the cars on the avenues converging on the Etoile.

I knew the neighborhood fairly well, although I could never have afforded to live there. Now here I was, with a mind almost bursting at the seams, imprisoned at half-past nine in a small, old-fashioned, intimate, expensive hotel three minutes from the Etoile. I had seen the chestnut trees in full bloom between Le Bourget and La Villette from the airways bus, and the plane trees along the Champs-Elysées from the taxi window, and now, after sunset, the luminous colors of the town were changing every five minutes, and I was incarcerated without even a book.

Surely, I thought, I might already have bumped into any number of people on the plane, on the bus, in the hotel itself; and for all I knew Rayne might not return till the morning.

The bookshops in the neighborhood, I seemed to recall, kept open till midnight, and I vaguely remembered there was one by that intersection of the Avenue de Wagram; what the hell was it called—the street, I meant? In any case, I knew the way blindfold. Rayne would never find out.

But it was struggling with a guilty conscience that I descended the stairs and stole out of the hotel like a lodger leaving without paying.

I hurried along the street: in the atmosphere of gasoline vapors and cooking and radio music. Within a few minutes I had found a bookshop, even before I got to the one I had in mind, and as I entered I was aware of the smell of books and cheap scents. The shop was full of people, some trying out fountain pens or buying postcards, others, like a girl I noticed with hairy legs like a deer, and obvi-

135

ously from the Midi, browsing. The shelves were full of the white backs of Gallimard and Grasset and the yellow backs of Calmann-Lévy and Mercure de France. In a box marked *Occasion* I saw a large number of Maurice Leblanc and Rex Stout and Simenon and Peter Cheyney, and among them, its cover torn, dusty and lonely in exile, was Francis Jammes' *Clara d'Ellébeuse*.

"*C'est combien?*" I asked the assistant, and my voice must have sounded loud and excited and peremptory, for everybody looked at me. And as I paid and hurried out into the bright lights of the Wagram, I felt that there are times when the voice of nostalgia can sound like a cry of pain.

//

I WOKE, it seemed, a second or two before the *femme de chambre* knocked on my door with the breakfast tray. From the moment I opened my eyes I was fully conscious of the events of the previous day. In fact, in the slightly cool air and the blue and gold light of the morning, they seemed less dreamlike and more excitingly realistic than before.

The breakfast cup was enormous and had no handle: old memories of Paris stirred, and the smell of French coffee began to permeate the room, mixing with the smell of disinfectants from washstand and *bidet* and the harsh, hygienic smell of the bed-linen.

While I was eating, I looked at my watch on the nighttable; it was half-past eight. I saw the book I had bought. Rereading the tales of Clara d'Ellébeuse, Almaide d'Etremont and Pomme d'Anis was little more than an excursion into my past, and at this moment my past left me cold. At one time I had thought them the greatest thing in literature, but now little remained except the style. I pushed the book into the drawer. A moment later there was a knock on the door and Rayne strode in.

He wore a fawn-colored tweed jacket, slightly crumpled from having been packed, and I noticed that he looked rather flushed.

"I've already had mine," he said when I suggested his having breakfast in my room. "But don't you hurry." He brought over one of the straw-backed bogus Louis XV chairs and sat down facing my bed.

"Normandy butter," he muttered as he looked at the small earthenware jar on the tray. "I'm sorry I had to intern you. Now at last we've got time to talk. Several hours, in fact. Well, the two men are staying at a small hotel off the Place de Clichy. You know where that is, of course. . . ."

"Yes," I said. I was losing my appetite.

"They're at the Hotel Aquitaine, rue Biot."

I gulped down the remains of the coffee and left the second croissant and most of the butter uneaten. I placed the tray on the night-table and got out of the bed. Quickly I put on my shorts, socks and trousers. "Tell me more," I said.

"Fontanet," he continued, "expects you any time after one o'clock today."

I stopped with my shirt in my hand. "How does he know I'm in Paris?"

"He got a telegram yesterday from a man in London to say you'd be coming and would hand him a message. I've got it here."

From his pocket he took out and handed me an envelope. It was open. It contained a single sheet of notepaper with a printed heading: an address in Maida Vale.

"Dear Eric—Sorry I couldn't do it any other way, but everything else promises to work out well. Don't worry. I'll write soon.

"Yours in haste,
Jan."

"Who's Jan?"

"A man called Jan Barton."

I remembered Addyman asking me about him. "Who is he?" I said.

"We're not sure whether he's an Austrian or a Czech, but he's got a Czech passport. His real name is something unpronounceable, and officially he's a journalist. He's made his home in London now for quite a few years. Since the war, anyhow. He's a Communist agent and a friend of Fontanet."

"How do I come in?"

"You'll have to say Barton has asked you to come over and bring the money."

"But why should Fontanet think I know Barton?"

Rayne smiled. "As a matter of fact, Fontanet mentioned your name to him before leaving London. He actually told him it was you who had bought the railway tickets. He won't suspect anything if you turn up with the money Barton promised to send him, and a letter in Barton's handwriting to boot."

I still held my shirt in my hand. I decided I had better put it on, although I had not yet washed. "Well now," I said, "I must be slow on the uptake, but how do you know all this about Barton? Is he a member of your organisation or something?"

"Far from it. I understand, however, that he's decided to co-operate with us." Rayne paused for a second. "He was arrested two days ago and he told us the whole story. From what we've been able to check, what he said seems to be true. It ties in with your story, in any case. Apparently Fontanet didn't want to get the tickets himself in

138

case he was being watched, or because he was short of time, and Barton was the first person he asked to get them for him. But Barton had something rather urgent to attend to—I'm not sure what—and he asked Fontanet whether he knew someone else who could be relied on for the job. Fontanet mentioned you—that's how Barton knows your name—and this'll amuse you: Barton said, 'Are you sure you can trust him?'—meaning you, of course. 'Won't he talk?' And Fontanet said, 'No. I know how to keep him quiet.' As a matter of fact, he did, didn't he?" Rayne ended with a malicious but friendly grin.

"Never mind," he said. "You can make amends now. The important thing is to decide on some plan of action. It's probably better to pretend that Barton contacted you through an intermediary. In that case, you'll have to use your talent as a writer to invent someone whom you can say is a mutual friend of Barton and you. Let's call him X. He'd better not be a real person, even if you knew someone who might fit the bill. This man X is a friend of yours. Barton approached him to ask you to deliver a message and some money to Fontanet. It was, in any case, advisable for you to leave England."

"Why?"

"Because you yourself were implicated."

"Because of the tickets?"

"Partly that, but partly because, unknown to Fontanet, you've been a Communist sympathiser for years. That's one of the reasons you tried to get into the T.F.O."

"Fontanet'll never believe that."

"Oh, yes, he will. He'll be given corroboration later, in any case. I'd rather you didn't know about that just now. The main thing is that you're a sympathiser. But be careful." Rayne took hold of my left elbow. "Don't rush things. Don't blurt the whole thing out to him at once. You'll have to act the part of a man who's being cautious, who's a bit afraid; the fellow traveller who's in for more

139

Colon Township Library

than he bargained for. You're not an intimate friend of Fontanet, after all."

Rayne was silent now, and I had a chance to think about his plan. It was exciting, but it had an element of unreality, like a suggestion for a plot which seems very attractive at first blush, but which begins to strain credulity on further inspection.

I saw one major difficulty straight away. "If Barton's been arrested," I said, "the news'll get into the papers."

"Eventually," Rayne agreed, "but not yet. Not for a day or two, anyhow. For the time being, as far as Lockheed and Fontanet are concerned, Barton's free and is using you as a courier. You can sign and hand over the travellers' cheques I got for you yesterday. Believe me, that'll be your best letter of introduction. And don't forget you'll be able to give them a note in Barton's own handwriting. The whole thing's been fairly thoroughly thought out, and I don't think you've got much to worry about if you keep your head. Well, would you like me to go on, or shall we leave the rest of the plan till later? We've got plenty of time. It's only a quarter-past nine."

Amazed at first, then becoming slowly excited, I could only stare at Rayne. I could see that he believed in the plan and, for that matter, it now seemed plausible to me. So they could arrest a man and suppress the news for several days! Two days earlier such an idea would have filled me with rage; this moment I was almost enthusiastic about it. We all, I suppose, retain something of the schoolboy's love—and as yet untamed sense of cruelty—for such situations in life. The schoolboy in me was perhaps a little further removed than in most people, that was all.

"Altman," I said, thinking aloud. I saw an infinitely sad Jewish face.

"What?" Rayne asked.

"That's the name of the intermediary I've invented," I said finally. "Let me see; he's a friend of Barton's and

140

Barton knows of me through Fontanet. . . . But how does Barton know that Altman and I know each other? Of course, if the worst had come to the worst, Barton could always have contacted me directly. . . ."

Rayne narrowed his eyes. "That wouldn't have been necessary. He'd have had plenty of time to check up on you and discover you knew Altman. In fact, that would explain the delay in your coming over with the money. Yes; it fits well. But, in any case, you probably won't have to go into details. Barton needed a reliable man, and he knew of you from Fontanet. That's the important thing."

He smiled, "I must say I whole-heartedly agree with P.A. about you carrying this off successfully."

"P.A.?" I said. Rayne could not surely mean the Press Association.

"Addyman," Rayne said; then he laughed. "He said you'd do the job well when I went back to him yesterday afternoon. And he didn't ask me *not* to repeat it to you." Rayne gave me an attempt at a "confidential" look. "You see," he went on, "the old boy's marvellous. In ten minutes he finds out everything about you—at least, everything he needs to know. He told me: 'Edmonton is the best man for the job. A natural!' "

Rayne suddenly burst out laughing. "I can't help it," he apologised. "He was absolutely priceless. He mimicked you to perfection; the way you move, the way you hold your head, the way you talk. It's only now I can fully appreciate his take-off. He said: 'That's how Edmonton would do it.' "

"If he's such a master mind . . ." I said, a little amused, a little annoyed, a little confused and a little awe-struck. I broke off.

"Then why does he pick such fools for associates? Was that what you were going to say?"

"Well, not exactly."

I was pleased that Rayne continued without listening

141

to me. "The answer's simple enough. Our job attracts the wrong type, and the obvious right type isn't easy to find. . . ."

"Why not?" I was torn between my natural curiosity and my surprise over his intimacy. This was a piece of exciting indiscretion even from an impulsive Australian. "Why not?" I repeated.

"Various reasons. One being"—and he looked towards the wall at the radiator with its silver paint flaking off—"that the man who would make a first-rate agent usually uses his talents for something more lucrative. I mean, you yourself must know at least half a dozen who'd make wonderful intelligence agents, but who aren't available. There's Major Treloar. . . ."

"The M.P., you mean?"

"Yes. He's a junior minister now. He was with us during the war, and he was the best there is. But you can't expect him to give up a really promising political career, can you? Or there's Jimmy Tamworth. . . ."

"Who's he?"

"Oh, he's News Editor of the *Evening Post*. Enough said?" Rayne made a circular movement with his left hand. "There are hundreds of people, barristers, businessmen, advertising men, whom we could use if we could persuade them to join us, but there's not much chance when they're already earning top salaries, or are well on the way to them. We're thrown back all the time on officers in the Services, but even they can say 'No.' I mean, you can't force people against their will. But we must get back to this. . . ." Rayne pointed at the envelope he had given me, which I had put on the tiny writing desk, next to my wrist watch.

"Your real job is to get into the two men's confidence, and you've got about three days to do it. You'll have to keep up the act all the time, and it won't be too easy. The point is, you'll have to stay with them, or near them. Your

142

great advantage, of course, is that you're being helped from outside and to an extent that will force them to believe you. It's a perfect set-up that they both know you, but don't know you too well. That's what gave P.A. the idea of using you."

"Why the three days?"

"It may even be four, but we can't do anything sooner, unfortunately. If only we could arrange for them to be taken back to England this afternoon!" He shrugged a shoulder. "Our main hope is that they haven't got any other plan of escape, and that they'll stick to the one they asked Barton to arrange for them."

"What's that?"

"Barton was to put them in touch with someone in Paris. He told us he hadn't done anything about it at the time of his arrest, which is probably true. He was detained on Monday after receiving Fontanet's telegram, which gave him the two men's address in Paris. Since the previous Sunday morning he'd been watched, his telephone calls tapped, his mail, every move of his checked. He was very frightened when we got hold of him and made a full confession. I think he hoped to get away with as little as possible. My own view is that he's not a real Communist. He's probably just a crook who's working for them. A real Communist is a dedicated man and a tough nut. You wouldn't get anything out of him. In any case, we're assuming he told us the truth, and the fact that Lockheed and Fontanet are still here seems to confirm it. But," Rayne said uneasily, "he did have at least one clear day to make contact with someone, and there's just the slight possibility that he managed to do so; in which case the two men may have a plan of escape we don't know about. That's something you'll have to find out. . . ." He searched the ceiling for a second, then shook his head. "No; I really don't think there's much chance of Barton having contacted anybody."

143

"I should imagine," I said, "the two men must be champing at the bit. This is their fifth day in Paris."

"That's quite true, but they thing nobody except Barton—and now you—knows that they're here. You see, they left England with false passports, under assumed names. . . ."

"No?" I said.

Rayne nodded. "Incredible, isn't it? They had time even for that. It's a further proof of their guilt. We don't know why, but they went under the names of Constable and Baker. Normally, we don't keep check on British citizens entering or leaving England. But Fontanet presumably thought a false name would be wise. Or perhaps he only had a diplomatic passport, which, of course, might have been noticed at Dover. I dare say the principal reason he asked you to get the tickets for him was that he and Lockheed had too many things to see to in the short time before they left."

"How did they get the passports?"

"There are ways and means. Barton denied that he had anything to do with it, and I'm inclined to believe him."

"Perhaps one of them even knew someone in the Passport Office?" I suggested, on the assumption that if there are Communists in the Foreign Office, there are probably also Communists in other Government departments. But Rayne made no reply.

"When did you find out they'd left England?" I asked.

"Late Saturday night. A couple of hours after their departure." For the first time Rayne looked worried. "Just stupid incompetence. And it was partly the fault of my department, I'm sorry to say. Fontanet had been suspected for a couple of days and even watched part of the time, but nothing intelligent was done. The only sensible thing that happened was getting hold of Barton."

"How did you get him?"

There was no answer, but as I looked at him questioningly, he said: "Look, I really oughtn't to tell you. I know we can trust you. It isn't that. But if I tell you it'll make it difficult for you to pretend to Lockheed and Fontanet. The more you know, the more you're likely to reveal to them accidentally. In fact, you already know almost too much. It only helps to confuse you. There's one thing I must tell you, though. Yesterday at noon Fontanet received a telegram from Barton to say that you'd be arriving to-day."

"My job, then, is to get into their confidence." I said. "Then what? I presume you want me to find out why they ran away."

"That's secondary. I can see it intrigues you, but I think we more or less know the answer. Obviously, find out what you can, but the main thing is to keep an eye on them and find out if they've been in touch with someone un-known to us about leaving France. Whatever happens, you must prevent them from contacting anyone. But it's not likely they'll want to if you play your part properly."

The whole thing was still strange and confusing. I said: "You must forgive my ignorance, but wouldn't it be easier to ask the French to arrest them and apply for extradi-tion?"

Rayne smiled. "Certainly not. On what grounds? False passports? No. As far as we know, no important documents are missing from the F.O. and there's no conclusive evi-dence at the moment that either of the men has given away official secrets, whatever we may suspect. The situation is —please don't ask me why we assume this—that they're trying to go over to the Russians, asking for asylum and all that. There's no actual evidence at the moment of any im-portant crime having been committed. Lockheed's absent without leave, but that's not a crime. If we want to, of course, we can prove quite a lot, but we're not anxious to prove. If you get my point. We shan't be able to avoid some sort of outcry, but there's a chance that if we can get the men back, we may be able to play the thing down. But it'd be fatal to let the French or anybody else get hold of the news. Think of the uproar there'd be. Two important English diplomats found to be unreliable, suspected of treason even, and we'd allowed them to escape! What price British security? You can just hear Senator McCarthy on that one. *And* more responsible people than him! No, the less we publicise this business at the moment, the better it'll be."

"So I've got three days to get into their confidence and keep them from getting out of France while you're making arrangements to get them back to England?"

The full implication of what I was doing suddenly struck me for the first time.

Book Three

12

"IT was absolutely incredible," Eric said, "getting the wire about you—the whole thing." He shook his head. This was the second time he had said it within five minutes, and again I nodded. When I had telephoned him, half an hour earlier, I had realised the minute I heard his voice that Rayne's analysis of the situation had been correct. Although French telephones are often bad, I had distinctly heard Eric give a sigh of relief, and I had caught the accents of hope and impatience in the few words he had spoken.

The success now of my actual reception, the fact that I was accepted by Eric as a friend, had little to do with my skill or histrionic ability; mine had become a part that almost anybody could have played. It was just circumstance that forced him to believe me. It had been no surprise that he had practically embraced me as we had met on the staircase of the hotel.

We were silent now. The slight pause I suppose helped him to get over his excitement or perhaps to digest what I had just told him. I was watching his face quite openly, for there was no reason to hide my curiosity; it was legitimate and understandable. It was only now, in this momentary lull in the conversation, that I suddenly realised that Eric was no longer a trivial person. He was instead what he had not been, I thought, for fifteen years or so, a person one had to take seriously. What were the outward signs? He seemed less anxious now than on the Saturday afternoon, five days earlier, when I had last seen him; and, consequently, he looked younger. . . . But did he really?

149

Was it not perhaps only that I was looking at him through fresh eyes—that is to say, appalled and embarrassed eyes, frightened and excited and at the same time almost pathologically curious eyes? Was he a different person now? *Of course* he wasn't. And for the second time—or was it the third—I thought that seldom in the course of my life had I felt so intimately the presence of history.

"Things," I said now, and I felt I was smiling, "would have been simpler if you could have *afforded* to be frank with me last Saturday, but it's obvious you couldn't. In any case, everything's all right now. I hope you haven't worried too much."

"Difficult to say," he drawled. He looked away for a moment as if he had not quite heard what I had said. Then he raised his head. "Did Barton tell you why he couldn't arrange things sooner?"

"I've never met Barton, as I've told you already. On Tuesday evening a friend of mine called Altman came to see me and told me all about—"

"I know." Eric's voice was now a little impatient. "So you were given absolutely no message apart from this note?"

"No. What did Barton tell *you?*"

"He said someone would come and see us here on Monday or Tuesday. Today's Thursday . . ."

"He probably didn't know where to get hold of me at first. Then there was a certain amount of red tape, Bank of England, and all that. I had to make an application as a writer for an extra allowance of French francs. I've got more than just my ordinary allowance. Officially I'm writing a book on post-war Paris. . . ."

I heard the hissing sound from the washstand; a water-tap must have been released somewhere upstairs. In a place like this, one could not help hearing some of the other residents' activities. One could feel lonely without enjoying privacy.

150

"Where are you staying?" Eric said.

"I'll look for a hotel nearby. There are plenty. I think it's better for us not to make it too obvious, don't you?"

He shrugged a shoulder, "I suppose so."

"Where's Alan?" I said.

"In his room. Asleep, I think. He went out last night."

Alone? I wondered. He must have got drunk.

"We'd better go to the bank," Eric announced. He picked up the travellers' cheques from the dark green, baize-covered table and examined them. "You'll have to sign them," he said. "I'd better put on my shoes."

I noticed for the first time that he was wearing a pair of dilapidated sheepskin slippers which he must have picked up at some Oriental bazaar. While he was replacing them with light yellow, oil-stained suèdes, I looked round the room again. The choice of the hotel was almost certainly fortuitous, but nevertheless he seemed to be very much at home there. There was something in Eric that fitted so perfectly into this semi-sordid hotel of the Batignolles; the smell of harsh, French tobacco mingling with the undisturbed reek of the room, the shabby, *art nouveau* furniture, the gaudy pre-war jazz patterns of the carpet, the tin *bidet* behind the screen, the marble mantelpiece in the corner and above it the over-ornate 1890 bronze clock which must have stopped around 1920. There were no pictures, and the flowery blue and mauve wallpaper was greasy in places. There would doubtless be pages from an old telephone directory hanging from a nail in the lavatory, and doubtless also the *patronne* had never heard that the vacuum cleaner had been invented. Somewhere in my heart there stirred a vague echo; this was Paris.

"Right," Eric said. "I'll see Alan when we come back."

As we walked along the rue Biot and the Place de Clichy came into view, I said: "Which bank shall we go to?"

151

"It doesn't really matter. I don't suppose you know anywhere you can get more than the odds? There's a bank on the way to the St. Lazare."

The Place de Clichy was bathed in its early afternoon light; it was all pink and gold. The traffic was thick with cars, trucks and buses, advertising Byrrh and Cinzano. We crossed into the rue d'Amsterdam, and my past loomed up again. I had once known someone in this neighborhood, somewhere near the St. Lazare, a Swedish girl student with whom at one time, nearly fifteen years ago, I had spent some of my days and most of my nights.

But there was no time for nostalgia, although Eric was not very talkative on the way; and although I had only been there once since the war, I found myself wondering whether Alan was drunk all the time now. It was curious that in Eric's presence I could not think of the two men except as Eric and Alan; Fontanet and Lockheed now sounded strange.

A few minutes later I handed Eric a hundred pounds' worth of French francs. This was not on Rayne's instruction, but as a result of my own prudence. Had I given Eric all my money, my hold on him might have lessened; besides, he might even have lost it or spent it in a neurotic fit. "You'd better leave the rest unchanged," I said, and he nodded. The silent nod, I felt, was a further proof that I was accepted and perhaps trusted.

He pushed the bundle of notes into the inside of his jacket pocket. On the way back we sat down for an apéritif at Dupont's in the Place de Clichy.

"Have you any friends in Paris?" Eric asked.

"I'll have to find out. I haven't been here for two or three years," I said.

"Barton didn't mention the name of anyone in Paris?" he asked, and he looked uneasy.

"No. But I'm sure in view of the note that he's organising someone. Don't worry. There's no reason why he should let you down."

He shrugged a shoulder impatiently. "How does your friend—what's his name?—know Barton?"

"I'm not sure. All I know is that Altman's a good friend of mine."

"What does he do?" Eric asked.

"He works in Oxford Street."

"English?"

"Naturalised. He was born in Austria and came to England in 'thirty-eight. He was interned on the Isle of Man. I met him after the war." I felt a little uneasy lest I should involve myself too much with Altman. Rayne had advised me not to give Eric too many facts. I said, "Why does this Barton business worry you?"

"Why?" Eric said, and I saw the anger rising in his throat; then he suddenly calmed down and his voice became tinged with a suggestion of self-pity. "Time's getting on. My biggest worry so far has been money. Now the money's arrived, but at any moment something may happen to us, unless we get away."

"You mean the police?"

"Everything." He looked at me impatiently. "The French Deuxième Bureau, the F.B.I., M.I.5. Anything you like. There's nothing in the papers, I know, but that means nothing. . . ." He broke off as the waiter approached. "What will you have?" Eric said, but he ordered without waiting for my reply: *"Deux St. Raphaels, s'il vous plaît."* Then to me, "Give me a cigarette. I must buy some."

"You say it's meaningless," I said as I gave him a light, "that there's nothing in the papers."

"Of course it is. They keep these things back from the public, but at the same time I'm sure they're mobilising the whole bloody world to find us."

153

"They don't know you're in France," I said. "All they know is that you've vanished, and they don't know you're together."

"I know, but they may find out. You've no idea what a time I've had—we've had—since that day I last saw you."

The waiter brought the drinks. "Cheers," I said, out of habit. "Of course," I went on, "I'm still in the dark about the whole business. What I'd like to know is why you had to run away so urgently. I mean, I know now it wasn't sex and I don't blame you for not telling me. I mean, did you think they were really after you?"

He drank his St. Raphael at one gulp.

"I don't know, but I think so. How else do you explain that page you found?"

"It referred to you?" I hoped I looked surprised.

"Yes."

"How on earth did it get into my dossier, I wonder?"

"Nobody knows," Eric said. Somewhat to my surprise, he seemed not to be interested.

"The page made no sense to me," I ventured, "but I suppose you must have found it pretty compromising."

"The information very obviously came from the F.B.I. We wouldn't have bothered to get out otherwise. I'm sure that, apart from notifying M.I.5, the Americans had started to act on their own."

"What could they do to you? Outside America."

"Now don't be a fool, James."

"All right," I said. "Tell me."

"Don't you realise that England's full of their agents? They're almost running the country. We're practically occupied by the United States."

"Agreed," I said, trying to pacify him.

"You don't realise what a terror the F.B.I. is in America."

"I've heard something about it. Of course, Eric, I'm

154

strangely ill-informed." I thought this might be a good line. "Like George the Sixth, nobody-tells-me-anything."

But Eric brushed aside the joke. He said—and his voice was a little louder now: "You have no idea of the witch-hunts in America. Innocent people being accused, kicked out of jobs. Half the population suspected. Just like the Gestapo. And they want to extend the same thing to England."

"But they haven't got much against you," I said with a sudden inspiration; the challenge technique was a good one to use with Eric.

"Except that they've found out I've been working for a democratic cause."

He said this slowly, talking to the pavement. I was very glad he did not watch my face, for it might well have given me away. I was *not* a man ready for any situation in life. A moment later my face was again what I presume is known as "blank," but I was still feeling uneasy; this time I knew it was a pang of guilt. If I spoke, I might arouse his suspicion or cause him to change the subject. But keeping silent was just as suspicious. I decided I would have to try to pretend to be "agonisingly discreet" if he looked up at me.

But he spoke before he looked at me again.

"You know that I was suspended when I came back to England?"

"Altman said something about it."

"Now, that was largely at the F.B.I.'s instigation. They told me it was because I'd been involved with the American police over some minor driving accident, but that was all rubbish. The F.B.I. told them I was passing on information."

My heart froze. I felt the full astounding impact of self-confession, although what he had said was not in the least unexpected. But there is a vast difference between the anticipation and the realisation.

155

The shock was caused by the commonplace phrasing or, perhaps more important, the commonplace intonation. He had spoken as if he attributed very little importance to his words, to the facts he had disclosed. And my sense of shock did not vanish even when he crushed out his cigarette on the ashtray and said, "We have to go," although I suddenly knew then that what I felt was not so much shock as excitement.

"What is it?" I said mechanically.

"I ought to see Alan. He may be up by now."

"He did know I was coming?"

"Yes."

He caught the waiter's eye and paid. Neither of us spoke as we walked back to the hotel. I was too overwhelmed by what he had told me, and in a way I also felt somehow guilty. I had given way in reckless fashion to my natural curiosity, and asked questions point-blank—questions I could have asked later, questions in which Rayne was not interested, and questions which might have made Eric suspicious. When we reached his room I felt I had to say something before leaving.

"Look, Eric," I began, "you mustn't worry. It's only a matter of three or four days before Barton fixes things for you. In any case, I'll do whatever I can for you myself."

He suddenly looked at me with a silent gaze which I had not seen before. For a moment I had the impression he was mimicking someone.

"I still have to get over your being here, doing things for me. Tell me, how long have we known each other?"

"Twenty years." I tried not to look away, but I was embarrassed. I felt a strange conflict, and, despite everything, I suddenly began to dislike myself for what I was doing.

"There were gaps, of course," he said. He was now looking at my shoes. Yes, there were gaps, and my sense of

156

guilt faded as if by magic. There was no need to think of Addyman's pep talk.

"It wasn't our fault," I said.

He walked towards the door and began to search his raincoat for cigarettes. Finally, he found some.

13

"AND where was Lockheed?" Rayne asked. We were sitting in a little café on the Avenue de Wagram, not far from his hotel.

"I haven't seen him yet," I said. "He had a late night, which probably means he's been drinking heavily. I'm meeting him—both of them. We're going to an Arab place for dinner, or after dinner. . . . You don't mind my coming back so soon?"

"Not in the least, although I'm surprised you weren't there longer." He looked at his watch. "So Fontanet was agitated. Well, that's pretty understandable, isn't it?" There was a faint mockery in Rayne's smile. "Your line is to rub in something about the essential slowness of Soviet bureaucracy. They'll both believe it, because they're civil servants themselves. Don't forget that. Only don't overdo it yet. There's time—I hope."

Rayne had been looking at the drink in front of him for a time. "Now, you will remember there's one thing we must make absolutely sure about?" he said.

"What's that?"

"That they've made no contact with the Soviet, or with anyone except Barton. It's absolutely vital. I've already told you that from what Barton said it's unlikely that they've approached anyone, but I'm taking no chances.

They've been here five days, and that's a hell of a long time, especially in the circumstances. What Fontanet told you—or at least conveyed to you—rather supports my hope that they're relying exclusively and absolutely on Barton. But in a job like mine it's just lunacy to take chances."

"So my job is to find out. . . ."

"But not today; at least, don't ask questions directly. Not yet. Of course, if you discover something or even have a hunch or a suspicion, let me know at once. I'll be out the whole evening, but you can telephone and leave a message." He closed his eyes for a moment. "I hope you won't need to 'phone. There's such a thing as luck. And we need it. You'll be able to find out safely some time tomorrow. In the morning, perhaps. . . ." I heard quite clearly the note of excitement in his voice; for a moment I thought it was the sportsman's, then I realised it was the hunter's.

"Why tomorrow?" I said.

"Because Fontanet's going to get a telegram."

Rayne's search for dramatic effect was unmistakable, but I only liked him for it. I played up. "What will it say?" I said.

"It'll ask him to warn you that you must stay with them and not return to England. The idea is, of course, to help you to get further into the two men's confidence. Now, listen carefully. The idea is that you yourself are suspected by M.I.5, or what you will, and not only because you acted as a courier for Barton."

"You've already hinted at this."

"Yes, but I didn't want to say too much, so as not to confuse you. You have had a so-called dirty past, politically. Not as dirty as theirs, because your opportunities weren't as good, but dirty enough to be incriminating. If you want, you can hint at this tonight—that is, if you're good at being carefully indiscreet; if not, better wait instead until tomorrow, or after they get a letter we're getting Barton to send, giving more details. Then you can break down and confess that you've been in contact with Soviet agents and passed some information over. You can start being agitated, worried and so on. I'm sure they'll believe you, only please don't overact."

"I was just thinking. Wouldn't it be a good idea for me to *underact,* to try to pretend that I'm innocent?"

Rayne raised a hand. "That'd be hopeless; you'd either confuse them or lose their confidence. . . . Sorry. It may be a good line in fiction. This is life."

"Is it?" I said.

Rayne burst out laughing. "I'll remember that one."

He took out his old-fashioned pipe, and for a moment there was silence. He must have noticed that I was caught up with my thoughts, because he asked: "What is it?"

"Oh, nothing," I replied; "at least, nothing to do with the—job. I was just thinking how strange it was that last week I was under suspicion and now I'm being entrusted with an Important Government Mission. . . ." I saw that Rayne noticed the capital letters. "Why are you so sure you can trust me?"

"Don't worry. We've checked up on you," he smiled. "Don't forget it wasn't my department that suspected you in the first place. It was an outfit known as General Survey. P.A. formed a good impression of you, and you fit into our plan perfectly."

"Thank you."

"Now don't be cynical. I may tell you we spent an agitated fifteen hours checking up on you. We contacted your publisher, your former C.O.; then there was Twining, and one or two other people."

An agitated fifteen hours, indeed, I thought to myself! They had probably had to make up their minds about me in two hours. Twining had not telephoned Addyman until quite late in the evening, and they could hardly have made many enquiries until the next morning; yet by the time I saw Addyman before lunch the next day, he had already decided to enlist my help. I could not help feeling it was Twining and possibly Hackwood with his "Court Circular" wife who had guaranteed my reliability. But there was no need for me to be ironical over this, for suddenly I remembered my first questions on reading my dossier.

"By the way," Rayne suddenly said, "there's one more thing I must tell you."

2

I was now in the Avenue de Wagram. It was difficult to decide which was better: to spend all my available time with Eric and Alan or as little as possible. If I stayed with them too much, I might give myself away; if I stayed away too much, I might arouse their suspicion. Being with them meant, of course, that I should be in on any unexpected development; on the other hand, I knew that Eric's impatience might easily get on my nerves if I had to share his company a lot. In the end I decided that, in view of the telegram which Eric would receive the next day, it would probably be better if I kept to my original plan and stayed away until dinner. I had, in the circumstances, a few hours to kill.

I walked past the Etoile and entered the Avenue Kléber. It really made little difference which of the many avenues I chose. The Kléber would take me to the Trocadéro and the river.

I became aware of how fast I was walking; a few more yards, I thought, and over the plane trees and the square white blocks I would surely see that graceful and evocative giraffe-neck of steel which since the beginning of the century had been the best-known symbol of Paris.

I suddenly felt a pang at my heart, but I was already lost among my memories. I was "writing" now as I walked, and the phrases were evoked by the rhythm of the street, the warm and slightly second-hand air, the nervous tootings of fast Renaults and Citröens; the whole thing was floating, almost impermanent, on the point of flying away.

Oh God, why did I feel like this, in what was possibly the most unrepresentative part of Paris, in the Avenue Kléber, with its embalmed and uninteresting antique shops and dressmakers and dentists and *immeubles à louer,* in an atmosphere which was so clean that it was almost sterile?

But, of course, I knew the answer to my own questions. This was Paris just the same, and by some mysterious chance everything was implicit in the Avenue Kléber. You could feel or at least sense the Second Empire elegance of the rue de Bellechasse, the seediness of the Filles-du-Calvaire, the bottle-green sadness of la Cité, the shabby vitality of Clichy, the melancholy beauty of the Place des Vosges, the blatant Americanism of the Boulevard des Italiens. Everything was implicit, and even here in a near-new avenue you could somehow feel the presence of the ghosts of Condorcet and Laplace, Ampère and Michelet, Littré and Lenôtre. It was unfortunate that Stendhal did not know the Avenue Kléber, and even more unfortunate that the man who did know it was Henri de Régnier.

I walked on. Perhaps all this was the inevitable impact of Latinity on the Nordic, Protestant mind; gauche, romantic, intransigent and evangelical when young, becoming vulnerable with middle age and thinking of the past as a series of missed moments.

I had to wait for a flood of cars to pass at the corner of the rue de Longchamp. Why all these thoughts when I was in the middle of the greatest adventure of my life; the sort of event that happened, if at all, once in a lifetime? Why did I think of Littré and Condorcet, when the proper "Representative Frenchmen," the proper terms of reference, should perhaps have been Babeuf and Saint-Simon

161

and Fourier and even—not illogically—Julien Benda and *The Treason of the Clerks?* But no doubt I needed breathing space, a few hours to file and store away and digest what had happened in the last couple of days.

Then I was already on the top of the staircase between the clean, white monoliths of the Palais de Chaillot and the Musée de l'Homme. This was, I remembered, the Mount of Chaillot, one of the seven hills on which Paris had been built. The Mount of the Martyrs, the Mount of Parnassus, St. Valerien, Ste. Geneviève, I forgot the rest. . . . I looked down on the curve of the river and the Champ de Mars. I stood there a long time. There was quite a crowd looking at the monoliths: a less frightening Stonehenge of the Age of Loneliness than Rockefeller Center; and a *bateau mouche* cut across the river as if rolling on castors.

Then I descended slowly to the Pont d'Iena and saw the youth of the neighborhood with their short, bandy legs, long bodies and good hair and teeth, attractive for five brief years, diving into the Seine.

I decided to walk as far as the Ecole Militaire. There was a break in the heat of the day. How little seemed to have changed. On the benches, in the sandy lanes, I saw the same old women with the same poodles, the same retired civil servants; they all dressed and moved and talked as if the Third Republic had not vanished with Pétain's surrender.

3

As I entered Eric's room I saw Alan first standing against the mantelpiece. I said "Good evening," and he came forward with something like a faint, social smile and held out his hand without a word. Some years ago he had decided that I was a man to whom he must be particularly polite, and although he may have since forgotten the actual reason, the attitude had become a force of habit. He wore a grey flannel suit; the English diplomat on a country week-end. He looked tidy and a man of consequence.

He spoke at last. "It was very kind of you to help us," he said—a conventional enough phrase. I felt that it had been rehearsed, just like my own behavior, though for different reasons. I could see and hear the effort he was making to keep up a façade, to hide all the confusion and embarrassment he must have been feeling ever since Eric had received the bogus telegram yesterday announcing my arrival. His voice sounded wooden and curiously lifeless; then I noticed a thick vein standing out just over his temple. This was the first time I had seen him for a year or so, except for those few seconds at Victoria Station.

"It was nothing," I said. "I was only too glad to help."

I saw now that his eyes were red and swollen; for the first time, he looked much older than his age. There was a sudden hint of refugee Polish officers in his expression, the sort of look one associated with middle-aged exiles one had met during the war in London, except that in their cases hope seemed brighter and there was excitement in the air. But did I know much about hope?

"You mustn't worry," I whispered, then I turned away from him. It would have been unwise to show too much curiosity, although I had every reason to be curious, but we were going to spend the whole evening together, for one thing.

Eric, I saw now, was standing by the window trying, it seemed, to extract a splinter from his finger with a pin. But by the time I reached him he must have succeeded, for he pushed the pin into the lapel of his sports jacket. "What have you been doing?" he said.

"I spent most of the afternoon trying to contact a friend,

163

a schoolmaster I know. I can trust him, and he might help me if necessary. But he wasn't in, so I left a message."

"You've known him for some time?" he asked, but it was more of a statement than a question.

"Since the time of the Spanish War. I thought I might as well see him, just in case you don't hear from Barton, but I'm sure everything'll work out all right."

There is a way of inclining the head and looking at someone slightly sideways which I have always thought a middle-aged habit; in England at least it can convey anything from polite doubt to resignation. I was surprised to find Eric doing it, and in his case I decided it was probably meant to convey something like "Wait and see, but there isn't too much time to wait."

Eric now moved towards the mantelpiece. "Do you want a drink before we go out?"

"Please," I said. I had already noticed the bottles. There had been only one that morning, with some brandy in it. Now there were half a dozen. "May I have a Dubonnet?"

"You will have to drink it quickly," Eric said. "We've only got two glasses."

"I won't have anything," Alan said. "I think we ought to go soon, or there won't be any room at Cousteau's. Like last night."

"You want to go to Cousteau's?" Eric said.

"It's probably our best place."

From force of habit I was about to raise my glass to say something conventional and foolish, but I saw that Eric was already gulping down his drink. He put down his empty glass. "You're staying next door, aren't you?" he said.

"Yes, room seven, on the first floor." I turned to Alan. "I think it's safer for you. . . ."

Alan nodded. I made a mental note not to try to involve him too much, not yet, even if I *was* more interested in him than in Eric.

The restaurant was in one of the side streets of the Avenue de Clichy. It was tightly packed with small tables. I wondered what had brought them here: perhaps the fact that it was cheap or that it was obscure. It was one of the innumerable small restaurants of each *quartier* which are known only to local inhabitants.

There were only three vacant seats at a table where a soldier was already sitting. The table faced the square hole in the wall behind which I saw the enormous copper pots of French kitchens.

"Vous permettez!" Eric said to the soldier, who was sitting there reading the evening paper between two courses.

"Mais je vous en prie," the man said in utter surprise, rolling the *r* like a provincial. For a moment I thought he would get up and stand to attention, then he changed his mind and repeated the entreaty, *"Vous en prie,"* and gaped at us through yellow teeth as if we had walked straight out of a novel about a mythical and slightly awe-inspiring upper class.

We were served quickly, and the conversation was forced even after the soldier had left us. Eric said practically nothing, but Alan spoke a few words to me as if he felt it was a social duty towards a dinner guest. The address of the place had been given to them by their own hotelier, and it was cheap and consequently always packed.

I noticed that Eric was eating very fast, as if he had to catch a train, and once he looked at his watch. I said nothing. By the time we had finished the meal, there were two or three people in the entrance waiting for a table.

When we left, Eric hailed a taxi in the Avenue de Clichy and told the man to go to the rue "Stéphensone." Though he pronounced it the French way, I recognised it as the rue Stéphenson, which I vaguely remembered was somewhere on the far side of Montmartre, quite appropriately facing some ancient railway line.

"Where are we going?" I said.

"Oh, just some Arab place," Alan said. There was some disapproval in the way he spoke, as if to say: "Oh, just one of Eric's strange ideas. Sordid and dangerous. But he must have his fun. He's leading and we're following."

It was increasingly obvious that Eric was the leader, as always; others had to follow and were rewarded or punished accordingly. I remembered now that he had told me in the morning that we would be visiting an Arab place, but I had thought he had meant for dinner.

The taxi ran along the Boulevard de Clichy, past the Place Blanche, the Pigalle, the Place d'Anvers. There were crowds outside the cafés, the seedy *boîtes* and the expensive and inferior restaurants, and there was target-shooting in the little booths facing them in the centre of the boulevard under the trees.

This had been, I supposed, the gayest, the most colorful and exciting part of Paris thirty years ago. But after the slump even Montparnasse was dead and now the Champs-Elysées was invaded by commerce, and "invisible exports."

We passed a few *boîtes* that had once been famous in another generation, but which had sadly deteriorated and now meant nothing. I had not been there for years; it was the one part of Paris I had always tried to avoid.

Past what I recognised as the Boulevard Barbès, the taxi swung sharply into an ill-lit street, somewhere, I fancied, at the back of the Gare du Nord. Eric knocked on the glass partition, and the cab came to a halt.

We got out and followed Eric along the cobblestones to a side turning, where we entered a *bistro*. It was sordid and full of Algerians, who wore what looked like their first Western dress as though it were an attractive stage costume, or the Uniform of Emancipation. I vaguely remembered that this was an Algerian neighborhood: large, lost, derelict blocks of flats, teeming with young men, dirty shops, sordid cafés and none-too-secret brothels, and play-ing cards on the pavement.

The zinc on the counter was cracked, and on it stood a rusty coffee-machine which did not seem to work. On the shelves behind the counter there were bottles of unknown and obscure brands of drink. I presumed that the trade was largely in red Algerian wine. As we seated ourselves at the back, on a broken-down red-plush couch, with a glass of Pernod, I heard the talk around us: loud and in Arabic. To my surprise, our entry and our presence did not create the stir I had at first expected. Around the tables there were perhaps a dozen young men, playing cards. Another group surrounded the pin ball machine facing the bar, where a few middle-aged men were looking at some cheap fountain pens.

I wondered what excitement Eric found in this sordid café, which had little color and hardly any atmosphere. Was it that, being a fugitive himself, he felt a kind of dis-tant solidarity with these people, who looked as if they must at one time or another have been wanted by the authorities?

Whatever the reason, his presence there was surely un-wise; places like this were often visited by the police, and Eric had a false passport, to say the least.

"Have you ever been to North Africa?" Eric said now, and I told him, "Never." He nodded with the cigarette hanging from his lips, but made no comment. It seemed that he, himself, was feeling rather disappointed with his surroundings. He must have been expecting something else, a repetition of some adventure he had had before or perhaps the place was more exciting on other nights.

I felt a sense of relief when a few minutes later he sug-gested we should go to another place. My guess was the rue de Lappe, or streets around the Place Voltaire. But we only walked for two minutes. The new place was near

167

the boulevard, a little cleaner than the first, but quite as uninteresting. The radio was playing behind the counter.

Soon after we had sat down at a small table facing the bar, a young Arab in a dark blue lumber-jacket approached us suddenly from nowhere and offered his hand first to Eric, then to Alan.

"Un ami anglais," Eric said by way of introduction, and then the young man grabbed my hand, and sat down at our table.

"Eric met him last night," Alan said. Again I sensed a certain disapproval in his voice.

The two went on talking as if they had known each other for a long time. The young Algerian spoke good French, unlike the generation of Arabs I had known in Paris, who wore burnous and slippers and had no idea of the formal address and called everybody *"tu."* His name was apparently Ali, and he was a mechanic of sorts who had worked for a time for Simca, but who was now unemployed. Then Eric's voice became quieter and a few minutes later he rose and we all followed him into the street. Not until we reached the corner of the Barbès-Rochechouart, where the Metro comes up for air, did he speak.

"I don't know what you two want to do," he announced, "but I'm going home with Ali."

"I'll see you tomorrow morning," Alan nodded, and Ali shook hands with both of us while Eric signalled a taxi.

"I suppose it's nerves," Alan said when the two had gone, and it took me some time to realise what he meant.

It was difficult to judge whether his remark implied criticism or was merely an explanation of Eric's behavior, but I saw he was reluctant to discuss it with me further. It was all part of the attitude of the professional diplomat towards an acquaintance who has rendered him some slight service.

He looked at his watch. "Where do you want to go?" he said. He was all attention.

"Oh, anywhere," I shrugged, looking round. I saw the sign, *Chez Dupont tout est bon.*

We crossed the busy Boulevard Barbès and walked up the Boulevard Rochechouart towards the Place de Clichy. It was around ten o'clock and the streets were crowded with people; the poor of Ménilmontant and Belleville taking their nightly promenade.

I was a little embarrassed at having been left alone with Lockheed. I was burning to ask him questions, largely to satisfy my own private curiosity, but I knew this was unwise and probably unsafe from Rayne's point of view. Besides, I sensed a certain embarrassment also in Lockheed's reserve towards me since we had met that afternoon, perhaps because he felt I was in a superior position by virtue of the fact that, as far as he knew at the time, I was not a fugitive, whereas he was.

The blunt fact, of course, was that for the first time in twenty years he was down and I was up. Ever since I had known him, Alan had belonged to the mysterious, remote, concentric circles of power which had lorded it over the rest of us who were not so fortunate; indeed, in the last ten years he had undeniably become a prominent personality. Now, owing to a strange chance of Fate, our roles were reversed, temporarily at least. There was no doubt of my relative importance. For a few days I was a "key" man with the full authority of the State behind me, the State guarding its sovereignty as if it were an article of faith.

This, of course, Alan Lockheed did not know, but nevertheless he found my company embarrassing. I wondered how much he remembered of our past in Oxford. Was it possible that he remembered little or nothing about me? On reflection, I decided that it was. For one thing, he was unlikely to have possessed that painfully, irritatingly precise, quite often unselective, photographic and phonographic memory which was my doubtful gift. For another, so much had happened to him during the last twenty years. His embarrassment was perhaps a natural reaction on the part of a man who was seldom given to exuberance towards a near-stranger in whose debt he suddenly found himself.

As we passed the Place d'Anvers I asked myself what Eric must have told him about me yesterday when the bogus telegram had arrived, and today when I had left their hotel after returning from the bank.

It was obvious that they must have discussed me, but I wondered in what terms, and what had been Alan's reaction.

We walked past the noisy *boîtes* of the boulevard until we came to a street crossing, where Alan suddenly said: "There's a quiet place up there." We turned left into the rue des Martyrs.

He had seen a small café, a few blocks away from the boulevard. It had a bar in front, and was quite empty save for three firemen and a small group of laborers in blue overalls. We walked to an empty table at the back, and a man in shirtsleeves, who looked like the owner, came up to take our order. Alan asked for two Pernods without consulting me. I looked up; this was one of Eric's tricks.

But Alan said nothing. Then the drinks arrived and we mixed them with water. I murmured something conventional before taking the first sip. All he said was, "Thank you."

I pretended there was nothing unusual in our being there together, despite the fact that he seemed to have nothing to say. I had a sudden recollection that he had not been very talkative at Oxford; not like Eric at any rate. But surely his silence now was quite strange. To an outsider we must have given the impression of two anxious patients waiting to be admitted to a doctor's consulting-room.

He finished his drink very quickly and I asked him if he would like another. Again he just said, "Thank you." I called the owner over. Finally, I could bear the silence no longer and, having thought about a "good line of approach," I said:

"That F.B.I. business seems revolting. Actually, I knew very little about it till Eric told me this morning."

He nodded. "Nor do most people till they see it at close quarters. And it's spreading. . . ."

That was all he said. The way he was looking in front of himself, apparently seeing nothing, made it quite clear that the subject was closed, for the time being at least.

The Americans may be hysterical, but in his case their fears were justified, I thought. It was strange that our own intelligence services suspected nothing about Alan until the Americans had sounded the alarm.

Yet in a way, I supposed, the explanation was simple enough. Why should anyone suspect a high official of treason? Alan Lockheed had an important position, not only a so-called brilliant future, but a brilliant present as well, a good income, a well-to-do wife, two children, a "happy home." That he was personally unsettled and unhappy was no cause for suspicion; most people of a certain intelligence and sensitivity are unsettled nowadays by the speed and pressure of public events, even if they do not drink heavily or engage in fist fights or furniture wrecking in Cairo. These minor scandals in which he was involved, in fact, probably served only to kill suspicion—in the same way that a murder story on the front page of a newspaper distracts public attention from really important events.

One had also to bear in mind the probable existence of a form of national Couéism. For so long we have repeated

171

the line, "We English never become traitors to our country," that now we believe it. For that matter also, there had, at least in the recent past, been little cause for any Englishman, other than a half-wit, to turn traitor. The Englishman's enemy has invariably been poor and has been unable to afford really rich rewards, for one thing; for another, the English have never had enough intellectual curiosity easily to be won over by ideologies. Then there is England's peculiar geographical isolation, its mistrust of foreigners and their ways; one result of which has been that the ruling class has managed firmly to establish itself as a defence against the foreigner, and since its members have been firmly in the saddle, there has been little reason for them to treat the masses in a really outrageous fashion. This explains why the masses in England have never in modern times violently hated the ruling classes.

Alan now finished his drink and he signalled to the owner to come over. He ordered another round, but still said nothing more. Now I accepted his silence. It was only a couple of days ago that I had thought about Alan's past, his adherence to Communism and his subsequent turning away from it. I had decided that emotionally he may have been a Communist, but consciously he could not help associating himself with the status quo, with the ruling class whose official attitude was naturally anti-Communist. It was obvious I had been wrong about that. Alan had either been a Communist since his Oxford days or had "lapsed" for a few years and then returned to the fold. Dr. Eldin had been impressed with Alan's radicalism in Egypt. Perhaps it was the poverty of the country, coupled with the contrast of his own position, that had created a guilt-feeling in him. The return to Communism had probably occurred within the last few years.

14

$\mathcal{I}$ REPORTED to Rayne the following day just before half past twelve in the afternoon. The sun was playing on the blue and white striped wallpaper in his bedroom.

"So you found Lockheed in a 'morbid condition'?" Rayne smiled.

"Well, conversation was something of an effort," I said. "He wouldn't speak without prompting and I didn't want to go too far."

"Quite right. There's no need to hurry things. Well, now, what about the other bright boy?"

"I saw him just before coming here. He's already had the telegram. It didn't seem to surprise him."

Rayne was watching my face. "If anything," I said, "he seemed mildly disappointed. I think the message was too brief and cryptic. It just said: 'James must stay on with you. Writing. Jan.'"

Rayne nodded. "There was a good reason for that," he said. "But go on."

"I took your advice and pretended to be worried, but I made it clear that I didn't much want to talk about it. I did ask Fontanet what he thought it meant. He said at first that Barton might not have wanted to communicate with him direct, but he dismissed the idea almost at once. Then he said I ought perhaps to move to his hotel, but he thought better of that too. It was odd that he didn't there and then realise that I might be criminally involved myself. In the end he asked *me* what I made of the whole

173

thing. I said I hadn't the faintest idea, but I spoke as if I had, and as if I were frightened."

"D'you think he noticed your fear?"

"I doubt it somehow. Maybe my acting was at fault. Or perhaps he thought that if I was in trouble, that was my funeral and was no concern of his. That's quite in keeping with his character, by the way. In any case, the receipt of the telegram seemed actually to have relieved him to some extent."

"That's exactly what we expected, but on what do you base your impression?"

"Well, he became quite cheerful, and said he was going out to buy a pullover. A man who's frightened out of his wits doesn't usually buy clothes, but of course . . ."

"Yes. . . ." Rayne said with his New World smile.

"A man as complicated as Fontanet, someone who's such a mass of contradictions—at least *apparent* contradictions . . ."

Rayne nodded, the smile still on his lips, seeming to suggest: "We'll got into the psychological motivation later." My interpretation of his attitude must have been correct, because he interrupted to ask: "What else did you find out?"

"Nothing much. He talked about the F.B.I. again, and said he was absolutely certain they were putting pressure on the Foreign Office. Then he said: 'But apart from all that, they're quite capable of acting on their own, especially now we're no longer in England. Even murder's not beyond them.' I suggested—unwisely—that his idea was a little bit like *The Four Just Men,* but luckily he didn't flare up. I said that Barton's letter was sure to arrive tomorrow."

Rayne asked: "Where does Fontanet think you are now?"

"I didn't say anything, but if he asks me what I've been doing, I'll say I've been trying to contact my literary agent and publisher. That's quite on the level, by the way. I really have a publisher and an agent here. As a matter of fact, there are some royalties due me—two pounds ten. Or it may be ten pounds two; I never can remember. I ought in any case to telephone my agent later. I should have done so already, but I got up so late. Which reminds me: I think Lockheed takes sleeping pills."

"I'm not surprised," Rayne said. Just then the telephone rang and he got up and went to the tiny writing desk by the window.

"Yes," he said. "Speaking. . . . Yes. Very kind of you. . . . Three-thirty this afternoon. . . . Well, it couldn't be helped, I suppose. . . . No. . . . Good-bye."

He was looking at his watch as he came over to me. "If you're not doing anything," he offered, "come and have lunch with me. I'm free till about three o'clock."

I got up, but the telephone rang again. Frowning, he picked up the receiver. "Yes," he said. "Oh, thanks for calling back. I *did see* him this morning. He came here at nine. Yes, he's trying Bordeaux, but you ought to go in with your own idea. Yes, I'd leave him out of it. . . . No. . . . Not before five or six. Could you leave a message. . . . *Message,* I said. . . . Thanks. Good-bye."

He replaced the receiver, and I saw him smile.

"Good news?" I asked.

He nodded. "About time. The worst thing about this whole affair is that I'm practically single-handed. . . ." His face became dark for a moment, then he changed the subject quickly. "I'm taking you to a small place I know."

As we walked out of the hotel I said: "I suppose Fontanet is right about the F.B.I. prodding us?"

"Up to a point. The first information about him did come from them, which was only natural; after all, they had a better chance to enquire into his activities in America than anybody else and, let's face it, they had the right to. They got on to us a few days after Fontanet was recalled." Rayne shook his head. "It's a painful business. We thought they were exaggerating. They are a bit hysterical at times, but in this case they were absolutely right, and it's we who were at fault for starting to investigate Fontanet too late."

"I suppose now the F.B.I. will come up to you triumphantly and say: 'What did we tell you, you calm, iron-nerved, alarmingly well-informed, effortlessly superior, practical, single-minded Englishman?' "

Rayne laughed. "They haven't so far. For one thing, I doubt whether they yet know that Fontanet has escaped and that Lockheed's with him. The trouble is they might. They're very efficient. . . ."

"You have to 'hand it to them,' " I said.

"Yes," Rayne smiled. "You have to 'hand it to them.' " The smile suddenly disappeared from his face. "It could be very unpleasant if they did know. I can just see Colonel Van Neff—he's one of their boys—talking to P.A.: 'Waal, I guess, *Sir* Paul, we're a nation of immigrants of low origin and limited historical experience, and we jump to conclusions.' " He shook his head. "The danger is that, if they discover the two men have escaped, they may start searching for them on their own. And if they find them, they're likely to broadcast the story of our 'incompetence.' "

We had to stop at the intersection of the Avenue Kléber. "What can they do that we can't to prevent the two men from escaping?" I said when we had managed to cross over.

"Nothing much—except that they might be more ruthless."

"Fontanet said they'd go as far as murder."

"I suppose it's *possible*," Rayne replied. "They could always say the Communists had shot them. But let's try to get them ourselves, shall we?"

But I decided not to let him change the subject.

"Incidentally," I said, "there's something that's been puzzling me. I don't think I ever told you, but when I first went to Fontanet's flat in London, I met a young man called David. Fontanet thought he was spying on him."

"What made him think that?" Rayne asked.

"Well, he didn't really at first, but he had a very strong suspicion. I asked him about it again this morning, and he said Barton also thought the man was a spy. Fontanet met David in rather odd circumstances, at a night club of sorts to which he goes, only a couple of days before I found the dossier. Somebody introduced him, but he had the feeling that the chap had asked to be introduced."

Rayne was looking at me closely, as if trying to make up his mind about something. I said: "I believe David played up to Fontanet all right, and for a couple of days Fontanet was quite keen on him. Then I came along with the dossier business and Fontanet at once began to suspect David. He suddenly remembered that the fellow was too anxious to find out everything he could about him."

"He may have had his own reasons," Rayne suggested. "After all, David needn't have been an agent to want to find out all he could about Fontanet."

"That's what I told Fontanet, but he's no fool, and somehow I feel he's too experienced about that sort of thing to make a mistake. And I don't mean about agents."

"What did he tell you about it?" Rayne said, and from his tone I began to suspect that he knew about the affair.

"That David was overdoing things," I said provocatively. "He asked Fontanet out to dinner and the theatre the night after they met and rang him up twice a day. But when it came to essentials, to quote Fontanet's exact words, 'David showed an extraordinary lack of talent.'"

I saw Rayne smile, then he shook his head. "Someone sold the idea to P.A. We knew something about Fontanet's personal tastes; he never made much secret of them. And we put up the man you called David—he's a good all-round chap, very versatile—to try to get into Fontanet's confidence. It's a twist to the old trick of the beautiful blonde as a decoy or as an agent. The idea was neither good nor bad. It came too late."

"You, of course, know," I said, "that Fontanet actually invited David to dinner at a Soho restaurant for half-past eight last Saturday night to get him out of the way."

"Mm. And David waited two hours. By that time Fontanet was almost at Calais."

The Place Victor Hugo came into view. "I only hope Fontanet doesn't tumble to *you*," Rayne said. "You'll have to make your 'full confession' to the two men tomorrow, by the way, when they get the letter."

"I think I've got my story pat," I said.

"I'm sure you'll do it well . . . if only nothing goes wrong with the ship. . . ." He broke off.

"You're not worried?" I said, feeling certain that he was.

"Things are moving too slowly. We're not in England and I'm practically single-handed, apart, of course, from yourself. I could do with a few more people."

2

"The legend," Rayne said, "of the British Secret Service still survives abroad. British Intelligence has probably never been as good as foreigners believe, but, like the Parliamentary system, the police, the public schools and Savile Row suits, it was considered beyond reproach, because England was the first nation of the world. And we believed in our own institutions, because we believed in ourselves. Today we don't. We try to cover things up for home consumption, but we don't always succeed. Policemen are brought to court for theft, and when defending counsel in a criminal case calls a police witness a liar, the judge looks at his own fingernails or at the point of his

178

pen. When it comes to our so-called Intelligence Service, we let scientists run away with our greatest secrets. We nearly lost Lockheed and Fontanet even. . . ."

"How do you explain it?" I said. "What's the main cause?"

"A pathological self-complacency, and, I think, a *mistimed* sense of humor.

There were many reasons for which one could like Rayne. To me his most endearing feature was a seriousness which never for a single second made him look pompous. Like many Australians, he had managed to retain some fine old English traits which are less noticeable in contemporary England. He had vitality and a sharp critical sense, but above all he had an intelligence of which he was neither over-conscious nor ashamed.

"It's difficult," he said later, "to estimate the real importance of the Secret Service in contemporary society."

"It is," I said. "Your function is to defend sovereignty, which in our time is more vulnerable to the forces of history than ever before."

"Except when present-day sovereignty was born."

"Yes." I thought for a moment. I said: "You mean when one nation conquered others and finally one sovereignty emerged out of two or three or four. All through the Middle Ages, in fact. We're living in a similar period now."

"But the whole world's on a larger scale today," Rayne interposed.

A little later I said: "Do you think there's a chance that the Americans will wake up and put up a real and acceptable alternative to Communism? Or will they just imitate our bad example?"

"By 'bad example' you mean the preservation of the status quo: democracy is a private tea-party of the rich?"

"Precisely. The poor are kept out of the party and from time to time lend themselves to a charlatan, like Hitler or Stalin, who gets hold of really splendid ideas. Mind you,

179

I'm the first to admit that the charlatan is in an easy position because he's got practically nothing to lose by distributing the wealth of the rich—I mean rich *nations*—but do you see one single sign that the Americans will put up a better alternative than Communism?"

"Materially speaking, they can hardly afford it, even if they marshal the British Empire and what's left of Western Europe."

"They would rather spend their resources on trying to defend themselves."

"That's another aspect. The more I think about America's role in world affairs the more I'm frightened. In production, in technology, in organisation, in many other things, the Americans are fully fledged adults; but in politics they are adolescents. . . ."

He closed his eyes for a moment. "Look at it in terms of the theatre. . . . The old star of the play is taken ill and his young understudy is called upon suddenly to play the part; he's gawky, of course, all legs and pimples and full of adolescent characteristics: naïvety and premature wisdom, an anarchic charm, sudden optimism and sudden hysteria, excessive generosity and sordid meanness. And—this is important—contrary to outward appearances, he's *not* over-ambitious to play the star role. He knows he's provincial and that he's had little experience. He doesn't know his lines well. . . ."

And the braces on his front teeth make him self-conscious, I thought.

"And the old star, sitting in his invalid chair in the wings, watches. He is torn, for the young man is a remote cousin, not a complete stranger, but the old boy is nevertheless jealous. Like all ageing actors, he is conscious of his ebbing strength; he knows he has all the experience in the world, but he also knows he can no longer take the initiative, but he is exasperated by the young man's inex-

180

perience and indecision. He thinks of his own past, and what a past! What star parts and what performances and what applause, the whole world applauding! Should he give useful advice? The young man's father is a good-for-nothing gambler; no relation, a foreigner; but the mother is a hard-working, self-sacrificing, God-fearing, kind woman and a niece. Should he give the boy the benefit of his magnificent experience? And if he did, would the young man listen?" Rayne now looked much older than his years. "Still, the play must go on. I suppose both of them would see that."

"Yes," I said; "the play must go on, but as regards the present play at least, there aren't many acts left. The decision must come within a generation or two. I don't think we can talk today about 'the distant future.' Thirty, forty, fifty years. . . . I wonder what'll happen. I suppose it's more probable that the world will be united by one of the two combatants during the next fifty years than that it should remain disunited, at any rate. . . ."

"Would you be happier in a united world?" Rayne said.

"I've no idea. Probably not. You see, I'm a member of the post–H. G. Wells generation. Not disillusioned, but sceptical. The thing, in a way, is *above* us, beyond our control. It will come into being perhaps against our will, and we'll be forced to accept it. And later on history will accept it. I'm not an optimist, but a fatalist; a part-time fatalist, I suppose. When it comes to such things, for example—"

"What are your grounds for thinking there'll be One World?" Rayne interrupted.

"Oh, the usual two," I said. I was now quoting an old article of mine. "First: the administration of the world as one single unit is now possible as it has never previously been. Second: the new weapons look as if they are able to compel lasting decisions."

181

"And the human element?"

"I don't expect a basic change in human behavior in one generation or two, but, all things being equal, a new order of things, a new science, may impose a state of peace on the people of the world, in the same way that the conditions of their existence in the past have kept them in a state of war. . . ."

3

It was a quarter to three. As the waiter brought back Rayne's change and we walked out into the sunshine of the Avenue Victor Hugo, I said, as if I were talking to myself: "What will happen to Fontanet and Lockheed after they're brought back?"

"They have to be brought back first."

"I'm assuming that."

"It all depends whether we can keep it secret. If so, then I don't think there'll be a trial. They'll be dismissed, of course, but in a case like this the Government usually acts on the principle which banks often adopt towards the cashier who runs away with the cash. They write the money off and keep quiet about it. There's no point in shaking public confidence."

Rayne said nothing further till we got nearer the Etoile; then suddenly he stopped and turned to me. For one single second he looked at the asphalt; then he began to talk as if to himself. " 'And I wonder' "—he raised his right hand slightly—" 'how they should have been together! I should have lost a gesture and a pose. Sometimes these cogitations still amaze the troubled midnight and the noon's repose. . . .' "

"The troubled midnight," I thought, "and the noon's repose." I saw Rayne's wistful smile.

"What is it?" I said.

"T. S. Eliot." He looked at his watch.

15

"*D*EAR *Eric,*" I read. "*I hope James arrived and contacted you. Please tell him that he must stay on, because he would be involved in serious trouble if he returned.*

"*As regards the other matter, I expect you must be getting impatient. (I hope not too impatient.) As you must already have guessed, the reason for the delay is that my original plans could not be carried out. In a few days' time, however, a friend called Kovac will call on you. He will explain everything. Best wishes.*

Benjy."

Unlike the other letter I had handed to Eric on Rayne's instructions on the day of my arrival, this was on a plain sheet of paper with no address on it whatsoever. But like the first, it was handwritten.

"Who's Benjy?" I said.

"A private joke," Eric said wearily. "Jan looks very much like a well-known English composer. He wrote 'Benjy' because he didn't want to sign his own name or for better identification, in case I didn't recognise his handwriting."

But all this was little more than making conversation. The way Eric handed me the letter, the way he watched me while I was reading it, made it quite certain that he believed that the letter was genuine. In a way, of course, it certainly was. The hand that had held the pen was indeed Barton's. Rayne's department was certainly competent and imaginative.

183

I saw Eric watching me. It was obvious that I would have to explain to his satisfaction how it had come about that I was so seriously involved that it was unwise for me to return to England. I remembered Rayne's instructions and my own decision about how to act. I had rehearsed my part more than Eric had his when he first came to see me. I hoped I was looking properly worried.

"Well now, you can start explaining." Eric gave me my cue. His voice was rather quiet and friendly, and I noticed the excitement and curiosity in his eyes—and was there just a touch perhaps of satisfaction? I looked deliberately at the carpet as if trying to avoid his face. Then I spoke. "Now it's your turn to help *me*," I said. "I didn't want to tell you because I thought nobody'd find out. I was advised to get into the T.F.O. in order to pass on information. But I'm absolutely certain nobody knew about it."

"Well, apparently somebody did," Eric shrugged. "And I can tell you who. This time you might believe me. . . ."

"The Americans?" I said. How difficult it was to express anger without feeling it.

"Don't shout," Eric said wearily. "What were you actually doing?"

"While I was in the R.A.F.—"

"But that was during the war."

"Yes; but I was already active. I wasn't asked to do much, though, until it was suggested I apply for the T.F.O. job."

He smiled. "So the things in your dossier were true."

"Not strictly."

"It amounts to the same thing. Like a man accused of a crime of which he's innocent who could have been accused of another of which he was guilty."

"You can put it like that, if you want."

"And you denied it to me. In fact, you were outraged."

This was not an accusation. Eric was merely enjoying a little fun at my expense.

184

"Wouldn't you have denied it?" I ought to have said, "*Didn't* you?"

"Certainly," he laughed.

"What can I do now?"

I saw Eric's slow grin. For quite a time he just looked at me with amused interest; then he spoke: "For the calm, level-headed man you are, you ask strange questions. You'll come with us, of course. At least that's what Jan obviously has in mind, and I'm sure he's right. You're in the same boat as we are now." Was it commiseration I read in his face or merely malignant joy? "You are as safe as we are, or as unsafe. You can't go back. Incidentally, who were your contacts?"

"A man called Dobbs. D'you know him?"

Eric paused, and for a moment I was anxious lest he might actually know somebody I had thought never existed. "A schoolteacher," I added.

"I don't know him." He went to the table and picked up a pack of Gitanes; he did not offer me one. "It's up to you, of course, if you want to come with us," he said. "But we must hang on now for Kovac."

"And if I came with you?"

"You'll be given a good job." He looked at me. "What are you worried about? What are you afraid of? Now, I ask you—what the hell are you leaving behind? A civilisation in decay, which doesn't appreciate you in any case." He shrugged a shoulder. "But still, you make up your own mind. There's no *guarantee* you'll be arrested if you go back to England. But. . . ." He smiled triumphantly.

"It isn't that," I said. I did not want to appear strongly to resist the idea of going to Russia, or to suggest that I was afraid; I wanted only to convey the impression that I was uncertain about what to do. "It isn't that," I said. "There's something else—"

"What?"

"It isn't definite that the Soviet Government will let

185

me in. Why should they? The services I've rendered haven't been important. If I'd got the job at the T.F.O. and passed on or collected information, then I'd probably be of some use to them. But I didn't. Quite frankly, what could I do in Russia? I can't speak the language, I'm not a scientist, a diplomat, an expert."

Eric smiled when I said I was unable to speak Russian. "There are hundreds of jobs you could do," he said, and he nodded as if to imply: "Nothing as important, of course, as the job I can do, but still . . ." He blew a smoke ring into the air. "You can be a radio announcer, and adviser on propaganda—any one of a hundred things. After all, James," he looked at me sideways, "Alan and I would *recommend* you."

He said this as if offering to propose me for his club. But the comic implication only touched me for a second. Then I had another idea. It was a risk to take, but I felt it was now or never if I was ever to satisfy my curiosity.

"That's very good of you, Eric. Very good, but . . ." I looked at the floor, hesitated, then said: "I shouldn't offend you by asking this, really—but just why are you so important to them?"

I felt I was hamming it, but a second later he was already on me like a ton of bricks: "My *dear* James," he said, and let loose a thunderous laugh. This was one of his favorite parts or at least attitudes: a studiedly masculine, belly-shaking, eighteenth-century roar. "You haven't changed one bit since Oxford; still the same Careful Enthusiast. You always remind me of the little boy who said to the chairman of Lloyd's Bank: 'Is your bank absolutely safe? I've got two pounds to invest with you.'" There was another roar; then he narrowed his eyes, the smile still on his lips, and I heard what I had been waiting to learn anxiously, hopefully, nervously for days.

"Alan and I are far more valuable than an atomic scientist. We know all the methods of the Foreign Office and

186

the State Department. All the joint plans of England and America. How their policy operates, what are the main points of friction between them. How to drive a wedge between them. Don't you see, our worth is enormous. Sciences changes, strategy can be altered, but the methods of the Foreign Office must go on for ever. It's not only that we know a lot about secret treaties or secret clauses; they're not important; they're impermanent for one thing, and every expert abroad guesses what's in them anyhow. But what we do know about are the methods and *permanent* principles that govern our policy. We are both key men, James. . . ." He added thoughtfully, "Especially Alan."

No doubt, I thought. Alan was Eric's passport. Alan, whose position made him intimately acquainted with American policy, really had the goods, whereas Eric was the salesman, the go-between, the impresario who would get his rake-off. It was possible, of course, that Eric also had valuable knowledge of his own, but it was typical of him to put up a terrific front.

I nodded, slowly, humbly, apologetically. I said: "Please forgive me. I never really had the slightest doubt about your importance. I just didn't know in quite what way. . . ." I suddenly looked at him. "But what will happen if they find out that documents are missing from the Foreign Office?"

"Nothing's missing," he said. He looked at me as if I were a particularly stupid child. So Rayne had been right. "I brought a copy of the Anglo-American plan for trans—Iron Curtain propaganda, and Alan's adding to it, but there's not much need for it. . . ."

No, I thought, except that it was doubtless a good idea to show the Russians something concrete. They liked documents in black and white, just as they respected men who wore glasses or carried a stethoscope.

Eric said: "That must have been one of the reasons why

the F.B.I. suspected me. They knew the Embassy had a copy of the plan and that I'd had a chance to look at it."

"Was that why they suspended you?"

"I don't know. . . ." His voice rose. "Well, are you satisfied now?"

It still seemed odd to me that Eric should so readily assume that he would be happy in Russia, for that was certainly my impression. How, for example, would a person of his emotional make-up and sexual inclinations get on in the Soviet Union?

He had come to a complete stop, so I decided after a moment's hesitation to ask him. I was apparently right to assume that he would not regard my question as either strange or impertinent.

"In the Soviet Union," he said, "they judge one by different standards. For one thing, I'm a foreigner; secondly, I'll automatically belong to the privileged group, one of whose privileges is that they accept your idiosyncrasies. They're very elastic. And they're beautifully human, you know. The admiration of the simple, young Russian, the sailor, the worker, for the artist, the writer, the intellectual . . ." His voice became almost nostalgic. . . . "They're not a smug, middle-class people like the English. They have no inhibitions."

No, I thought, no inhibitions. During the occupation of Czechoslovakia the Russian troops were said to have raped women of fifty or sixty. No inhibitions. I wondered if Eric really believed what he had said; it was efficient sales talk, but was his heart in it? I felt sure I detected some anxiety in his voice.

It was then that Alan came in. His eyes seemed tired, but he looked unusually elated.

"I'm just trying to knock some sense into James," Eric said. Alan came over and put his hand on my shoulder. He had never done that to me before.

188

"Have you seen this letter?" I said, trying hard to suppress my sense of triumph.

"Yes," he smiled.

"James has just told me," Eric said, "that it's all true." He licked his lower lip. The word "it" obviously meant that the two had discussed me after receiving the letter and had no doubt decided that I was involved, but that I had tried to be stupidly secretive about everything out of smug, middle-class fear, and that the help I had given them had not been entirely unselfish.

"I told him it's entirely up to him whether he joins us," Eric said.

"Well, in a way it is," Alan said in a middle-aged voice. He was silent for a moment, and with some amusement I began to feel something of the atmosphere of a conference between teacher and student.

Eric picked up a towel and left the room, and Alan said "Sit down, James," and pointed gently towards the armchair. He seated himself on Eric's bed. Yes, it was to be such a conference combined with advice from an older-friend-who-knows-best.

"James," he said in the same middle-aged voice, but it was full of genuine warmth. "Please forgive me if I'm too personal. I think I remember you quite well from Oxford. You were always hesitating, vacillating, playing for safety. And, if I may say so, you still are. In a way, you're a symbol for the attitude, the outlook of official England: biding for time, wait and see, orderly stagnation with the eventual hope of success in isolation; a romantic individualism. They haven't got an idea; they try not to think of the problem because it frightens them—just an agonising impasse and frustration.

"But you're a different person," he said after a little pause. "You are informed, you know the truth, you know that the Soviet represents the only one single hope of an eventually united democratic world." Suddenly he looked away, but I had no need to study his eyes. From the tone and the intensity, I knew what I had guessed before, that the man facing me was a believer pronouncing an article of faith.

He studied me carefully. "The world will get absolutely nowhere with people who go halfway. With spare-time enthusiasts."

Suddenly, for the first time, I felt uncomfortable. And it was not because of his words. I had heard them before. Twenty-odd years ago, I had even believed in them.

I said: "It's very good of you. Alan. You're more than kind. And what you're telling me is entirely true. It's just that I'm not feeling too well at the moment. I mean, you have to admit this letter was a shock to me."

He nodded grimly. He said: "You *are* coming with us?"

"Of course. But you see—I'm very upset. It's a very great decision. . . ."

"Didn't you expect to have to make it?"

"To be frank, I did and I didn't."

"Then it's time you made it now."

"I've already made it, Alan."

"Well, then." He nodded. I saw that he was a little upset that the conference was apparently at an end and that he could not continue to convert me. "Have you had breakfast?"

"No," I said.

"A miserable lot of frightened little clerks," Alan said. We were having breakfast and he was talking of his colleagues at the Foreign Office. "And lately some of them have begun to look like clerks, too. They may have had ideas once, but they sold them for a safe job and a little glamor. They're the first to laugh if someone tells them that the job has glamor, but the fact remains that it still

190

has a little. A diplomat's social prestige is still high." Not as widely recognised as a film star's, I thought, but more lasting.

"They're just as reactionary as their fathers," he said, "but they've lost their nerve and their confidence. Oh, they're a predatory lot. But what can you expect? They come from the upper class. They've already had the experience of privilege and a taste of the Good Life. . . ."

I nodded. I thought: The English diplomat is predatory because he comes from the upper class, the Russian because he does not.

2

My excuse for leaving Alan after breakfast was that I was going to see my French publisher to try to get some money out of him. I was for once really anxious to report to Rayne, and I was glad to get away. For one thing, Rayne's plan had been almost too embarrassingly successful.

The receptionist told me on the telephone that Rayne was out. This was an unexpected shock. Our arrangement had been that he could always be contacted in the morning.

I enquired whether he had left a message for me, and after a short pause I was told that he had indeed done so. "Monsieur will be back at two o'clock," the girl said.

It was now half-past eleven. I wondered whether it might be a good idea to return to the two men and tell them that I had made an appointment with my publisher for two o'clock. Then I immediately dismissed the idea. In the first place, I needed a little breathing space; and I also felt sure that, my credentials having been established by Barton's letter, it would not now create the slightest suspicion if I stayed away.

191

In the end I strolled down the Boulevard des Batignolles. The weather suddenly turned cool, and I decided to walk as far as the Parc Monceau.

There were many reasons why I had felt embarrassed while Alan had been lecturing me. *The Soviet represents the only one single hope of an eventually united democratic world.* That was what he had said. There was no doubt that the Soviet dream was grandiose, and, like all religions, Communism offered a strong element of hope. In fact, it offered the Promised Land; a new, materialistic variation on the promise of all great religions.

But there was some historical justification too, even if one tried to get away from the dialectic and tried to interpret history as independently as one could. There was no doubt that history could be regarded as the record of the gradual integration of mankind into larger and larger units. The old saying that "empires come and go" was not altogether true. I felt it more exact to say that they come and go *and come again.* In other words, the rate of progression was two steps forward and one step backwards. And in our time, this process was happening fast.

Yesterday, when I was having lunch with Rayne, I remembered having said that I was a member of a generation for which H. G. Wells had no message. Wells was the last nineteenth-century liberal who had survived into our time. I did believe that a united world was a more probable future prospect than a disunited one, but, unlike my parents' generation, I did not believe it would come about democratically, via enlightened self-interest, free discussion and consent. I believed it would come through strife, fear, bloodshed and treason, as it had always done in the course of history. And this time there were two or three new circumstances which the philosopher of the nineteenth century may have anticipated, but could not have known for certain.

Rayne and I had also discussed the enormous contrast

192

between the personalities of the two men, which had inspired him to quote T. S. Eliot. I had told Rayne that it was Alan Lockheed who really interested me. Eric, I felt now, was an adventurer who disliked the society he was living in because it did not give him the rewards he expected as his due. And, I thought, it was largely his own fault that he had failed to get them. I was not in the least certain that Eric was a dedicated or convinced Communist, and the more I thought about him the more I felt that his treachery was perhaps little more than an alternative to gun-running, dope-smuggling or black-marketeering. The only difference beween him and the man who turned to some less imaginative—and less serious—shady business was that Eric was better educated, had a little money of his own, had a better intellect and probably a greater vision; not to speak of the special opportunities which his position afforded.

Lockheed was a different proposition. He was a man of faith. For his Communism there was no other alternative except the monastery.

My mind suddenly went back twenty years: to Lockheed at Oxford. I saw him in slate-grey flannels and a sober tie, the young, devoted Communist; a type neither Fontanet nor I had ever been. Eric was too frivolous, too worldly, too cynical, whereas I was too much of an individualist.

Then my thoughts leapt six or seven years: to Lockheed at dinner at Southwick Crescent. Seeing him at table, smart and serious, sitting next to Selina, I had thought, with anger and envy, that he had shed Communism because of his career. Perhaps it had been mad jealousy that had made me see him in that light, but he himself may, of course, have thought for a time that he had given up his faith for a safer and perhaps even more "real" life.

Then came marriage to Selina and an almost fabulous success in his career. Perhaps too fabulous, in ten short years. Perhaps it had been too much for him. Guilt and

193

remorse must have struck some time or other; perhaps in Egypt, as Dr. Eldin had suggested; perhaps earlier, in America. The old infection which had been lying latent under the surface of the mind, under the layers of memory, must have become virulent again.

On the other hand, he may, of course, never have really given up Communism, except consciously. His life may well have been lived inside its dialectic, and no doubt when he was representing the official attitude of Britain against Communism, his attitude must have been a reflection of a painful inner struggle, the more painful because it was unconscious. It was only now that I began to find some explanation for his drunken brawls and his nervous breakdown.

When, and exactly how, the conflict had started, I could not be certain; and I could never ask him, because I was sure he himself had no idea.

3

A nurse, wheeling a pram and followed by a nervous little girl with a pale face, approached to ask me the time. It was half-past twelve. I lit a cigarette; I had no appetite. For the first time in the past three days, the fact that I was in Paris left me cold.

There was now no need to close my eyes in order to shut out the formal and elaborate prettiness of the Parc Monceau, and my mind went back to what I had been thinking about before the nurse had interrupted me. I had been considering the difficulties of the position of the intellectual in our time.

There had been a period very similar to our own— Rayne and I had talked about it only recently—a similar period of critical transition, when the sovereign, independent nation-state was born. The intellectual of the time had had an important part to play. He had seen that the old order was out of date and had to be destroyed, and he had helped to create the new order. "This happy breed of men," I thought; what magnificent advertising copy for the new sovereignty.

Today the intellectual sees again that the order in which he lives is ripe for change. In the testament of the nineteenth century there was only one clause—namely, that the task for the twentieth century would not be mainly to render into public hands the common means of life; that was a detail, an important detail, but a detail, nevertheless. The real task was to find a substitute for the rivalry of the system of nation-states.

But what can the intellectual do today? The substitute, the new order, cannot be created in a vacuum; allegiance has to be given to an already existing country. And the only country which has made a bid to create a new order is unacceptable.

It was no wonder, I thought, that the intellectual in our time had become frustrated or, by trying to avoid frustration, had become an escapist. I had been an escapist myself. One could, of course, say that the real cause of escapism was that the public was uninterested in politics. That was true. But as far as I could see, the public had never been interested; certainly not in intellectual speculation.

4

Rayne and I arrived practically simultaneously at his hotel. He waved to me as he paid off his taxi, but I saw that his smile was a little worried.

"They got the letter, I hope," he said, somewhat anxiously.

"Yes. . . ."

"How are they taking it?" he asked before I could go on.

"They're trying to persuade me to leave with them."

"That's good," he said. "Let's go up."

When we reached his room I said: "There's something more important. I'm now so much in their confidence that Fontanet has made a practically full confession to me."

But Rayne did not seem to pay attention. I spoke again. "A full confession. You might be able to arrest him on the strength of it."

"Yes," Rayne said. Suddenly he put his hand on my arm. "You'll have to forgive me, but there's something more urgent. Barton's arrest is in the papers, or will be in a few minutes' time. It had to be made public." He jerked a shoulder. "Luckily, he's not named. 'Alien detained'— that's all. But in a couple of days' time they'll have to disclose his name, and then our job becomes really difficult. They might get panicky and contact the Soviet Embassy or God knows what." He looked at me earnestly. "Yesterday you said they hadn't contacted anybody so far."

"That was what they said; and I believe it."

"Good." Rayne looked at his watch. "I've been out the whole morning, and now I've got to leave immediately for Marseilles." He gripped my coat sleeve. "From this minute on, you're in charge. Here are your instructions. You must do your best to prevent them from contacting anybody. Say it's highly dangerous and that you have supreme faith in Barton. I hope nothing awkward will happen." His tone was almost severe now. "But if it does, and if they do contact someone, find out exactly who it is. In that case, or if anything goes wrong, you'll have to contact this man." Rayne felt in his pocket and pulled out a piece of paper, which he handed to me. "He knows all about you and he's working for me."

The name on the paper was M. Kovac. His address was in the rue St. Dominique and he had an Invalides telephone number.

16

THAT evening I went again with Lockheed and Fontanet to their usual restaurant, after which we took the Métro to Barbès. As we came down the steps, just about to make our way in the direction of the Boulevard de la Chapelle, Ali hailed us from the terrace of the Café Rousseau. He was with another boy—a cousin, apparently —and we sat down at their table. It was quite early yet, and the boulevard under the dusty trees was busy with people, mostly North Africans, ambling slowly on their way towards the gaudy lights and second-hand air of the bottom of Montmartre, to see "life," to idle away the last hours of the day or to sell American cigarettes or dirty postcards to foreigners.

I prayed that I would manage successfully to hide my anxiety over the news Rayne had given me; or, alternatively, that I could make it appear an alarm over the fact that, like the two men, I was a fugitive now. As it turned out, they seemed to notice nothing. If anything, our relationship was now more intimate and they, for their part, were not so restless.

The boy with Ali was called Saïd. His coloring was unexpectedly light for an Arab, but he had the usual doe eyes, the curly, matted hair and the flat nose. Like so many young men in Paris, French or Arab, he wore basketball sneakers, faded blue jeans and a T-shirt. There was a conspicuous blue half-moon and star tattooed on his forearm.

"But he has another one," Ali said with a sordid grin, as if he were enjoying the point of a dirty story, and Saïd

197

obediently bowed his head forward so that we could see the back of his neck.

About an inch from where his hair ended in a dead straight line there was a number of small blue dots, and we managed to read the words: *coupez sur la ligne.*

"Instructions for the barber?" Fontanet said, not quite seeing the point.

"Mais non," Ali winked. "For the Public Executioner. The man with the guillotine."

"Cut along the dotted line!" What an instruction! This was a new line in toughness, I thought, a little morbid and masochistic; quite French. And Saïd seemed such a nice, quiet, affectionate boy, to whom Paris was still new. He worked, he told us, for a blacksmith near the Porte de Clignancourt.

Lockheed now turned to Saïd and said something I could not understand; then slowly, but quite clearly, word after word, he began to talk in a foreign language. I presumed it was Arabic, but only Ali seemed to understand it.

"You talk like the movies," Saïd said, but this was clearly a compliment to Lockheed, whom he obviously admired. Ali explained that they were conversing in the Egyptian dialect, the language of all Arab films.

It was only later that I saw that Lockheed had his own reasons for not speaking French or English. When Fontanet decided to take Ali to a cinema, Lockheed asked Saïd if he would like to go home with him.

Saïd pulled back Ali's sleeve to look at his wrist watch. "If I can see you at half-past eleven, monsieur," he said, his expression deadly serious, almost imploring. "I've got to see my brother. He lives in the rue des Couronnes. Would that be too late for you? Half-past eleven. We could meet here?"

Lockheed agreed, and Fontanet signalled to the waiter.

198

Lockheed and I were now sitting in the quiet little bar in the rue des Martyrs, to which he had taken me the other night. On the way neither of us spoke, which was perhaps just as well, for I was unsure which had surprised me more, the fact that he had arranged to take Saïd home or his complete matter-of-factness about it in my company. It was, if anything, a further and conclusive indication that I was accepted by him and that he had no need to hide things from me, for he was by nature reserved.

"Aren't these Arab boys charming?" he said after he had taken the first sip of his drink. Now that the shock of the surprise was over, I had more or less expected him to say something of the sort, so I just nodded.

North Africans in Paris, I had always heard and read in the papers, were considered dangerous, and I wondered if the two men were not taking unnecessary risks, especially considering their particular situation. Then I remembered Lockheed's comment when Fontanet had left with Ali the other night: "Nerves." Perhaps this was the explanation; or perhaps the sense of danger gave them an additional thrill.

"Eric met Ali last summer," Lockheed said now, "a few weeks before he was posted to Washington. Then we met him by chance one night near the Place Clichy. He's one of eleven brothers from somewhere near Oran. We took him to a café and he told us he'd had an accident last winter and was on the dope, which is about 7,000 francs a month, I think, and he has to pay 3,000 a month for his room." He shook his head. "But then poverty in Algiers is far worse. Eric gives him money, but I don't think there's anything bad about the boy. He's sweet and childish. The poor generally are."

I nodded. This blatant generalisation was so typical of Lockheed, with his guilt complex. It was so easy for someone who had never known poverty to invest the proletariat with virtues they did not necessarily possess or, if they did, that were due to their particular circumstances. And it was so easy for a man of his faith, despite his sharp intellect, to accept the myth that only the proletariat had that mysterious and unique quality which alone could save the world.

So, sexually, Lockheed was not much different from Fontanet after all. Their particular condition may have made them rebels, but not necessarily traitors. The distance between nonconformity and treason was infinite. I had to separate the two things, but it was a measure of my confusion at the time that I imagined a connecting link which, on reflection, did not really exist.

As if reading some of my thoughts, Lockheed said: "Eric is so much luckier. He's so well-integrated, with no complexes. . . ." Quietly he added, "Ruthless."

I felt so surprised that for a moment I could say nothing. Then I suddenly realised that in Lockheed's reticence and reserve during the past few days there must have been a certain amount of uneasiness about Fontanet's reliability. Yes; that was why Lockheed had been so keen on my going with them.

But I had to speak now, I knew, and I had to give him enthusiastic approval. "Eric's been ruthless all his life," I said. And suddenly I knew that here was my opportunity. There was no need for caution now. I had regained my balance. I felt I must know, and here was my chance. I said: "Until recently I hadn't seen either of you for some time. I didn't realise you were such great friends. Of course, you were colleagues."

I held my breath, but Lockheed noticed nothing. He said: "I hadn't seen Eric for a long time until a year ago. After Oxford we drifted apart. Quite frankly, I didn't like him then. I mean, you know what he was like. I met him a few times just before the war. Then last year I became ill and returned to London, and we bumped into each other again."

"I heard you were ill," I said.

"It was quite serious." He looked at me and nodded. "A lot of people advised me to leave the Service, and I thought about it. . . . Then I decided to stay on, after all."

I noticed the slight pause. What had been the real reason for his staying on? I could only hope that he might perhaps tell me later, although I assumed that his Communist friends had probably insisted on his remaining.

"I met Eric at the Poulteney Wheel," he said suddenly, and I looked up again surprised that a really distinguished member of the Foreign Office should have visited such a notorious pub which had repeatedly been raided by the police.

"I was quite drunk," he said, explaining the obvious. "Somebody told me about the place, and that night I was looking for something desperately. I knew it was a sink, but I never expected it would be quite so awful. It was so crowded you could hardly move. I was going to leave at once, but Eric suddenly came up to me. He took me to another place, a pub in Soho, which was half-empty. We had a long talk. . . ." Abruptly he continued: "It was only after that, the next day, that I told Bolger, who was treating me, about my sex life. He said he knew, had expected it, anyhow, and he was glad I'd told him. In any case, it was after that that I got better."

The strain of this confession must have been enormous, particularly for someone normally as reticent as Lockheed. Although he was, in a way, crying on my shoulder, I rather admired him for it, and I had another of those sharp doubts about the ethics of my position. Although logic told me that my real loyalty and self-interest lay in helping Rayne, at a time like this it seemed difficult to be logical; there appeared to be something mean about betraying a man who had such faith in one, even a man who had betrayed his country.

"I suppose," he said now, "I've been the way I am all my life. But I really was happy, awfully happy, with Selina for many years. It was the war that changed things. Actually towards the end. . . . And I love the children." He almost cried.

This was very embarrassing. Lockheed had been under the impression that I was a Communist, but I saw no reason why he should reveal to me what must have been his deepest and most shameful secret. In such a respect he was a very different man from Fontanet: secretive, aloof, reserved.

Then I saw one explanation. Lockheed must have thought that I was, like him, a fellow invert.

If so, the reason seemed plain enough. I had once or twice been called a "fellow traveller" during the war and even earlier. Men had never interested me, but inversion in itself always had. I found it absorbing and stimulating, as some highly respectable, law-abiding man might find murder. And I was honest enough to admit that this was not because I was a writer; the truth was quite the other way around.

"I love the children, James," Lockheed repeated. "Two beautiful children, a boy and a girl."

3

"Eric came to see me," Lockheed said, "the same day he returned from Washington. About a month ago. Of course, I'd already heard bits of the story; I knew about the accident at Concord and that he'd been sent back. He told me it was all the work of the F.B.I. 'I just couldn't care

202

less,' he said. 'I've got some private means and I can still return to journalism. If they let me.'

"I asked, 'If who lets you?' I remember he got up and went to the window. Then came back and stopped in front of my desk. He said, 'Alan, not so long ago you told me things about yourself. Now it's my turn to confess to you.' "

For a split second Lockheed looked at the empty glass in front of him, then he said: "When he spoke of *confessing* to me, I pretty well understood what he meant, and that it had nothing to do with his emotional life. I knew him too well not to see what he was leading up to. It was only then that I realised what his reference to the F.B.I. meant."

Lockheed was silent now, and after a time I could no longer restrain my impatience. I said: "What did he tell you?"

Lockheed looked at me. "In the first place, that he knew Alex d'Ormay."

"Who's he?" I said without thinking.

He paused. From the way he had spoken the name, I ought to have guessed that the man must have been somebody very important, and the fact that I had never heard of him might now make Lockheed suspicious or at least impatient. I was angry with myself for my clumsiness.

But he said simply, "He was a journalist," although his facial expression quite clearly suggested that the man was much more than just that. "Half French, half Russian. His mother was an *émigrée* princess."

I had the impression that Lockheed was struggling to be patient with me and that at any moment he might lose control. It is a painful thing when someone makes a dramatic statement and then, seeing the stupid, blank faces of his audience, must explain why the statement was dramatic.

203

But all that happened was that Lockheed suddenly grabbed my hand above the wrist. "You see, I had never told Eric that I knew Alex d'Ormay."

This time I was a little faster. I said: "You mean it was d'Ormay who had told Eric about you?"

"Yes."

The rest seemed clear. I said: "Was d'Ormay a contact of yours?"

"He was a friend. I first met him in Paris before the war, then later in Washington. Eric said he had kept him regularly informed. Then one day Alex suddenly left Washington without warning. Some time later Eric had a message that Alex had had to disappear. It was advisable, you see. That was the beginning of the purges in America, but the strange thing is that Alex's name has never been mentioned. Not so far, anyway.

"Eric, of course, was very worried. If the F.B.I. knew about Alex, it seemed obvious that they'd soon find out about his friends, who included me, of course, and Eric felt he ought to leave America before anything serious happened. The road accident with that young man, a few days later, was quite a lucky break. When Eric told me about it, I almost thought it was a deliberate plan to get himself sent home." Lockheed shrugged a shoulder. "Perhaps it was the result of wishful thinking."

I said: "So he told you in as many words that you yourself were in danger?"

"He said he wasn't sure how much the F.B.I. knew, but Alex had told him I'd helped him and the F.B.I. might easily find out about me."

"What did you say?" I enquired.

"I wasn't really worried at the time. I thought Eric was a little hysterical. I told him that now that he was back in England the F.B.I. couldn't very well investigate him, and in any case he'd decided to leave the diplomatic service of his own accord. This calmed him down, and in fact he didn't see me again for a whole fortnight."

"But what happened last Friday?" I asked.

Lockheed looked hard at me. "Without you we might never have got away," he said, "but Eric didn't tell me then. When he found a reference to himself in your dossier—or a reference to you in his; I'm still not very clear about that—he went at once to Jan Barton, who said it could only mean one thing: the F.B.I. was catching up with us."

The word "us" made me look up. I said: "How did Barton know about *you?*"

"He didn't, but my name was in the dossier. Don't you remember?"

I held my breath. The page relating to Fontanet had contained no reference to Lockheed; of that I was sure. *So Eric . . .*

But Lockheed seemed not to notice my surprise. He went on: "Last Friday—it was about five in the afternoon —Eric 'phoned me and said he had to see me at once. He only just caught me; fifteen minutes later I'd have been on my way home. I met him at Marylebone Station. I decided to take a later train. In the end, of course, I didn't take any train. It was then he told me about the dossier and of how he'd seen Barton, who'd said we must leave immediately before we got arrested.

"I must say Eric was remarkably calm. He said everything was organised. We were to leave the following day for Paris with false passports, and Barton was making all the arrangements. It was only after we landed in France that Eric told me he'd been watched for the previous two days. If I'd known earlier, I'd have been out of my mind with fright. And Eric helped me with Selina too. . . ."

He closed his eyes. "That was the most painful thing. . . . That evening I couldn't have faced her—it was dreadful. You see, Selina might have found out I was planning to run away if I'd spent the night in the house. And she'd have prevented me. She'd have guessed. Women are very dangerous, because they're not really intelligent. They don't reason. They just feel. In the end it was Eric who worked the thing out for me. He got through to our house and told me exactly what to say to her on the 'phone. But, of course, I still had to see her the next day." Lockheed shook his head. "Without Eric's help, I just couldn't have done it. He did everything." Suddenly he put his hand on my elbow. "And you. I'm really grateful to you."

"Forget it," I said.

"If Eric hadn't driven me down to Denham and back, I couldn't have faced Selina. But he knew, you see, if he was there, she wouldn't ask questions. He was quite right."

I suddenly thought of the Mystery Page. It had ended with a list of three or four names, of none of which I had ever heard. I wished I could have remembered them now. I spoke excitedly: "What was the name of d'Ormay's contact man? The man who told Eric that d'Ormay had to disappear?"

"I can't remember. Eric did tell me."

Perhaps it was not important. In any case, I could ask Fontanet tomorrow. But I felt sure the man's name must have been on the page, and that its presence there must have been the final reason why Eric had decided to run away.

It was now half-past eleven, and we got up, paid and walked out into the warm, still, undisturbed air of the boulevard. The crowds were thinner now, the booths with the clay pipes and the giant wheel of the Loterie Nationale neglected and only a few people were standing outside the *cafés chantants*.

We walked to the Café Rousseau, where Lockheed had arranged to meet Saïd, and, seeing the young man already waiting on the terrace, I said, "I'll see you in the morning," and walked away.

I walked down the Boulevard de Magenta, which was almost completely deserted. It was a little cooler, but I knew I would not be able to sleep.

So I had been justified in all the suspicions I had had about Fontanet while he had graciously offered to put in a word for me with the Soviet authorities. He had found out from d'Ormay that Lockheed had passed on some information while he was in Washington, and when the time came he exploited his knowledge, because he needed Lockheed as his passport, his trump card. When he discovered that he had to run away, he decided to take Lockheed with him, and, knowing his psychology, all he needed to do was to tell Alan Lockheed that the authorities had found out about him and that his name was on a sheet of paper which had got into my dossier. This simple little lie was enough.

Of course, for all I knew, the authorities might indeed have found out about Lockheed's contacts with d'Ormay, but that had nothing to do with Fontanet's treachery. Yes, that was the word—treachery to his country and to his friend.

But this was only one side of the problem. Alan's confession and the things it revealed had again touched off a feeling of guilt and doubt in me. Was I betraying a man? No such idea could possibly have been justified concerning Fontanet. He was just a frustrated, albeit an educated, adventurer. I had wormed myself into Lockheed's confidence—I noticed that I was trying hard to keep him at arm's length by not thinking of him as Alan—and now I intended to betray him. For a reward—the cushy job at the T.F.O.

It was true that he himself was guilty and that he would probably have betrayed his country sooner or later again, even without Fontanet's assistance, but I hated to be one of the executioners, or at least an instrument of his doom.

Everything had seemed so different in Addyman's office,

but then I was still full of hurt pride and a sense of injury and loss and self-pity.

I wondered whether perhaps my behavior had been conditioned by my attitude towards Selina. My wound had healed, or so I had thought until I had suddenly seen her again the previous week. But a moment later I realised how absurd this idea was. There was no need for revenge, even were I that sort of person. Alan had had enough. Assuming—as Rayne had suggested—there were no trial, his career was still finished. Even if the story were kept out of the papers, he was branded for life, for the people who mattered would know about him. As for Selina, she already knew why he had run away, and if she found out also about his emotional life, that might mean the end of his marriage too.

What should I do? Ought I to let him go? If so, Fontanet would get away also. Could I warn Alan only, at the last minute? I saw at least two possibilities. . . .

But as I reached the rue Lafayette I knew I would do nothing of the sort.

I disliked the conception of the Sovereign State, the Old Bitch who claimed everything for herself and exploited the body and soul of her children. I knew that history proved that bloodshed, violence and treachery were the only weapons to defeat her and to liberate man. But what was the alternative to sovereignty?

England, my own country, was predatory, selfish and intermittently criminal, because otherwise she could not possibly survive. Those were the implications of sovereignty. Russia, the alternative, was even more predatory, selfish and intermittently criminal, because otherwise she could not carry out her major commitment. She was committed, all right, to a united world; that was no false promise, no mere propaganda trick. But a world based on Russian traditions—and Marx knew them—would be dreadful.

If one could be completely detached—but I was not, for faith was a habit and the blood and the heart had long become conditioned by climate—I would perhaps say that my choice was between the greater and the lesser evil.

But there was more to it than that. The democracies did at least hold out a tiny ray of hope. Perhaps the fact that England could no longer take the initiative would liberate or inspire America's potentialities, in spite of Rayne's brilliant but bitter parable.

But all this was intellectual argument to support or to justify a decision to which I had come and which had already been made on other grounds. What the other grounds were, I did not know. I only knew they had little to do with reasoning.

Book Four

17

*T*HE moment I saw Fontanet coming towards me in the pink-and-gold light of the early summer morning, I knew he was rattled. There was something in the way he walked into the café terrace, the way he hit against a cane chair, the unmistakable pout of his lips. It was half-past nine and I had just finished my *café crème* and two croissants.

Without greeting me, he pointed towards the *Franc-Tireur,* still folded diagonally as I had bought it, lying on the table. "Is it in that?" he growled.

"I haven't read the papers yet," I said. So had had found out. "What is it, Eric?" I asked. It was difficult to feign ignorance.

"Someone was arrested in London yesterday," he said impatiently. "There's no name or description, but I'm worried. It may easily be Jan."

"Where did you see it?" I was trying to gain time.

"In this." He dropped a crumpled *France Libre* on the table. It looked as if he had slept on it, and I picked it up to read the report. He had already unfolded my paper, turning his back on the sun and the Place de Clichy.

I saw a piece at the bottom of the front page—a Havas Agency report: *Un étranger détenu à Londres.* There were three lines, no name, no description, no mention of a charge, exactly as Rayne had forecast.

"It isn't in this one," Eric said, impatiently dropping the paper on the chair. "All the same, they've given the game away."

"Why?"

"By not giving any reason for the arrest."

"Perhaps they're not sure. You often see 'Later a man was detained' in the English papers."

"Yes; but only at the end of a report where some crime has been mentioned. No; this is quite the typical Secret Service trick."

"Why should it be Barton?" I said. "He's only just written to you."

He shrugged a shoulder, but I could see he was unconvinced. "The letter was posted earlier; the man was only arrested yesterday. It takes two days for a letter to arrive." He waved to the waiter. *"Café noir,"* he barked. He sat down next to me and pulled out his box of Gitanes.

"I must contact somebody at once," he said. "The chap Barton said would come hasn't arrived, and now he may not come at all."

"Just because you saw that bit in the paper?"

His voice became rather loud. He blinked impatiently. "I think the two things are connected. The man hasn't come and Barton's been arrested. We've been here more than a week now. Today's Sunday already. It's just sheer lunacy not to have contacted my friends long ago."

"Who are your friends, Eric?" I said. There was no need for me now to pretend to be anxious. I was genuinely worried.

"I've got plenty of friends. One's a Party member." He spat out the words. "He's the best man for me. I was a fool not to have gone to see him earlier." I thought that he looked at me accusingly.

"When did you see him last?"

"Six months ago. In Washington. But he's back in Paris." He moved his foot violently; the table leg luckily was not too solid. "It's preposterous. All Barton's fault. He said this man Kovac would get in touch with me. This is the eighth lousy day we've wasted. I knew he'd mess things up. Bloody fool. . . ."

214

"But your friend in Paris doesn't know Barton?"

"That's beside the point. He's got the contacts, and I think from now on I'll leave Barton out of it."

His sudden hatred of Barton surprised me. I saw it grow, and I was becoming desperate. "What I'm afraid of," I said, "is that if you go to see this friend of yours, you may give the whole thing away. If he's a prominent Communist, the French police are sure to be watching him."

The waiter came with the coffee. Slowly and deliberately, he rested his tray on the next table, put a breakfast cup in front of Fontanet, poured out the coffee from the metal jug, placed two small packets of sugar, wrapped in wax paper, on the side, then slipped the bill half under the saucer.

This gave me time to think. Weak though it was, my suggestion that the French police might be watching Fontanet's proposed contact was at least good enough to cause a doubt in Fontanet's mind. When Rayne had told me to prevent Fontanet from trying to contact someone on his own, he had suggested no course of action. It was always difficult to argue with Fontanet when he was acting on a hunch, and this time his hunch happened to be correct.

"I'm sure," I said, "the French police keep an eye on prominent Communists. And I think the F.B.I. have greater influence in France than in England."

I thought this was a good line, but the look he gave me convinced me that I had made things worse. "You're quite right about the F.B.I.," he said. "They can do what they like to us in France." His fingers trembled as he opened the sugar packets. "All the more reason to get out of France quickly." He looked at his watch. Then, decisively, as if he would brook no argument, he announced, "I must contact my friend at once."

I was now absolutely certain that, so far, he had contacted nobody. But what now was the value of that information? "How does Alan feel about it?" I asked.

"He's still asleep."

This was agonising. Rayne had gone and left me alone in a crisis like this!

"Eric," I said. This was a last feeble attempt. "Wouldn't it be better if *I* went to see your man?"

"Why should it?" he looked at me. Was he getting suspicious? "He doesn't know you."

He gulped down his coffee, then he got up. "Where's there a telephone?"

"I'll show you," I said. We went inside the café, where the indicator *Lavabos: Téléphones* pointed towards a passage at the back. Since I could not see no way of preventing the telephone call, and in the hope that it might help to get rid of his suspicion, I gave thirty francs for the slot.

There was only one small, yellow bulb in the passage, and it was rather dark, so I took out my lighter, and on pretence of helping him to find the name, I looked over his shoulder at the telephone directory. I was relieved that he did not seem suspicious. "Frondaie," he said and began to turn the leaves backwards, till he reached the page which had the name Duclos on top in bold type. He began to comb the right-hand column, moving a nicotine-stained index finger upwards. Suddenly he stopped. *"Ducretet, Marcel,"* he read aloud, *"67 rue René Doumic,"* and disappeared into the telephone booth.

He inserted the slot and I saw him dial, then I heard him talk. His voice, though, was muffled through the glass partition and, hard as I tried to listen, I understood nothing. Within a few moments he was out again.

"I'm going to see him straight away," he said. He seemed rather relieved. I felt that if I now suggested he should not tell the man too much, it would only provoke an angry outburst and probably suspicion. I followed him

216

meekly into the broad daylight of the terrace. Then he said briefly, "See you later," and left his bill unpaid, apparently for me to settle.

I went back to my seat and picked up the newspaper. I saw him hail a taxi. As soon as it disappeared, in the direction of the St. Lazare, I went back to the telephone and dialled Kovac's number. It was nearly ten o'clock. If I missed him now, I was sunk. I realised that I was sweating.

But he was in. I told him my name, and he immediately changed to English. "Yes. . . . Good morning. What is it, . . . please?" I heard his thick, deep voice; an extrovert's voice.

"Could I see you at once?"

"Yes. Where are you now?"

I told him.

"That is good," he said. "My apartment is near Solférine Métro Station. . . . But you should take a taxi. It would take fifteen minutes."

2

"This is very serious," Kovac said, and then repeated himself. "Very serious."

He looked very much what his voice had suggested, a thick-set, hairy, primitive man from the Balkans who had half assimilated himself to Paris. He wore a heavily striped suit and grey suède shoes. He might have been anything between thirty and forty, but he dressed like a prosperous, middle-aged man. His flat was in an expensive-looking block, the entrance hall of which was all mirrors and the ironwork of the banisters the last word in interior architecture; but the apartment itself consisted almost entirely of a few pieces of gimcrack furniture.

"Ducretet, you said?" he asked me.

Alors, bon voyage." He offered his hand to Fontanet and nodded to all four of us; then we started out and got into our taxi.

4

This was bad, very bad, I felt, as the taxi turned into the Avenue de Clichy and tore down the narrow streets towards the Opéra. I dared not look at Kovac. But I felt he was very calm—as calm and authoritative as during the interview in Fontanet's room that morning.

"We also," he said now in his thick voice, "would like to know who the mysterious alien in London is. Soon enough we shall find out. But the chances are that he may just be a—*ballon d'essai,* how do you call *that* in English?"

"The best translation is 'put-up job,'" Lockheed said. "But you're not suggesting that the British authorities would go quite so far as to report the arrest of a man who doesn't exist?"

Kovac raised both hands level with his shoulders, palms extended inwards; he smiled.

"I can believe anything," Fontanet said. Kovac seemed in some way to have inspired him with confidence. This was, I felt, due not only to his last-minute, dramatic entry into the proceedings, but probably more to the fact that Kovac was not an intellectual, but a man of action: tough, competent-looking, efficient. Personally, at first sight of Kovac, I might even have been frightened, had he not been my last hope, so to speak. He looked the sort of man who would not hesitate to go to great lengths to achieve his ends. Fontanet, who admired that type of person, probably had the same impression of him.

Although he had doubtless lived for a number of years in the West, Kovac had few of the outward signs of a liberal culture: mechanical logic, a graceful scepticism which allows man to question what he does not understand, the

220

ability to look at things from both sides, a romantic individualism, a sense of humor. He seemed to me a man who saw everything as either black or white, and he was somewhat forbidding, especially when he attempted to be amusing. He looked more the type of what I imagined was a Soviet agent rather than a British one.

Probably, I thought, he once *had* worked for the other side. Assuming he was thirty-five, he had been born at about the time between Lenin's arrival at the Finland Station and the beginning of the "New Economic Policy." But where? The name Kovac sounded vaguely Slavonic: Bulgarian, Serb, Russian? It might easily have been a code name, of course, but it suited him. He struck me as a mixture of childish simplicity and adult cunning. He had probably started life as a Communist student in Belgrade or Sofia, and had then left the Party; and, being a man of conviction and drive, he had joined the rival group. It was a conversion from faith to faith. Rayne had said nothing about him; there had been no time.

There was a traffic jam just before we got to the Châtelet, a long row of taxis and trucks and green buses tooting. I looked out and saw two policemen gesticulating; it was nearly twenty to two. Normally, it would have taken no more than ten minutes from there to the Gare de Lyon, but apparently the pavement was torn up and only a single file could pass.

Then, finally, we got through and the taxi tore across the rue Saint Antoine towards the Bastille. We caught the train with five minutes to spare. There was no compartment anywhere with four empty seats. We managed to find one with three vacant places, so I volunteered to sit alone in the next carriage. It was with a sense of great relief that I felt the train begin to move, and saw it slowly leave the station.

There was the inevitable assortment of passengers: a commercial traveller, probably in silks from Lyons; a

221

country priest with yellow eyes, magnified by powerful lenses, reading *Le Monde;* and two sergeants with *Extrême-Orient* shoulder flashes. I tried to read *Cinémonde,* the only magazine I had had time to buy, reflecting how long the journey took. Nine hours—or was it ten?

Later, as we left Dijon, there was a knock on the compartment door and I saw Kovac signalling. I got up, clambered over the outstretched legs of one of the sergeants, who was sleeping, and joined him in the corridor. There was a smell of tinned mushrooms, which I inevitably associate with French railway carriages, mixed with the harsher odor of Régie cigarettes. Trying to balance ourselves against the nervous speed of the train, we walked as far as the end of the coach and stopped in front of the toilet.

"We'll have dinner after Lyons," Kovac said; then he added in an undertone: "I told you it was serious when you came to me. That man at the last moment . . ."

"Yes," I nodded. "I knew it would worry you. . . ."

"Worry?" he said and looked at me as if I had accused him of cowardice; then his face lit up. "No; but we must hurry as much as possible. I'm sure the man is suspicious. But who was the second man?"

"Who?" I looked up. "There was only one man, surely?"

Kovac blinked: "One man came into the hotel. That must have been Ducretet; but the other man stayed in the taxi. I don't know him and probably he doesn't know me. Probably . . ." Kovac shrugged one massive shoulder. "If I saw him again, I would recognise him. I could draw it for you on paper, only I can't draw. He looked like a German, blond hair, cut short like a *forçat*—I mean, a prisoner. About thirty. Probably a tall man if he stood up." Kovac moved close to me, then said in a throaty whisper: 'M.V.D. or any other organisation." He nodded twice, watching my face. "Could be."

"Did you talk to Lockheed and Fontanet?" I said. "You probably haven't had a chance."

Kovac shook his head. "The car is full. But it is wise to think that Fontanet told everything to Ducretet." He suddenly pointed a finger. "Luckily, they don't know where we live in Marseilles, but it's a small place." He shook his head angrily and said between his teeth: "And Fontanet *would* tell him we're going to Marseilles." I saw his face turn red. "Just that one particular word: Marseilles!"

Kovac turned away from me and for a moment I thought he was about to tear something off the wall, or smash a window. Instead, he gripped my shoulder and closed his eyes. He seemed to meditate for a moment, as if weighing up the wisdom of letting me into a secret, then he said slowly, as if quoting a classic: "You can depend on me."

18

IT WAS rather late when we arrived at Marseilles, but it was still quite warm and humid. I sensed the sea, and the conscious anxiety that had been with me all through the journey suddenly gave way to a new feeling. The sea was a door that opened on to the dark places of the unknown. It was stimulating and awe-inspiring, but on this occasion I felt little stimulation.

I had not been to Marseilles since before the war, but I remembered that the St. Charles Station was on a hill-top and that, as you came out on the terrace, you could see most of the town; I had once counted the ninety-five steps to be climbed down before reaching the tree-decked roadway of the Boulevard Athénée.

"A fine place," Kovac said while we were waiting for the train to stop, and I wondered what he meant. Was he merely making conversation, or was it an expression of his confidence? He had hinted that there was a strong chance that we might be sailing the following day.

Then a little later he pushed us into a taxi and I heard him give an address in the rue des Grandes Carmes. The journey took exactly four minutes, and we got out in front of a small hotel in a narrow, slanting Mediterranean street. I imagined that the Old Harbor was quite near.

It was another of those semi-sordid little French hotels which increasingly nowadays are invaded by Levantines, if not yet by North Africans. What was the idea? A hideout obviously, but why so near the station and why in a place like this? There was a large, ageless parrot in a cage behind the dilapidated reception desk. The fat receptionist, who looked more Balkan than French, apparently expected us. He was probably one of Kovac's compatriots, which may have explained the choice of hotel.

We were given two double rooms on the first landing. The stone floor, the distempered walls and the beds, with their functional candlewick spreads, looked surprisingly clean, and were in sharp contrast to the street outside, with rotten sackclothing against the gutters and the spiral staircase, which looked as if it might collapse overnight.

"Very good so far," Kovac said in undertones as he put his small aluminum suitcase on one of the beds. "I went through the whole train and I don't think anybody followed us. Nor from the station. But, of course, that may not mean anything. They are very well organised. I won't be calm till all of you are on the boat. And even then . . ." He shook his head. Then he looked at his watch. "I must telephone," he said and darted out of the room.

Were Ducretet and his companions really suspicious, or

224

was it merely my imagination, which had found support in Kovac's suspicions? Or, again, was Kovac overdramatising a danger that was small or problematical? If Fontanet had told Ducretet everything—and it was likely that he had—he must have said that Barton's letter had announced Kovac's impending arrival, and that he was worried about the report he had seen of the arrest of an unnamed alien in London.

Why had Ducretet come so quickly to the hotel? Fontanet had seen him around ten in the morning, and within not much more than three hours he had already turned up at the rue Biot. What had he wanted to do or say?

When Ducretet had seen that we were ready for our journey to Marseilles, he had looked very surprised, but whether pleasantly or unpleasantly I could not say.

Kovac had said that he had never seen or heard of the man, but did that work both ways? And even if it did, was it not sensible to assume that Ducretet suspected something?

It was quite plausible that between half-past ten in the morning and one in the afternoon he had discovered that the mysterious alien in London was Barton; and he might also have found out that Barton, in fact, had been arrested nearly a week earlier. In that case, Ducretet probably knew more or less what Kovac and I were planning. It was of no significance that he either could not or had not wanted to warn the two men. The fact that he had learnt that we were going to Marseilles was enough.

On the other hand, why must I automatically assume the worst? Was the Communists' intelligence service really so much better than ours? Kovac had said so, but did he know?

Kovac returned. He seemed less concerned now, almost confident.

"What is it?" I said.

"One piece of good news. . . . You may have seen it in

the papers; there was a sailors' strike and dockers' strike threatening." He shook his head. "It could have killed us. But it's all right. The unions are giving the Government ten days. . . . I couldn't speak to the Captain, so I'm leaving at once to see him." He must have seen the expression on my face. "Don't worry," he said, and placed his large hand on my shoulder; then, almost before I knew it, he was gone.

I wanted badly to ask Fontanet what he had told Ducretet that morning, so I went to his room.

"I was just coming to see you," he said, and for the first time for many days there was a confident smile at the corner of his mouth. "Have you got any money?"

"A couple of thousand francs," I answered, "and the rest of the travellers' cheques. Why?"

"That's good. Let's all go out and have a drink. It's so frightfully stuffy here and it's not yet eleven. I haven't been to Marseilles for ages."

I do not know what appalled me more, the idea of leaving the hotel and thereby risking the collapse of everything which Rayne and his department had worked out so ingeniously and carefully, or the undergraduate nonchalance with which Fontanet announced his plan.

"For God's sake," I said. Then, for a moment, I was speechless.

"Now what's wrong?" he challenged.

"Kovac has just told me that Marseilles is one of the most dangerous places from our point of view. It's tiny. We may easily have been followed by the F.B.I. all the way from the station. I mean, you yourself know. . . ."

This was the worst line I could have adopted. Fontanet only smiled. "Nightmares, James," he interrupted. "We're leaving tomorrow. . . ."

"All the more reason . . ." I said.

"Let's consult Kovac."

"He's gone," I said. I felt cold sweat on my forehead.

"Where to?"

"To see his contact man. For God's sake be reasonable, Eric."

It was Lockheed who spoke now, and his voice was agonisingly slow and calm. "I can't see why we shouldn't go out for an hour or so."

That decided it. I had already seen the expression on Fontanet's face. "You can stay in if you like," it seemed to say, "but we'll go. . . ." There was nothing I could do, under the circumstances, but to accompany them.

"All right," I said. At least, I suppose that was what I said. I thought I would leave a note for Kovac on his bed. "I'll just get the money."

Back in my own room, I looked round hurriedly but unsuccessfully for a piece of paper. The magazine, I thought, but its margins were ridiculously narrow. Then I saw the tariff card by the light switch on the wall. Quickly I tore it down and wrote two lines on the back: *Fontanet decided to go out for a drink. Will try to get them back soon. Edmonton.* I placed the card on Kovac's suitcase, which lay unopened on the bed.

Now that the note was written I was a little more relieved, but I was still anxious. I was angry with Lockheed for supporting the plan to leave the hotel. As likely as not, he wanted a drink or two. Or had the sense of hope, which Kovac's sudden arrival and the journey had created, completely intoxicated him? I returned to the other room, bitter, worried and resigned.

A few minutes later the three of us were walking down the cobbled street in the semi-darkness. Fontanet was the leader, and he seemed to be making a beeline for the most sordid and dangerous quarter of the town. There was, I remembered, that little square, which served as a bus terminal, with a diminutive triumphal arch at its centre and around it a number of more than doubtful *bistros* and cafés. I had once been told that it was a dangerous place at night. But there were other places and Fontanet was sure to have found them, in any case.

"You know Marseilles pretty well, don't you?" This was Lockheed's voice, and his remark was addressed to Fontanet. Lockheed sounded calm now, as if he had cast off all his doubts and maudlin fears. Fontanet murmured something I could not hear because in my anxiety I trod almost ankle deep into the water which was running down in the gutter in a small cascade.

We came to a main road. "La Republique," Eric said. "Shall we go to the Belsunce or to the Vieux Port?"

It was so obvious that the question was meant for Lockheed that I said nothing. For me, it was hell either way.

"All I want is a drink," Lockheed murmured, and we turned to the right. We walked along the wide avenue towards the port. It was a little cooler now and the dimly lit avenue was almost deserted. Then we suddenly came to the Old Harbor with its dozens of tiny fishing craft and excursion steamers which invited you to visit the Château d'If, accompanied by gramophone music. The Mediterranean was dark and shiny and still.

We stood there on the corner for a few minutes, but to me it seemed like hours. Every passer-by seemed to watch and discuss us. I had never hated Fontanet more than at that time.

"Let's go across to the café," he said, and we crossed the road and sat down on the terrace. He could not have chosen a more exposed spot or behaved with more idiotic recklessness.

While we were having a drink, it became clear to me why it was that they now had little to say to me, or to each other for that matter. They had heard the good news of their imminent departure that morning. They were obviously completely relaxed after the strain of the past week, and they were no doubt trying to pretend that what was happening was in the normal course of events, and

228

that they had never for a moment really been in doubt about the outcome. I felt that at any moment Fontanet would come out with a remark like "Marseilles doesn't seem to have changed very much," or with an opinion on the Mediterranean tradition, and I would explode.

I decided to speak, and I no longer cared if I sounded agitated. "I must say Ducretet was quick off the mark," I said.

"It only shows how wrong you were about him," Fontanet sneered, lighting a cigarette on the stub of another. "He's first-rate. . . ." He turned to Lockheed. "Marcel knew Alex, by the way, in Washington. But I could see he didn't think much of Jan. I mean, he didn't say anything. There's discipline, after all. And he was quite right. It's all very well Barton's man arriving at the last moment, but we were kept waiting more than a week. All we need have done was just to have arrived and gone to see Marcel. If we had, we'd have left France ages ago. . . . By the way," he turned to me, "did Kovac say why he couldn't turn up earlier?"

"No. To be quite frank, I was so pleased to see him that I didn't bother to ask. In any case, I haven't had much opportunity so far."

Fontanet nodded absently. He was now more interested in the fair, which was in progress further along the quayside, with its illuminated booths and radio music and small crowds encircling someone in a top hat, apparently a street entertainer. "Let's go and look at it," he said.

We paid and walked over. It was a seedy affair. There was a lot of noise and bright and smelly acetylene lights and tinned music coming from a miniature merry-go-round. The fairground was poorly attended and the barkers' cries were unconvincing and lacked confidence. Lockheed seemed a little bored, but I could see the interest in Fontanet's face. We stopped at the rifle-shooting booth with its clay pipes and fluffy dolls and bottles and bottles of cheap champagne. There were two young soldiers aiming at a ping-pong ball balanced on a jet of water, and I was now irritated, instead of being amused, to see Fontanet inspecting them with a quick, well-practised glance, like the connoisseur in a junk-shop, who does not need to handle the articles. We moved just in time to avoid the huckster's invitation to try our luck.

There was sudden but half-hearted applause from the people who had been watching the antics of the man in the top hat, and most of his spectators moved over to the mechanical horse race. We joined them and Fontanet quickly took stock of the crowd. "An amazing lack of talent," he announced in a bored voice. "Shall we go back?"

To my great relief we turned back towards the café and the avenue. The clock of the whitewashed church in the corner of the harbor struck midnight.

2

I felt the excitement was too much for me as we walked up the circular staircase of the hotel, past the out-of-date calendar, the dilapidated reception desk, the key-stand and the barometer advertising Dubonnet.

The key was in my door, and I remembered that, in my anxiety, I had left it there when we had gone out. Kovac was not in the room. My message was still there, but perhaps nevertheless he had returned and was now searching for us all over Marseilles. It was all Fontanet's fault. How I loathed his self-satisfied nonchalance, his aggressive sense of relief, his almost gay mood; I felt I wanted to go to his room and hit him.

How could I for one single moment have felt the slightest sympathy, the slightest remorse, for him? He had always done the most outrageous and insane things because of some momentary whim, and every time he had got away with it. It was the same at Oxford, and now I remembered someone telling me many years ago that it was the same at Eton too. He got other boys in trouble and he himself went unpunished. I had once been told that there was talk of a boy from the same house being expelled on his account. I was not much interested at the time, but now I believed it. He would get away with murder, I felt with bitter envy. Take the dossier, for example. By a stroke of luck, he had discovered that he was in danger of arrest, had involved Lockheed in his plans and had escaped from England. Now events were again playing into his hands. Instead of being allowed to go to Russia, he would be returned to London. And that was as much to his advantage as to Britain's. After a time, Fontanet would either have outlived his usefulness to the Russians or they would have seen him for what he was and liquidated him. Instead, he would be brought back to England, where, to avoid a public scandal, he would not be tried and would lose only his job instead of his life or liberty. I should not even be surprised to hear in three years' time that he was in charge of anti-Soviet propaganda in some Ministry or other.

And Lockheed? But just then I heard a taxi drive up, and I ran to the window. It was Kovac.

I wiped the sweat off my forehead and hastily prepared some line of defence in case he held me responsible for the fact that we had left the hotel in his absence. But there was a broad smile on his face as he came in. "I saw the Captain," he whispered as he entered the room. "Chances are that we are leaving tomorrow at noon. But we are leaving." He gave me a wink. "The Captain calls me early in the morning." His face suddenly turned dark. "They gave out the man's name in London," he said. "So it will be in all the newspapers tomorrow morning." He shrugged a shoulder. "Perhaps it doesn't matter now. . . .

And the Marseilles papers may not print it." He was looking bright again.

"Fontanet forced me to go out," I said. "We were away for a whole hour. Along the quay. I could have murdered him."

Kovac nodded and raised both hands to indicate that I should speak more softly. Suddenly I realised that the window was open. Then he smiled again, and seemed to reflect, as if looking for an English expression. "Boys will be boys," I thought bitterly, was probably what he wanted to say. That seemed to be the world's reaction to Fontanet.

But Kovac said: "I just go to see them," and went next-door. He was not gone many minutes and soon he was back again. "I told them," he announced when he had shut the door. His expression was calm and confident. Kovac was a professional—competent, efficient, energetic, probably ruthless. Now he took off his jacket and put it on the chair, then he unlocked the aluminum suitcase and began to rummage in it. Finally, he produced his toothbrush and paste.

I undressed slowly. There was no doubt that he inspired confidence. In any case, we were sailing tomorrow. It looked like a last-minute miracle. He had no idea of our destination. Malta? Cyprus? If it was a small tramp steamer the journey might take several days. I was anticipating the worst journey of my life. This was war; cold war possibly, but the constituents were the same: boredom and horror. I really must get a few books. First thing tomorrow morning.

After the landing, there would be a formal arrest and probably an aircraft back home. Now, lying in bed, listening to Kovac's snoring, discreet at first, then steadily increasing in volume, I was not so sure as I had been only a short while ago that the case would be hushed up. Now that the report of Barton's arrest had been made public, things might take a different turn.

And if there were a trial, could they avoid dragging me in as a witness for the prosecution? This was something I ought really to have discussed with Addyman. My job may have been a "patriotic duty," but I wanted to remain an unknown patriot.

And I thought with bitter disgust how much more publicity I would get if I became a witness in this case than I was ever likely to get as a writer. . . . The first thing I must do was to ask Addyman to leave my name out of it. A patriot, after all, was sometimes entitled to a small reward.

19

LIKE most of my dreams, this one was incoherent. Selina was in it, much older than in real life: a kind of projection into her future, with greying hair, but she looked attractive just the same; and there was the bridge over the Regent's Canal in Paddington, and Rayne, for some reason barefoot; finally, there was a girl from my childhood whose name I could not remember.

But I knew immediately that the hand which shook me was Kovac's and I was wide awake at once, although I had not fallen asleep until around three in the morning. Kovac was fully dressed and smelt of some lotion. "It's half-past eight," he said, and I sat up in bed to show I was awake and attentive.

"I've just spoken with the Captain," he told me excitedly, "and I must go and see him. He's near the quay.

. . . But I'll be back soon. I don't know exactly when, but soon. Please go somewhere and have breakfast with them, but don't go too far. We may have to start in the forenoon. There's a good café in the corner of the Avenue National." He looked at the enormous wrist watch and said: "I must find a taxi."

I rose and opened the shutters, and as the bright sunshine burst into the room, I saw a shiny black beetle dart across the stone floor and disappear under the door.

I shaved in cold water, and through the open window I could see practically the whole length of the street as it climbed the hill above the Old Harbor. It was full of people, clattering up and down the cobblestones, and an oversized blue lorry with "Esso" painted on its side rumbled down the road. A man was singing somewhere across the street, then he stopped abruptly and shouted: *"Hé, Emile, ça va?"*

I looked at my shirt, which was rather soiled. I did not have a clean one left. Perhaps I could have it washed on the boat, I thought, and at once my mind became filled with a sense of adventure, such as I had not experienced since my early childhood, not even during the war.

Yet, a second later, I was already thinking of the men in the next room. They too must have been feeling the spirit of adventure. But I was no longer concerned with the morality of my behavior towards them. Fontanet's arrogant and triumphant sense of safety had finally cured me. And Lockheed, too, seemed cold and reserved after his confession to me. Would Rayne come with us on the boat? Probably not, I thought. It was more likely that he would go by plane; in which case I would not see him till we arrived at Malta, or whatever was our destination, or perhaps even not until I reached England. I remembered that I intended to buy some books for the journey when we went out for breakfast.

I felt a slight pain, probably a touch of indigestion,

234

and walked along the corridor with its thick, dirty carpet to waken the two men. They would probably still be asleep.

I was just about to knock on their door when I heard a voice inside the room saying, "About ten minutes." I stopped to listen, because it was not Fontanet's voice, nor Lockheed's. "That is why you have not much time," the voice went on, and my heart missed a beat, because it was a high, throaty voice with a precise foreign intonation. I put my ear to the door, but a sudden noise in the street outside muffled everything.

I was sweating. Then at last I heard a voice I knew. It was Fontanet speaking: "I wouldn't take a chance. Remember last night how he tried to keep us back. The story he told me was cockeyed in the first place, and all yesterday morning he tried to . . ." There was a sudden sound as if a chair were being pushed on the stone floor, and my heart froze. This was the end, and it was just my luck that Kovac should have gone out at the last minute, leaving me alone against three men—possibly more. What could I do? I could hardly call the police. They would never listen to me. It was obvious that Ducretet had sent someone to help Fontanet and Lockheed to run away. I could not go with them. To follow them would be extremely difficult. No; there was only one thing to do—go in and pretend I had heard nothing, treat Ducretet's man as a casual visitor—I hoped against hope that there was not more than one stranger in the room—and delay them until Kovac returned.

"We know for a fact that he has been caught a long time. . . ." I heard the man's voice again, and I knew at once with agony that he meant Barton. There followed the sound of a low thud, and I bent down to look through the keyhole, but the key was in it; it would be. The room was very quiet now for a moment, then I heard one single footstep and a second later the door opened and I found myself facing the outlines of a tallish, slim man. The whole thing happened so suddenly that I just had time to straighten myself out.

"Good morning," I said pretending desperately that I had not been listening, but it was clear at once that Lockheed for one had seen me. He was standing slightly behind the man at the door, his eyes narrow and his nostrils wide with suspicion.

The man backed politely to let me in. He had fair hair, cut short; a tall, slim man with a jesting, conceited mouth, and in his hand he held a pair of sunglasses.

"I just came to see if you were awake," I said to nobody in particular. I had no idea how my voice sounded, nor what my face must have looked like, but I heard my heartbeats in my ears, in my mouth, all over my body. Then I saw Fontanet straighten himself up from one of the chairs. I noticed his suitcase on the floor. His lips curled in a sneer. He was trying to catch Lockheed's eye.

There was a brief, ghastly silence—very brief and very ghastly. Then the man spoke in a slow, peremptory English. He was obviously as startled as I at first, but he had a better experience of how to behave in an emergency. He already had the calm and assurance of a film actor. He was now going through the motions of a smile. I saw he was wearing a brown gaberdine jacket.

"The gentlemen," he said, pointing to the two men, "are going out to see a friend." I saw now that his voice was much younger than his face; perhaps the face was prematurely old. I then caught sight of Lockheed's fibre suitcase, already packed, but open on the bed.

"But you can't," I said desperately, turning to Fontanet. "I have a message for you from Kovac." I nodded idiotically towards Ducretet's man. "Who's this?" I asked.

The man was still standing in the same position, but nobody spoke and I said: "And you're taking your bags."

That was a painfully bad mistake. I was a dangerous

fool, I knew immediately. "Kovac," I said, seeking for something sensible to say; his name must have sounded like the beginning of a prayer; but I could not continue. I turned towards Fontanet, who was now standing with his hands on the back of the chair. He was still sneering. There was no agitation in his sneer. He looked calm, triumphant and nasty.

It was his face that should have told me what was happening; perhaps it did, but everything happened in a split second. I believe I did see him looking above and behind me, then he suddenly turned his face away as if caught in some wrongful act, as if afraid he might give the game away. I turned round, I think, numb with surprise, and saw Lockheed with the china waterbottle raised in his hand. . . .

2

My first sensation was a vague feeling of water all over me, and perhaps because of the water I felt like coming up to the surface from a high dive. Now all of a sudden I heard street sounds, and the room was bathed in harsh sunshine which lit up the large mauve roses of the wallpaper. I had an impression that I had seen the room earlier from the floor; I seemed to remember the legs of the bed and the skirting round the wall. But now I was lying on the bed, and I knew it was Kovac who had put me there.

I reached out with a tired hand and felt the side of my head. It seemed large, very large, and at my touch a stab of pain shot through my whole body. I felt it even in my feet. Now I saw Kovac's face above me, anxious, almost tender, with its blue chin and bushy eyebrows. He looked as if he were afraid of me.

"It was Lockheed," I said, and my voice sounded small. I wanted to prove that I was alive and that all was well. I spoke more loudly. "Lockheed," I repeated. "He hit me."

Kovac smiled. For an instant I thought he looked almost pleased, but before I could become angry his face was serious again.

"You are all right," he said, spacing the words as if quoting a line from Shakespeare.

"Yes," I shouted angrily. "But you must hurry. . . . They only left a few minutes ago." I made a move to get up.

But Kovac tried with all the gentleness of a cut-throat to restrain me, and, angrily spitting out his words, he said: "It's almost eleven. You were unconscious for . . . a long time. Nearly two hours, maybe. I've been here some time. . . ." He shrugged a shoulder; then suddenly he turned towards the door.

I heard the door open, and saw Rayne rush in; Kovac had obviously telephoned him. "How is he?" Rayne said. His face was dark red, as if he had bathed it in hot water.

"I was hit by Lockheed," I said before Kovac could reply.

Rayne stood by my bed. He seemed not to hear what I said, and he looked closely at my face; his own red face was perspiring. He said: "Do you feel strong enough to sit up?"

"Yes; of course," I said, somewhat angry that both of them should treat me like a dying child.

I sat up. There was a slight pain in my head from the too sudden move.

I saw now that Rayne's face was bathed in sweat. Had he run all the way on hearing the news from Kovac? "Now, raise your arms level with your head." His voice sounded like a command.

"But . . ." I said.

"Oh shut up," he said, then he smiled and spoke gently: "Do as I tell you. Good boy."

Feeling ridiculous, I raised both my arms.

"How does it feel?" he asked.

238

"Fine," I said; "just fine. What's the idea?"

"I just wanted to see if you had concussion, that's all." He made a move as if to pat me on the shoulder, but changed his mind at the last moment. "You seem to be all right," he said, and added in an undertone: "I want to avoid sending for a doctor, if we possibly can."

"There's no need," I said. How could he be so dumb? "But aren't you going to follow them?"

He shook his head. "It's too late." It was only when he said that that I saw his underlip was trembling. I had already heard the note of pain and frustration in his voice. I looked away, so as not to embarrass him.

"You'd better come to your own room," he said a little later.

3

"It was childishly easy," Rayne said. There was still some bitterness in his voice. The first-class compartment, all heavy and nostalgic Edwardian luxury, blue plush and antimacassars, was empty, and I was lying across the three seats. "Childishly." He repeated the word masochistically. "It was a losing game from beginning to end. I had more than one hunch this would happen. We had a miracle on our side, but unfortunately we couldn't make use of it. . . ."

"A miracle?" I said.

"The fact that the two men contacted nobody for a whole week. We should have been able to do something in that time." He got up to take off his jacket, which he put over his suitcase above his seat, and I saw there was a patch of perspiration under his arm. "The moment Fontanet contacted Ducretet, all was lost. I should have got the men out of France before Barton's arrest was announced in the papers. Anyhow, thanks to Fontanet, Ducretet knew you were going to Marseilles, and his friends must have been suspicious of the whole set-up. The Communists are tragically well organised in France; and the Russians don't have several rival intelligence organisations like we do. Now you know why I was so anxious to find out whether the two men had contacted anybody in France. I've no doubt that within a couple of hours of Fontanet's calling on Ducretet, they found out all about Barton and knew that you and Kovac were not what you pretended. In any case, they took no chances. They knew you were taking the two o'clock train to Marseilles, and the rest was child's play.

"Either somebody took the same train and travelled with you, or they telephoned your description to Marseilles and you were followed from the station. Or someone could have flown down. . . . Anything. The only thing that puzzles me now is that they apparently waited till this morning before seeing the two men."

"It might have been too conspicuous to have approached them at night," I said. "After all, we didn't get back from our little outing until after midnight."

"By now," Rayne said, "the two men are probably out of the country—possibly already behind the Iron Curtain. Because we didn't want the French authorities to know, we couldn't arrange for a special plane to fly the men home, or anything like that. Instead, we had to keep the two men happy while we made very complicated arrangements for a ship to take them to British territory. How much easier it must have been for the Russians, with their network in France . . . they could probably have organised a private plane, or some other means of escape, without the French authorities knowing anything about it. They had nearly twenty-four hours to work out a plan and put it in operation, and a whole army of men at their disposal and all the money they needed. And we were so short of help, and there were so many snags that Kovac even had to leave you at the worst moment." Rayne's voice

240

suddenly rose. "D'you know that we *couldn't* have sailed today?"

"Suppose the men are still in France?" I said.

"It's not very likely. But even if they are, I still can't tell the French police. Think of trying to explain why we didn't tell them in the beginning." He looked away as if he were in pain. "The whole thing," he said, "broke down because of insufficient organisation." I felt Rayne was already writing his report or rehearsing his speech to Addyman.

"What'll happen now?" I asked. I was sorry for Rayne. Defeat made him look like an undergraduate.

"I shall try to fly to London tomorrow morning, but you"—he put a hand on my knee—"I'd stay in Paris a couple of days, if I were you. . . ."

"I don't mean that," I said. "I mean, is this the end of the affair, or . . . ?"

Rayne shrugged his shoulders. "One thing's certain. The fact that the two men are missing will get into the papers before long. It's odd they haven't got hold of the story already." He shook his head and looked up at the electric light. "If I were the Foreign Office," he said, "I'd release the story now, before the papers find out on their own."

"What would you do? Call a Press conference?"

Rayne smiled—for the first time that day. "I don't think so. That's not the way. What, I think, the F.O. would do would be to make a Carefully Calculated Indiscretion. Somebody would 'babble' to the Press. The Press would call the F.O. and the F.O. would issue the usual formula: 'We can neither confirm nor deny the report' which in plain English means: 'It's true.'"

He leaned over me for a second and looked at the right side of my face. "How's your head?" he said.

"All right," I said. I did not really know what was responsible for my headache, for my lethargy. All of a

241

sudden I felt as if I were dreaming: a passive and impotent spectator.

"It doesn't show much," Rayne said.

We were silent now. I admired his self-discipline in the face of what must have been a very serious personal disaster, all the more because he was lovably impulsive. He was a first-rate man and he probably enjoyed Addyman's confidence. As far as I could judge, he was not responsible for the failure of the affair, but I wondered, all the same, whether he might be blamed for it.

Rayne might not yet have realised the full implications of his position, or perhaps he was trying to keep up a brave front for my benefit. Certainly he was amazingly calm; outwardly at least. Or was it not just a temporary relief, after several days of strain? I knew that he was engaged to be married. He had shown me her photograph: a nice girl with an intelligent, humorous face. She was doing industrial research. I wondered if she knew much about his occupation.

The door of the compartment slid open, and a man in the tobacco-brown uniform of the Wagon-Restaurant said: *"Vous prenez du thé ou du café, messieurs?"*

20

I SAW that Mrs. Graham had not been near the flat in my absence, apart from pushing my mail through the letter box. It was Wednesday: a dull day in London, almost stiflingly warm, with the sun hidden behind a haze, and it was around two in the afternoon. I had lunched in Westbourne Grove, and bought some of the papers I had not yet read that morning on the bus from London Airport.

The news of the missing diplomats had broken the previous morning—that is, the day after their escape from Marseilles—but I only saw it in the evening papers in Paris where I spent the afternoon largely in bed. Rayne and I parted on Monday at the Gare de Lyon, and I went to a small hotel in the rue Gay-Lussac near the Panthéon, where I had once stayed many years ago. But now, as far as I was concerned, the place had lost its evocative powers, and within a couple of hours I had come to feel that the same applied to the whole of Paris. The following morning, rather half-heartedly, I strolled across the Jardin du Luxembourg and had lunch at a place near the Saint-Sulpice where they still knew me from the old days. I was on holiday, I told myself, but I did not believe it. Everything was unreal and boring. I could have spent a couple more days, maybe a week, perhaps even at Government expense. In any case, I had the remainder of the travellers' cheques still in my pocket, and Rayne had said I could spend them. But suddenly I felt very lonely. It was the same feeling as when I had been told at the Base Hospital that I had been discharged from the Air Force. I also felt sad and quite lethargic. Perhaps I really had concussion. I retired to bed for the afternoon and later sent out for the papers. I decided to leave the next morning.

I was now reading the report of the affair in the *Clarion,* a paper on which Fontanet had once worked for a short time. I wondered how anyone had discovered that the two men had gone to France, but I remembered that Rayne had spoken about the possibility of a Foreign Office hand-out.

There was a description of Fontanet's flat in Bayswater. The reporting was colorful, but on the whole less lurid than I had expected. "Interviewed yesterday, Mrs. Ada Spiritt, the charwoman, said, 'Mr. Fontanet was a nice gentleman, but very artistic and untidy; he dropped cigarette ash all over the place. . . .' "

Then there were interviews with various people, including one with Arthur Beaufort. Apparently someone on the editorial staff must have known that Fontanet was a friend of his. "Surrounded by his famous collection of modern French paintings, Mr. Beaufort said: 'I knew Fontanet largely through official contacts and very casually. . . . It is unkind to condemn a man in his absence, but I must say the news hasn't come as too great a surprise to me. . . .' "

I loved the words "very casually" and kept wondering how many people knew about Fontanet's intimate and long-continued friendship with the man to whose house he had brought his undergraduate friends and who had helped him into the B.B.C. and into the Foreign Office.

The *Clarion* reporter also knew that Fontanet had been friendly with C. C. Gallen. The "famous novelist" had just arrived in London for his usual few weeks in Jermyn Street. He said that as far as he remembered Fontanet had been a friend of his nephew, but he had never really known Fontanet personally. The nephew in question had most conveniently been killed in the war.

The reporter had apparently made an unsuccessful attempt to interview Sir Aubrey Fontanet, Eric's father. This rather surprised me, because I thought the father was already dead. Having been snubbed, the writer enlarged on the fact that the former Court official was now living in a smallish and inexpensive hotel in Bournemouth. There was a photograph of the hotel and a reference to what Sir Aubrey paid for his full board.

There was far less in the paper about Lockheed. From the guardedly venomous tone of what there was, it seemed obvious that the family had refused to be interviewed and that the reported had failed to discover the identity of Lockheed's friends. It was news to me that Lockheed's mother had remarried shortly before the war. Her husband was a retired admiral. Nor had I realised that Phoebe, the eldest of Lockheed's sisters, was the wife of Lionel Spratt, who was almost certain to be in the Cabinet again if there were a change of Government.

One of the papers printed a photograph of the Lockheeds' house, near Denham, but there were no interviews with Selina. The *Chronicle* report said she was ill.

It was amazing how I seemed to have forgotten about her during the past forty-eight hours, but as I crossed over to the telephone to call her I realised that my mind had been more or less of a blank altogether during that time. It was as if I had been under an anaesthetic.

I really ought to have written from Paris, I thought, but it was a maid who answered the telephone with peevish weariness. After cross-examining me, she said that Mrs. Lockheed was away and she had no idea when she would be back. I asked her to take a message that I had returned from France, suspecting that Selina might be at home just the same, unless perhaps she had gone to stay with friends or with Alan's family.

While I was still at the telephone I rang Miss Welgar and asked to be put through to Sir Paul Addyman, although there was really very little to discuss with him. He had, however, promised to look into the business of my dossier. After a long wait Miss Welgar said she would ring me back as soon as possible; she had my number.

I suddenly felt lonely. Should I go out, and perhaps buy the afternoon papers, or else try to contact Rayne or Twining? Or should I stay in and take up the novel again? But the mere thought of the novel repelled me. I was not even in the mood to write a letter.

In the end I rang Keith, the painter. "Wasn't it a strange coincidence," I said, "my talking to you about Eric just recently?" But as I spoke the obvious deception filled me with nausea, so much so that I was almost

245

tempted to tell him the whole story. It would probably come out one day, anyway.

"Yes; wasn't it?" I had the impression that Keith was grinning as he spoke. "Why don't you and I offer an article on Eric to one of the evening papers?" he said. "I've just heard from someone in Fleet Street that the papers are simply besieged by all sorts of people who claim to have known Eric and the other fellow—Lockheed. Most of them have never even seen them. We could do a really exciting story," he roared.

"Were it not for the law of libel," I said.

"And obscenity."

"What do you think of the interview with Beaufort?" I asked.

"The best joke of the week. Somebody really ought to send Beaufort a poisoned choirboy. . . . I say, have you heard any of the rumors?"

"What rumors?"

"That they're really British agents, and that that's why the Secret Service hasn't done anything. . . . Actually, you know, I wouldn't be a bit surprised if M.I.5, or whatever they call themselves, were busy planting rumors that the two men are really British agents in disguise. It would be a good way for our security forces to save face, and it might lessen confidence in Eric and his friend in Russia too. If that's where they've gone."

A minute or two later, having replaced the receiver, I felt as if a sudden change had overtaken me, perhaps quite independently of what Keith had told me. It was as if the anaesthetic were wearing off and I was regaining my reasoning power and interests.

Keith was astute to have realised the implications of a whispering campaign, I thought. But even if the Russians recognised it for what it was—an attempt to discredit the reliability of their new acquisitions—the position of the two men was precarious. Even if they never actually out-

246

lived their usefulness, a political change might bring them into disfavor, and changes were always violent in the Soviet Union. A sudden and dramatic swing of the pendulum is typical of all conspiratorial societies, even if their ultimate aims remain irrevocably the same. So punishment for Lockheed and Fontanet, in the long run, would only be delayed, not avoided.

From the point of view of Britain, the implications of the escape were far more difficult to assess. The actual harm the two men could cause might not be great, in spite of the fact that I believed every word that Fontanet had told me about his and Lockheed's usefulness to the Russians. Treason may or may not have been a historical force, but isolated treason has never decided history, and there was little to worry about unless the escape was the prelude to further defections.

From the point of view of national prestige, their flight might have been a serious blow had the two men's private behavior been above reproach. Fortunately, this was not the case. In fact, they easily lent themselves to a successful smear campaign. The newspapers had already pounced on this, for reasons completely independent of the so-called national interest, but the effect was the same. The fact that they could allege without the men being able to defend themselves that Fontanet had lived in sordid, Bohemian surroundings, that Lockheed had engaged in drunken brawls and needed the services of a psychiatrist, and that both men had frequently been drunk, was first-rate evidence of unreliability. The fact that it could also be hinted that one at least of the men was a homosexual would also help to discredit them. In fact, Fontanet's undoubted inversion would, I felt sure, lead to a large-scale witch-hunt against homosexuals.

An hour later, the day was still quite warm: the sun had broken through the haze, and it was now a really magnificent June afternoon such as is rare in England. I had nothing to do, and I finally decided to stroll in the Park and buy the evening papers. I expected nothing important or exciting, but reading them would pass away the time.

I was in the kitchen cleaning my shoes when the telephone rang. As I lifted the receiver I heard the button being pressed at the other end and the pennies fall.

"James"—it was Selina—"I've tried to get you several times, but there was either no reply or you were engaged. When did you come back?"

"This morning. I spoke to your maid about an hour ago."

"I'm at the station," she said, as if she had not heard me. "Marylebone . . . Could I come and see you?"

"Of course."

I went back to the kitchen, picked up a rag and dusted the furniture in the study. I would have to tell her that my charwoman had not cleaned the flat in my absence. But what else should I tell her, and what would she tell me? When I had rung her earlier, I had done so largely because I felt lonely and she was the person I most wanted to see. But now that it was she who had rung me and was in fact on her way in a taxi to see me, the situation was very different. She had obviously heard something from Twining or Addyman and would want me to tell her what I knew.

Then soon enough the bell rang and I hurried to the hall. She wore a frock of black lace, and I suddenly felt shy and awkward as we went into the study. This was the first time she had ever been to my flat.

But she did not look round. "Are you all right?" she said with a mother's tenderness and anxiety.

"Yes; of course," I said. She must have heard, I thought, what happened in Marseilles. I was embarrassed.

"It was sweet of you to have written," she said as she

248

sat down facing the mandarin and gave my study a very brief glance. I had quite forgotten the note I sent before I left London.

"You realise, of course, I couldn't write to you from Paris."

She nodded. It was only now that I saw her against the light. She had changed in the past few days. Her face somehow looked thinner, and there was a tired uncertainty around her eyes. Bromides, I thought.

But my real surprise came while I was giving her my version of the whole story. It seemed obvious that she was not very interested, although she politely listened as I related how I had met the two men in their hotel. Before I could tell her about my second day in Paris, she interrupted to ask for a cigarette. I got up apologetically, because I did not realise she smoked. Then I fetched the remains of the bottle of sherry.

"I wanted to see you," she said now. "I can't stay at home a moment longer." She was smoking her cigarette very inexpertly. "The last few days have been quite awful. Every few minutes the telephone rings and some journalist wants to talk to me. As I was leaving this afternoon, two of them drove up to the house—some morning paper. I told them I knew nothing. . . . James"—she looked at me—"you've read all the papers?"

"Most of them."

"You've seen the hints about Alan?"

"Yes."

She saw my embarrassment. "Look, James. Don't try to spare me." She placed the sherry glass clumsily on the table; I heard it as it knocked against the wood. "You've been doing that all the time. It's very sweet of you, but the point is: I've got to know—the worst." A slight tremor seemed to run through her body as she shook her head. "I'm past crying," she said. For a moment I thought she was actually smiling, then she suddenly spoke again: "You *did* know all about Alan, didn't you?"

It was not easy to give a direct answer, any answer.

"How shall I put it?" I said.

"Simply yes or no."

"That's not the point," I said. I added, "Selina. . . . If you're asking me whether I knew before I saw Alan leave from Victoria with Fontanet, then the answer is no. You must remember I didn't know Alan very well. We weren't friends at Oxford." I avoided her eyes. Must I tell her everything, including the story of Saïd, and Alan's confession at the bar in the rue des Martyrs? I spoke again trying to side-track the subject: "Did *you* know . . . ?"

She looked away: "I wasn't absolutely sure. Perhaps I didn't want to be sure. . . . It's so very difficult to explain."

The way she spoke, far more apologetic for her own inability to assess her knowledge than embarrassed, made me feel that my question had made things worse. It was, I saw now, only partly the desire in me to side-track the issue that had made me turn the tables on her. Unconsciously, I wanted to find an answer to a question that had excited my curiosity ever since I had seen Selina, for the first time after many years, exactly ten days ago. I had the answer now; my curiosity was satisfied; but the humility with which she had replied made it obvious that I ought not to have asked the question. I was ashamed of myself.

But she suddenly spoke again: "There's one thing, James, I've never told you."

"What is it?" I said, confused. I could not interpret the way she was looking at me. It was frightened and humble. I thought of the bromides again.

"You may not remember. It happened so long ago."

"Yes . . . ?"

250

"We were great friends, you and I. You wanted to marry me. . . ."

"Oh, my dear . . ." I felt I was blushing, but my surprise was far greater than my embarrassment. "Why do you remember?"

"Because one must. . . ."

"I was an absolute nobody at the time. I had no right to ask you to marry me."

"That's not the reason I didn't marry you," she said. "Do you remember? I went away to France, practically without a word. You must have been hurt. . . . What was the name of the musician in *The Man in the Moon?*"

So she knew it; so she had recognised me in the book. But why bring it up, why now . . . ?

"You still don't know why I went away and didn't marry you?"

"Yes, I do." I felt hot and cold with anxiety. "Besides being an absolute nobody, I was the most disagreeable mixture of a conceited and timid, cocky and depressed, monomaniac bore. In short, the textbook example of a struggling writer. . . ."

I saw a faint—very faint—smile around her lips, then all of a sudden the smile disappeared. "That wasn't the reason, and you weren't a bore. . . ."

I had to look at her. It was a strange face I saw, worried, attractive and virtuous. Then she spoke, a split second after I had begun to ask myself what she could possibly have in mind. "Alan told me you were a pansy."

The penny dropped. So that was why she had asked, the last time I saw her, what had broken up my marriage. I knew at the time she was not just making conversation.

She gave a tiny snort. "I found out later it wasn't true, of course, but it was so typical of poor Alan. . . ."

"Poor Alan," I echoed. What else could I have said?

"One really must feel sorry for him," she said, but I did

251

not quite know what she meant. There was a long silence. Did she still love Alan in spite of everything? Could she still forgive him? There were the children, I thought, and there was her own almost devastating sense of pity. Then why had she told me what she had just said? Did she want me to understand that her life with Alan was all over, *in spite of* the children and that her pity was now for me?

Many years before I had allowed her to slip away from me. I still did not know what had paralysed me then. But now I knew at least why she had left me. *This time,* I thought, and I suddenly felt I could be happy with her. Not as if nothing had happened, but in spite of what had happened. But could she be happy with me? That was far more important.

I was still a selfish monomaniac bore. Could she still change me? Was it not too late? Too much had happened to me in the last few years; the last few days, the last few hours, for that matter.

Then Selina spoke. "Do you mind if I use your telephone? I must book a hotel room. Brown's or the Hyde Park, I think." She adjusted the sleeve of her frock. "I left my cases at the station," she said slowly. "I don't want to go home—for a few days at least. It's been quite impossible there. The telephone . . ." She made a move to get up.

"Then what do you plan to do?"

"I don't know. I spoke to Mother a couple of days ago. She wants me to go and stay with her in America. Perhaps I even will."

We were facing each other now. "Of course," I said, "you can always stay here, Selina. For a short time . . . for ever. . . ."

With my heart in my throat, I was watching her face now, waiting for her answer. . . .

The End